Murder at Blackwood Inn

Also available by Penny Warner

The Party-Planning Mysteries

How to Dine on Killer Wine
How to Party with a Killer Vampire
How to Survive a Killer Séance
How to Crash a Killer Bash
How to Host a Killer Party

The Connor Westphal Series

Dead Man's Hand
Silence Is Golden
Blind Side
A Quiet Undertaking
Right to Remain Silent
Sign of Foul Play
Dead Body Language

The Food Truck Mysteries
(writing as Penny Pike)

Death of a Crabby Cook
Death of a Chocolate Cheater
Death of a Bad Apple

Murder at Blackwood Inn

A HAUNTED DEAD AND BREAKFAST MYSTERY

Penny Warner

NEW YORK

Books should be disposed of and recycled according to local requirements. All paper materials used are FSC compliant.

This is a work of fiction. All of the names, characters, organizations, places, and events portrayed in this novel are either products of the author's imagination or are used fictitiously. Any resemblance to real or actual events, locales, or persons, living or dead, is entirely coincidental.

PUBLISHER'S NOTE: The recipes contained in this book are to be followed exactly as written. The publisher is not responsible for your specific health or allergy needs that may require medical supervision. The publisher is not responsible for any adverse reaction to the recipes contained in this book.

Copyright © 2025 by Penny Warner

All rights reserved.

Published in the United States by Crooked Lane Books, an imprint of The Quick Brown Fox & Company LLC.

Crooked Lane Books and its logo are trademarks of The Quick Brown Fox & Company LLC.

Library of Congress Catalog-in-Publication data available upon request.

ISBN (hardcover): 979-8-89242-185-0
ISBN (paperback): 979-8-89242-285-7
ISBN (ebook): 979-8-89242-186-7

Cover design by Rob Fiore

Printed in the United States.

www.crookedlanebooks.com

Crooked Lane Books
34 West 27th St., 10th Floor
New York, NY 10001

First Edition: September 2025

The authorized representative in the EU for product safety and compliance is eucomply OÜ Pärnu mnt 139b-14, 11317 Tallinn, Estonia, hello@eucompliancepartner.com, +33757690241

10 9 8 7 6 5 4 3 2 1

To my brilliant critique group,
I couldn't do it without you!

Colleen Casey, Margaret Dumas,
Janet Finsilver, Staci McLaughlin,
Ann Parker, and Carole Price
And my plus one: Tom.

"Mother Nature provides a cure for many afflictions, including ghosts and
 evil spirits. If you're ever in a bind with ghostly entities, sprinkle a little basil
 around your bedroom, hang a blackberry wreath on the door, and place cumin
 on your windowsills to keep them away. Then have a cup of ginseng tea. It has
 a calming nature and will soothe your soul if the spirits just won't leave."

—Hazel Blackwood, herbalist

Chapter One
So Not Nancy Drew

"Welcome to Pelican Point!" the sign read as I drove into town on a late fall afternoon. "Established 1853."

Although the coastal fog had lifted from the Northern California seaside village, I shivered and took a deep breath, bracing myself. I hadn't been to my ancestral town since I was ten, which was twenty years ago. That sign immediately brought back memories of the time I poisoned my father.

I only hoped my two eccentric aunts had forgotten about "the incident."

I tried to shake off the chill as I drove through the five-block downtown area. *This is a new beginning*, I told myself. I was looking forward to starting fresh after a year of emotional upheaval. I scanned the buildings that lined the one and only main street through town—Victorian, Greek Revival, Renaissance, Gothic, Italianate, and other vernacular structures. I'd read that the eclectic architecture dated back to when the first shop was built in Pelican Point—a saloon, of course. Now brew pubs had replaced the saloons, and the town was filled with shops to bring in the tourists, selling everything from T-shirts to taffy and surf gear to swimwear.

I turned up the hill, away from the breathtaking views of the Pacific Ocean, where longtime residents lived next door to short-term renters. The larger homes, tucked behind redwoods and cypress trees, allowed for privacy, peace, and serenity. Just what I needed after my ugly divorce from my cheating ex, Sergio the Sleazeball.

I spotted the sign I'd been looking for—"Blackwood Bed and Breakfast Inn." Underneath it, a smaller sign dangled precariously by one hinge: "and Herbiary." I thought of my Aunt Hazel, a master gardener with a penchant for odd and unusual plants. I turned my Mini Cooper onto the long driveway and pulled up to the front of the house.

My breath caught when I saw the decades-old structure. I'd expected to see the aging but still proud home that my grandfather and his ancestors had lived in, but it didn't look at all like I remembered from childhood. My dad had called it a classic Italianate with "square belvederes instead of round cupolas, wide eaves with cast-iron brackets, and a U-shaped crown in the center with rounded windows on either side."

To me, the house looked more like a tiered wedding cake, with six small rooms on the first floor—a kitchen, dining room, parlor, foyer, entryway, and walk-in closet—plus five bedrooms on the second floor for guests, four rooms on the third for my aunts, and a roomy attic at the top. Nestled among local wildflowers—poppies, forget-me-nots, thistles, mustard—and flanked by coastal redwoods and cypress trees, it had felt magical to me at a kid. My father had told me that in its heyday, the house was quite a showplace. But after my grandfather died six months ago, I had a feeling the place might have fallen into disrepair. My dad mentioned that his father had been having trouble keeping up with the repairs, so I'd pictured peeling paint, rickety staircases, and abundant weeds.

I wasn't even close. As I stared at the newly renovated bed and breakfast inn, I wondered, *What on earth have my aunts done to the family home?*

Instead of a stately manor for a distinguished family, it looked more like a haunted house from a movie set. The once white exterior walls were now painted black, accented by purple and green trim on the windows, doors, belvederes, and eaves. Purple curtains covered the two front windows, and a couple of carved gargoyles perched on the belvederes. I noticed a murder of crows lined the edge of the roof, adding the perfect Gothic touch.

Before I could wrap my head around all this, I heard someone call my name.

"Carissa! Carissa Blackwood!"

I looked out the windshield of my Mini to see my sweet-natured Aunt Hazel standing on the wide porch. She pulled off her gardening gloves and then held onto her straw hat as she rushed down the steps to greet me. At sixty, she was puffing by the time she reached my car, her cheeks rosy, her eyes glistening.

"I was beginning to worry!" she said.

I got out of the car to meet her. She embraced me so tightly, I had to pull back in order get a breath.

"Sorry it took me so long, Aunt Hazel," I said when I could talk again. "There was a lot of traffic driving up from the city. It seems everyone wants to escape to the coast."

My aunt held me at arm's length and looked me over. "Well, I'm just glad you made it, safe and sound. That windy, narrow road can be treacherous."

I looked down at her five-foot-five stature from my five-ten height. "You haven't changed a bit!" I lied.

I wished it were true, but she had changed considerably since the last time I'd seen her, nearly twenty years ago. Gone was the slim figure, the long blond hair, the form-fitting dresses she'd worn. She'd put on some weight, her hair had turned white, and she wore stretch-waist jeans and a red camp shirt embroidered with cats and embellished with fresh dirt from her treasured gardens. On her feet, she sported a pair of well-worn, once white athletic shoes. But the sparkle in her eyes hadn't diminished a bit, nor had the sly smile accented in red lipstick.

"Well, *you* have!" Aunt Hazel said, looking up at me. "The last time I saw you, you were, what—nine or ten? I can't believe it's been that long. You've grown into such a beautiful young woman, just like your mother. Tall, slim, same long brown hair and green eyes. Thank goodness you didn't get the family nose from your father's side."

I heard a loud creak that came from the front of the house and glanced over, expecting to see my Aunt Runa. The door was ajar, but there was no sign of her. Instead, a small orange streak bolted out from the open doorway. The cat leaped onto a nearby cypress tree, scaled the trunk until it reached the roof of the house, then disappeared behind the belvedere.

I caught a glimpse of a lacy lavender curtain fluttering in a third-floor window. Behind it I thought I saw the outline of a figure. I couldn't make out the features, but I guessed it was Aunt Runa, Aunt Hazel's older sister and her sometimes nemesis.

I pointed at the window. "Is that Aunt Runa up there?"

Aunt Hazel followed my gaze. When she turned back to me, she seemed puzzled.

I looked again. The curtain was still. The figure had disappeared. I frowned. "Sorry. I thought I saw someone."

Aunt Hazel shrugged. "Never mind. Come on in. I'll show you around, give you a cup of my special herbal tea and one of Marnie's delicious caramel-pecan brownies. Runa and I are so glad you're here."

"Just a sec," I said as I popped the trunk and started to retrieve my suitcases.

"Leave those," my aunt said. "Noah will bring them up to your room."

I looked around for someone named Noah, but the yard was deserted.

"Come on, now," my aunt insisted. "I want to show you what we've done to the place, then we'll have tea."

Well, I thought, *if the outside of the house is any indication, they've done a lot. Maybe too much.*

I knew moving to Pelican Point would be an adjustment, but I had no choice at this point in my life. My dad had warned me the former logging and fishing community had changed a lot since my grandfather's day. These days the town thrived on tourist money, offering remote getaways from the bustling city and boring suburbs. He'd called it a "quaint little town," with cute cafés and ice cream parlors. Quaint—and quiet—were what I needed after all the divorce drama, not to mention watching my career as a ghostwriter take a dive. I looked forward to a change of scenery and a chance to reboot. When my dad told me my aunts were turning the old homestead into the Blackwood Bed and Breakfast Inn and needed help with the startup, I packed my bags.

Stepping over a black cat lying in the entryway, I found my Aunt Runa waiting for me inside. If she had just rushed down three flights of stairs to greet me, she was in better shape than I was. I would have been hyperventilating.

"Carissa!" Aunt Runa said, her voice two octaves lower than her sister's higher, babyish voice. She gathered me in an awkward, stiff embrace, then stood back and tilted her head. "Look at you!"

She gave me the once over and I did the same to her.

Aunt Runa couldn't have been more different from Aunt Hazel. Granted, they both had the slightly bumpy Blackwood nose, but aside from that, they were like night and day. At six feet tall, Aunt Runa was as thin as a rail and towered over Aunt Hazel. She wore her dyed black hair in a severe short bob, parted down the middle, with heavy bangs, and a streak of purple on one side. Although the day's fog had lifted, she was dressed in a long black jumper over a gray shirt, and wore black flats. A necklace with an interesting pendant hung from around her neck.

"You must be in great shape," I said. "You got down the stairs so fast."

Aunt Runa shot Aunt Hazel an odd look I couldn't read, but my dad had warned me that the sisters always had a special unspoken connection he never understood. I broke the awkward silence that followed. "Anyway, it's so wonderful to see you both again."

I looked back and forth between them, drinking in the memories that flooded my brain. Aunt Runa was a year older than Aunt Hazel and had never let her younger sister forget it. Their mother had died suddenly when they were young, and Aunt Runa had taken on the role of parenting in spite of Aunt Hazel's constant objections. My dad, the adored baby in the family, said the two girls fought throughout their childhood and were never close even as adults. Now that they were both widowed, they'd finally come together again in their old home. After the death of their father, Abraham Blackwood, they and my dad had inherited the Pelican Point property. He wanted nothing to do with the place, and decided he and my mother would prefer to travel the country in their newly purchased RV. Since neither of my aunts was willing to give up their share, they decided to move in together and turn it into a themed bed and breakfast inn. According to my dad, the renovations, along with the arguments, had begun immediately after.

I stepped through the entryway and glanced around at the remodeled foyer. I had only fleeting memories of the last time I'd visited the place as a kid, and I recalled dark rooms with busy, flocked wallpaper and heavy, florid furniture. There had always been hints of secret passageways and hidden rooms which, unfortunately, I never found, as much as I searched. Now it looked as if the inside of the house had been decorated by the witches of Disney.

"Amazing!" was all I could say about the dramatic changes, taking in the purple and green striped wallpaper, the spiderweb throw rug, and the hanging antique Tiffany lights.

"We couldn't have done it without our handyman Noah and our housekeeper Marnie's help," Aunt Hazel said. "Marnie helped us pick out the antique roll-top desk for you to use, the embroidered loveseats, and the Art Deco side tables. You know, she was dad's housekeeper for years. We're lucky to have her."

"And Noah did most of the renovations," Aunt Runa added. "He's a master at carpentry and can fix anything electrical."

"I think you'll like him," Aunt Hazel added with a wink.

What was that about? I wondered.

"Well, it's really . . . amazing, what you've done," I said again. What else could I say? I nodded at the vintage Ouija boards and tarot cards that were framed and hung on the walls. "Aunt Runa, I see you're still a fan of the occult. And Aunt Hazel, your displays of antique medicine bottles and herbal plants are . . . fascinating." I eyed the items propped on the small tables.

"Oh, thank you," Aunt Hazel said. "You know, my herbs can cure everything from eczema to irritable bowel syndrome. Let me know if you need anything."

TMI, I thought, wincing.

The Tiffany lamp swayed overhead, catching my eye. I glanced up to see what looked like a shiny black rock the size of a Ping-Pong ball dangling from the chain attached to the stained-glass light fixture.

I took a step back. "Goodness. What is that?"

"Oh, just one of my crystals," Aunt Runa said matter of factly, as if everyone had crystals hanging around.

Aunt Hazel scoffed. "Silly New Age stuff, if you ask me."

"No, it's not," Aunt Runa said, obviously taking offense. "Crystals have healing powers, just as much of your medicinal plants. And they've been around a lot longer."

Aunt Hazel shook her head. "You'll spook the guests with all the rocks you've got tucked around the house. Is that the kind of energy you want for our inn?"

"I've always loved your gemstone collection, Aunt Runa," I offered. "When I was a kid, I used to play with them and pretend they were special treasures with superpowers."

Aunt Runa grinned. "There, you see?" she said to Aunt Hazel. "Even Carissa believes in my crystals."

I was about to say I wouldn't go that far, when she added, "And by the way, they do have superpowers, as you called it.

Different crystals can do different things, like promote positive energy and get rid of negative energy, and heal the mind, body, and spirit."

"Really? What does that one do?" I pointed at the pendant around her neck.

She grasped the purple crystal and rubbed it with her fingers. "My amethyst? It promotes serenity and emotional balance, among other things." She shot a look at Aunt Hazel, who rolled her eyes. "Never mind her, Carissa. I'll give you a clear quartz crystal. It releases positive energy and removes negative energy, and balances emotional and spiritual places. Or maybe a smoky quartz. It not only will protect you, but it will help you get rid of any emotional baggage."

Wouldn't hurt, I thought. I had plenty of baggage from my divorce.

"Well, those jagged black rocks you've sprinkled around the house look like cat poop," Aunt Hazel said. "If one of the guests steps on one, it'll probably slice off a toe."

Aunt Runa sighed. "For your information, black obsidian is an excellent tool for increasing one's psychic abilities."

"Is that what's hanging from the light?" I asked. "Black obsidian?"

"No, that's black tourmaline, not volcanic glass," Aunt Runa said. "It's probably the most powerful crystal of all because it not only creates a protective shield and blocks out negative energy, but it also keeps you from having psychic attacks."

Psychic attacks! What the hell?

"Listen, Runa," Aunt Hazel said. "If you want to keep evil away, you need to let me hang up more blackberry and clove wreaths instead of using those silly rocks. I'm telling you, you're going to creep out the guests."

Yep, still bickering after all these years. I wondered if I'd made a mistake coming here. But I really didn't have any other place to go, since my divorce had left me with virtually nothing and my ghostwriting gigs for mystery authors had dwindled down to nearly nothing.

My dad knew I was good with marketing, creating websites, and promoting the authors I had written for. That was another reason he'd suggested I help manage the B and B. Hopefully I'd have some time left over to write my own mystery novel, and maybe even support myself with my writing. That was my plan, anyway.

A loud thump interrupted my thoughts. It had also come from overhead—above the ceiling. Was someone on the second floor?

"Do you have guests already?" I asked. "I thought you weren't opening the inn until the weekend."

Aunt Hazel shrugged. "It was probably Noah, dropping off your suitcases. Your room is upstairs."

"Or maybe it was one of the cats," Aunt Runa added with a raised eyebrow. "They're always coming and going."

I glanced toward the staircase on the right side of the entryway. "Really? I didn't see anyone come in."

Aunt Hazel shot Aunt Runa another odd look. "Oh, well," she said. "That's easy to explain. There's a back entrance, dear, for the staff, with a hidden staircase."

"Seriously? Just like in a Nancy Drew mystery!"

Aunt Runa raised any eyebrow. "Oh, you just wait," she said cryptically, the Blackwood twinkle in her eye.

"By the way," Aunt Hazel said, "we've got all the ghostwritten books you've collaborated on."

I blushed. "Really? All of them?"

"I think so, unless we missed one," Aunt Hazel said. "Your dad kept us up-to-date on all your publications. They're on a shelf in the parlor. We're hoping you'll sign them for us."

"Of course," I said, touched by the gesture. "I had no idea."

"My favorite was the one called *Murder in a Locked Room*, from that series by what's-her-name—that bestselling author. You know—the one who wrote *Murder in a Cozy Village* and *Murder on a Dark and Stormy Night*."

"Ah, Patricia Patterson," I said. It stung a little to say her name, since she'd recently replaced me with a new ghostwriter.

"I have to say, however," Aunt Hazel continued, "I figured out the killer after the first chapter in that last one."

"Aha," I said, smiling graciously. "I'll have to be more careful next time." If there was a next time.

Aunt Runa shook her head. "Oh, ignore her. So, tell me. Was that scene in *Murder in the Graveyard* inspired by that time you poisoned your father?"

"Runa!" Aunt Hazel cried, shooting her a daggered glare.

Runa shrugged. "I'm just asking."

So they *did* remember, after all.

Back when I'd visited as a kid, Aunt Hazel had told me about the special gardens she grew at her own place, filled with curing herbs and botanical remedies. I was so excited by what I'd learned from her that when I returned home, I collected a few local herbs of my own, along with some wild mushrooms and a handful of pyracantha berries for color. I blended everything together with a little soda water and served this tasty brew to my father in one of his shot glasses. He'd already had a few drinks by then, so throwing caution to the wind, he downed it and declared it "oddly tasty, with a hint of something musty." An hour later, he was in the emergency room having his stomach pumped.

How was I to know I'd made a poisonous cocktail?

Sometime later, I learned more about my aunts and their peculiar hobbies via whispered familial asides. Besides growing therapeutic herbs, Aunt Hazel also grew deadly poisonous plants in her "special" garden. Meanwhile, not only was Aunt Runa into crystals, but she also gave tarot readings, created astrology charts, and used a Ouija board.

Like I said, they were a little woo-woo.

And as it turned out, I didn't know the half of it.

Chapter Two
What Was That Noise?

"Follow me," Aunt Runa said. "I'll show you to your room. You'll probably want to get settled in after your long drive." As she led the way up the creaking stairs, Aunt Hazel, trailing behind me, said, "Watch your step."

I looked down just in time to keep from squashing the orange cat I'd seen leaving the house earlier—or were there two of them? Startled, the cat darted up the stairs and out of sight. How had it gotten back into the house so fast? Was there a secret passageway for cats? I had to zigzag the rest of the way to avoid two black cats, both lounging on the staircase.

"As you know, we open next weekend," Aunt Hazel said. "We've already got a full house. All four rooms are booked, and there's a waiting list. But we do need help with so many of the details, running an inn."

"A full house? That's wonderful," I said, joining her on the second-floor landing. "As for the details, as you call them, that's what I'm here for." I glanced at the sign that hung on the left bedroom door. It read, "Sleepy Hollow." A framed picture of a dark rearing horse was tacked underneath.

Aunt Hazel opened the door and I peeked inside.

"Wow," I whispered as I entered.

The room was filled with early American antiques, along with images and objects from one of my favorite childhood stories, *The Legend of Sleepy Hollow* by Washington Irving. A quilt featuring a fall scene with scarecrows, pumpkins, and hay bales covered the queen-size bed, while ceramic pumpkins sat on the twin nightstands. The scent of pumpkin wafted up from a gourd-shaped room defuser, enhancing the New England autumn ambiance. Painted portraits of Ichabod Crane, Katrina Van Tassel, and Beau Brummel hung on three walls, but what caught my attention was the silhouette of the Headless Horseman that took up the entire wall behind the bed. I wasn't sure I'd want to sleep in a room with a headless dude watching over me. The story had scared me as a kid, and I shivered at the memory of that dark figure who'd filled the townspeople with fear.

"This is amazing!"

"Thank you, dear," Aunt Hazel said. "At first we thought about using a strictly mystery theme with rooms featuring Miss Marple, Sherlock Holmes, Jessica Fletcher—"

Aunt Runa cut her off. "Then we figured a ghost theme would be better. You know, like *Ghostbusters*, *Beetlejuice*, *Casper the Friendly Ghost*, *The Haunted Mansion*—"

"And then I thought it would be fun to use horror movies," Aunt Hazel continued, "and take ideas from *Poltergeist*, *The Exorcist*, *Halloween*—"

"But then we decided that might be too scary for some people," Aunt Runa said, "so we each just chose our favorites and went with those. Wait until you see the other three guest rooms."

Murder at Blackwood Inn

I walked around the room admiring the details my aunts had put into creating the decor, then stopped at the window that looked out the front and pulled back the lacy curtain. I noticed a tall, muscular-looking guy wearing classic jeans, a form-fitting black T-shirt, and a black baseball cap over his dark hair. He stood near my car, then suddenly looked up at the window.

I dropped the curtain, a little embarrassed I'd been caught watching him. I turned to my aunts hovering in the doorway and asked, "Who's the guy down by my car?"

Aunt Hazel joined me at the window and peered out. "Who, dear?"

I looked down again. The man was gone.

"Oh, I thought I saw someone . . . a guy," I said, frowning. "He was by my car. He's gone now."

Aunt Hazel patted my shoulder. "We get a lot of that here."

I raised an eyebrow at her. "What do you mean? You get a lot of men looking up at your windows? Or people who suddenly disappear?"

Aunt Hazel giggled. "Come along, now. We don't want to let the Headless Horseman out, do we?"

Oookay.

While I knew my aunts were eccentric, I didn't know to what degree. They'd been raised by their "spirited" father, Abraham Blackwood, who later in life was rumored to hold fake séances, "read" palms, and pretend to tell fortunes using tarot cards—mostly to women. At least, that's what my dad had said. Now that I was here, I sensed Aunt Runa was a chip off the old block with her interest in the occult. My dad had also said my grandfather had become a bit paranoid near the end of his life. He claimed the house was haunted and that he "saw things." My dad attributed it to the onset of undiagnosed dementia.

But did my aunts also believe there was something supernatural about this place?

That was just crazy talk, wasn't it? Still, it seemed like a great gimmick to lure in tourists, since the inn was already booked to capacity and had a waiting list.

"All right, you two," I said, as I closed the bedroom door behind me. "I know you want your guests to think this old house is filled with ghosts and spirits and whatever. Granted, some people love the idea of staying in a haunted bed and breakfast. But you don't need to try to convince me. I'll play along."

My aunts locked eyes just before we continued down the hall.

They showed me the remaining three guest rooms with door signs that read, "Ghostbusters," "Scooby-Doo," and "The Birds." Each one had a framed portrait to go with the name plate. And each room was more intriguing than the last, embellished with Hollywood-style objects and images related to the various themes. I'd read about the popularity of macabre events like horror camping and zombie trains, and overnights held at abandoned prisons or places like Lizzie Borden's house, so it wasn't exactly a surprise that people would actually pay to stay in these creeped-out rooms.

My aunts were either insane or brilliant. Maybe both.

"How did you get the idea for all this?" I asked.

"Easy," Aunt Runa said. "We both like horror films, and it turns out a lot of scary movies have been filmed in this area—*The Birds, The Fog, Halloween, Scream*. But like I said, we didn't want it to be too spooky, so we kept it family friendly."

"Carissa, your room is at the end of the hall," Aunt Hazel said as we left the last guest room. "You have your own private bathroom, and you can use the secret staircase at the back of the hallway to come and go, if you want to avoid the ghosts . . . er, guests."

I rolled my eyes. "Very funny."

"I hope you like your room," Aunt Hazel said with an odd grin.

Uh-oh, I thought. What horrors had my crazy aunts prepared for me? A gory scene from *Carrie*'s prom night? The bleeding bedroom from *Amityville*? Or would I just see "dead people" under the bed?

Aunt Runa stopped at the last door. The sign read: "River Heights—Private Residence." On the door was a black silhouette of a girl holding a magnifying glass. It was set inside a wreath made of dried blackberries and some kind of twisted vine.

Aunt Runa unlocked the door with her key, then stepped back so I could enter.

My breath caught as I took it all in. "Oh my God. This . . . is . . . incredible!"

I felt like I'd just arrived in Nancy Drew's bedroom. The Girl Sleuth was evident everywhere I looked, beginning with the blue color scheme right off the cover of the original Nancy Drew mysteries. The comforter featured images of the young detective from her early books when she wore ankle-length "frocks" and cloche hats that covered her titian hair. On the wall hung painted portraits of Nancy over the years, along with her chums, Bess and George, and her dreamboat boyfriend, Ned Nickerson. Displayed on a shelf were items from

Nancy's sleuth kit—a magnifying glass, binoculars, a flashlight, some candles and matches, even a bottle of "Smelling Salts" in case someone fainted and had to be revived. It happened all the time in Nancy Drew mysteries. Naturally there was a bookcase full of classic Nancy Drew mysteries. From the tattered edges, they looked like originals.

"Unbelievable!" I cried. "After all these years, you remembered!"

"Of course, dear," Aunt Runa said. "You were such a big fan of the girl from River Heights. That's probably where you got your love of writing whodunits. Although at the time, I thought you might become a Girl Sleuth yourself."

Me too, I thought wistfully.

"Hazel bought the comforter from Etsy and collected the sleuthing supplies," Aunt Runa continued. "Marnie did the artwork. And Noah painted the room and built the desk, bookcase, and window seat."

"And the wreath?" I asked, not remembering it from any of the Nancy Drew mysteries.

Aunt Hazel shrugged. "I added that, just for extra protection."

From what? I wondered.

Aunt Runa shot her a knowing look. *What was with all those looks?*

"Well, I'm touched by the details and your obvious care. It's perfect. Thank you." I gave them each a hug.

Out of the corner of my eye, I thought I saw the bedspread ruffle move. A chill ran down my back. I leaned over and slowly lifted the ruffle. The orange cat—the same one?—darted out from its hiding place, startling me. It leaped onto the padded window seat and dashed out the half-open window.

Murder at Blackwood Inn

"Sorry about that," Aunt Runa said. "That's just Pyewacket. Did he scare you?"

I fake-laughed at my uneasiness. *What had I been expecting? Actual dead people under the bed?*

"No," I lied.

Aunt Hazel sighed. "Poor Pye. He must have gotten trapped in this room again. He's always hiding in here, no doubt waiting for Father to return. He died in here, you know, in that bed. We try to keep Pye out, but he always finds a way to sneak in."

"Grandfather died in this room?" I asked, somewhat surprised and a little disturbed.

Aunt Hazel nodded. "Mysteriously, you know."

Aunt Runa glared at Aunt Hazel. "No, he didn't," she scoffed. "He died of natural causes—old age."

Aunt Hazel shrugged. "Maybe. All I know is, he thought he was becoming a little paranoid at the end. Thought for sure the house was haunted by the original owner, an old sea captain. At least, that's what we heard from Marnie. She came over from Scotland years ago and has—had—been with him ever since."

Aunt Runa shook her head. "It's all nonsense. Spread by a few of the townspeople."

Aunt Hazel bit her lip. She looked as if she had more to say, but before she could add anything, Aunt Runa said, "Just be careful of Pye. He's not the friendliest cat around."

I was more of a dog lover than a cat fan, so avoiding Pyewacket wouldn't be difficult. I just hoped he stayed out of my room and there were no more surprise visits. Of any kind.

"Are those two black cats on the staircase friendly?" I asked.

"Oh, yes. And so are the others," Aunt Runa answered.

I blinked. "Others?"

"We have seven cats total," Aunt Hazel said. "All rescues, I might add." She began counting on her fingers. "Let's see, there's Azrael, Glinda, Lucifer, Hermione, Maleficent, and Wendy. All black except Pye."

"Seven cats?"

"Seven is my lucky number," Aunt Runa said.

"Not thirteen?" I asked, teasing.

Aunt Runa frowned. "Thirteen cats? Now that would just be crazy."

Of course it would. "You gave them such cute names," I said, not knowing what else to say.

Aunt Hazel nodded. "They're all named after famous characters."

"I figured that," I said. "I think you've covered the *Smurfs*, *The Wizard of Oz*, *Cinderella*, *Harry Potter*, *Sleeping Beauty*, and *Casper the Friendly Ghost*."

"Don't forget Pyewacket from *Bell, Book, and Candle*," Aunt Hazel added.

"So how do you tell them all apart?" I asked.

"It's easy. Just look at their eyes," Aunt Runa said.

Well, that made no sense.

"I'm glad you know your mystical characters, Carissa," Aunt Runa said.

"How could I not, with a grandfather like Bram Blackwood and the two of you."

My aunts exchanged another cryptic look. If I didn't know better, I'd think these two had some kind of sisterly ESP. I frowned. "Did I say something wrong?"

Aunt Hazel sighed. "It's just that we don't use the nickname Bram for Father. It makes him sound like . . ."

"A vampire or something," Aunt Runa added, finishing her sister's sentence. "The townspeople may still call him Bram behind our backs, but we prefer his given name, Abraham Blackwood. It sounds more . . . distinguished."

That will take some getting used to, I thought. I'd never heard anyone at home call him anything but Bram.

"We'll leave you to settle in," Aunt Runa said, bringing the discussion to an end.

Aunt Hazel nodded. "When you're ready, come down to the parlor and we'll have some of my special ginseng tea and chat."

"That would be lovely," I said. "Thank you both for all you've done for me already." I gave each one another hug before they left and closed the door behind them.

As I explored the room, I thought I smelled a hint of basil. *Some kind of room deodorizer?* Or one of Aunt Hazel's special herb concoctions to keep me safe. I couldn't help but appreciate the care and thoughtfulness that went into the decor, everything from the iconic sleuth stuff to the girl detective's favorite color blue. They'd also hung a vintage trench coat, silk scarf, and cloche hat on the coat rack in the corner, all ready and waiting for Nancy to wear while solving one of her puzzling cases. My aunts were truly creative, even if they were a bit peculiar. I had a feeling the Blackwood Bed and Breakfast Inn—and Herbiary—would be a hit with Pelican Point tourists.

"Time to unpack," I said to myself as I scanned the room for my two suitcases. I assumed the guy I'd seen by my car had brought them up. Noah, was it? But after a thorough search in the closet, bathroom, and under the bed, my bags were nowhere to be found.

I opened the bedroom door to go track them down and came face-to-face with the man I'd seen from the window. He stood just outside the doorway flanked by my suitcases, his right fist raised as if ready to hit me.

I jumped back. "Oh! You scared me!"

"Sorry," he said. His voice was low and smooth. "I was just about to knock."

I sized him up as he stood in front of me. Thirtysomething. Tall, maybe six feet two to my five feet ten, with chocolate-brown eyes that seemed to look right through me. He'd removed his hat, revealing thick dark hair that matched his neatly trimmed beard. I couldn't help but notice how his black T-shirt outlined his muscular chest and arms.

He extended a large hand. "I'm Noah."

Deciding that he wasn't a serial killer—not with my suitcases propped next to him—I took his hand. It felt strong and callused—a working man's hand—and it gave me a slight jolt when he gently shook mine.

Where had that come from?

I stood there for an awkward moment, his eyes holding mine, before he finally said, "So, where would you like these?"

I swallowed and swept open the door to allow him inside. "Oh, anywhere is fine. Thanks for bringing them up."

"No problem." He lifted the suitcases as if they were weightless and placed them on the padded window seat, a cozy spot for reading, writing, or just gazing at the view of the sprawling gardens. When he was done, he turned to me. "Do you need anything else?"

For a moment, I thought about tipping him before I remembered I wasn't at a hotel and this was no bellhop. "No, thanks."

"Okay, then . . ." He headed for the door.

"Are you . . . do you work for my aunts full time?" I asked, curious about him and his duties at the inn.

"I help out when they need me, which seems to be most of the time. Carpentry, electrical, plumbing, repairs, that kind of thing. There's always something to fix in this old house, especially now that the Blackwood Inn is about to open."

"Have you always done handyman work?"

"In some form or another," he said mysteriously. He reached into his pocket and pulled out a card, then handed it to me. "If you need anything," he added. The card read simply, "Noah O'Gara," with a cell number underneath.

When I looked up from the card, Noah had vanished. I stepped into the hall, but there was no sign of the handyman. Still, the sensation from his touch remained. I reentered my room and closed the door, then remembered the loud thud I'd heard when I'd first entered the Blackwood Inn. My aunts had said it was probably Noah dropping off my suitcases.

But Noah had only brought them up a few minutes ago.

So what had made that loud thud on the second floor? One of those darn cats?

And who had fluttered the curtains in the third-floor window when I'd arrived? Another one of the cats? *Right.*

I thought about Pyewacket, the orange cat that had been hiding under the bed in my room. What was it Aunt Hazel had said? Something about how he seemed to be waiting here for his master to return? The room where my grandfather had died.

My room.

Aunt Hazel had let slip that it might have been a mysterious death, but Aunt Runa had quickly vetoed it. I'd have to check into it, that is, if I planned to get a good night's sleep in this creaky old place.

Maybe Noah the Handyman could tell me more about the Blackwood family home, the death of my grandfather, and what had happened in this room.

If I could catch him before he disappeared.

Chapter Three
Stranger in a Strange Land

A peaceful night's sleep eluded me the rest of the week, thanks to things that went bump in the night. I hoped the noises were made by cats. The days were filled with the minutiae of preparing to open the inn, which kept me too busy to do much research on the house, my grandfather, or the mysterious handyman. I caught glimpses of Noah from time to time, but he seemed to vanish as quickly as he appeared.

My aunts and their team of housekeeper and handyman had done a lot to make the house unique and inviting, in keeping with their theme of scary-but-not-too-scary movies. To welcome the guests, Aunt Hazel had prepared her special green tea with lemon (to remove toxins), cinnamon blueberry scones (for energy and antioxidants), and local honey (to prevent allergies). Aunt Runa bought local wines and cheeses for happy hour. And Marnie whipped up adorable white chocolate ghosts to present at bedtime.

While my aunts had spent considerable effort on these details, they'd let the business end of the B and B slide. Thanks to Google, Reddit, Quora, and Wikihow, I soon had a fairly good grasp of the inn-keeping trade. But when I opened the registration book, it looked more like one of Aunt Hazel's scrapbooks than a ledger. Instead of carefully listing information about each of the expected guests, she had just jotted down names, dates, and credit card numbers on random pieces of paper—old napkins, torn envelopes, the backs of recipe cards—then simply jammed them between the pages of the book. It took me hours to properly organize and record the information in my laptop. And that was just the beginning.

By Friday I was mostly caught up with the books and the website, but the late hours and restless nights had taken their toll on my energy level, and Aunt Hazel's special tea had yet to do the trick. When I padded into the large, cozy kitchen one morning wearing Nancy's scarlet slippers and the blue chenille robe my aunts had left for me, they noticed immediately.

"You look tired, dear," Aunt Runa said, frowning at me as she put down the local newspaper she'd been reading. She was dressed for the day in a dark blue skirt and matching shirt, and was wearing a different crystal pendant, this one a stunning iridescent play of colors. "Here. Wear this."

She pulled a pendant from her pocket and handed it to me. I examined the delicate pink crystal, then slipped it on over my head.

"Clear quartz," she said. "It should give you some energy."

"Thank you," I said, feeling the weight of it. "It's beautiful." I gestured toward hers. "Yours is beautiful too."

"Labradorite," Aunt Runa said, touching it. "Good for enhancing intuition as well as energy. I have a feeling I'm going to need it now that opening day is upon us."

Aunt Hazel, still in her pink-striped bathrobe and puffy slippers, stopped steeping her tea and stared at me. "Well, I think you've been working too hard, Carissa. Peppermint tea should do the trick."

I wanted to say, "I look tired because you left the business end of this place in a mess," but I didn't. Instead, I said, "I'm sure things will get easier now that I've updated the guest book, registration, and website."

"Are you sleeping all right?" Aunt Runa asked, eyes narrowed, her frown deepening. It was as if she'd read my mind.

"Not really. I've been having these weird dreams—" My words were interrupted by a black cat leaping off one of the kitchen chairs. My thoughts wandered to visions of stealthy black cats, vanishing ghosts, and weird creatures from beyond the grave. I snapped myself back to reality before my aunts actually *did* read my mind.

"I'm sure you know how it is," I said. "Sleeping in a new bed in a strange place. But I'll get used to it."

In truth, I wondered if I'd ever get used to those "bumps in the night." There was nothing quite like staying in a supposedly haunted house to discourage a solid night's sleep. I wrote off the creaks and moans to the continued settling of the old place, and decided I'd buy some earplugs and an eye mask to help me sleep. But I doubted I could stop my imagination from conjuring up more creepy scenes. Not to mention the thought of my grandfather dying in what was now my bed.

"Hmm. Maybe pomegranate tea would be better for you," Aunt Hazel said. "It's full of antioxidants, plus it helps prevent cancer, heart disease, and erectile dysfunction."

I frowned. *What was she suggesting?*

"Got any coffee?" I asked, a request for my drug of choice.

"Try one of the apple-pecan muffins Marnie made this morning," Aunt Hazel continued. "They're better for you than caffeine, and the pecans will give you some energy. The nuts came from our trees out back, all organic, of course. The tea leaves are from my garden."

"Which garden, exactly?" I asked her, as I accepted the warm cup of fragrant liquid. I was obviously making a reference to the garden where she grew her "special" plants.

"Well, not the one you're implying," Aunt Hazel said.

"You mean her poison garden, don't you," Aunt Runa said. She turned to her sister. "You know, Hazel—the one where you cultivate killers like belladonna, oleander, dieffenbachia, castor bean, monkshood, lily of the valley, foxglove, elderberry, nightshade, and hemlock. Did I miss any?"

Aunt Hazel scoffed. "Hush, Runa. You know I keep those plants locked up so animals and whatnot can't get to them."

Whatnot? Like people?

She handed me a small, delicate china plate that held a warm, fragrant scone. I stared at it a few seconds, eyeing the suspicious green flecks.

"Don't worry, that's just bits of sage," Aunt Hazel said, again reading my mind. "From my *herb* garden."

I took a bite. It was a melt-in-your-mouth combination of savory and sweet. I'd never been a big fan of scones. They were usually dry and tasteless. But this was a whole new experience.

Aunt Runa cleared her throat again. "Personally, I think it's ridiculous to keep a bunch of poisonous plants on the property." As she folded up the *Pelican Point Press*, I caught a glimpse of the headline.

"New Haunted House-Themed Inn to Open This Weekend." The article was written by someone named Aiden Quincy.

There was a picture of him next to his byline—thirtysomething, nice-looking, glasses, a friendly smile, chin-length wavy brown hair. I'd have to thank him for the publicity if I ever got a chance to meet him.

"Like I said, Runa," Aunt Hazel countered, "my special herbs are no more ridiculous than those crystals you've hidden throughout the house."

"They're not *hidden*," Aunt Runa argued. "They've been strategically placed to balance the energies of the inn and bring us good luck. I doubt if anyone will even notice them."

Hazel sighed. "If you say so."

After the past week, I was getting used to the bickering and barbs my aunts volleyed back and forth throughout the day. Why they'd decided to live together, let alone go into business together, was beyond me. While Aunt Hazel tended to be cheery, from her outfits to her outlook, Aunt Runa's dress and demeanor were more serious and severe.

According to my dad, although the sisters were both widowed when their husbands died of cancer within a year of each other, they had lived very different lives. Aunt Hazel had studied horticulture at the University of California and become a master gardener after completing the courses and passing an exam. She'd opened her own flower shop downtown for a while called The Red, Red Rose, but sold it after Alfred passed away.

Aunt Runa had pursued an education in metaphysical science, hoping to learn about holistic healing techniques. But she dropped out soon after she met and married her husband, Rodney. For a few years they owned a new age shop in town called Enchanted Elements, until a competing business, Tranquility Base, opened up across the street and drained most of their business. I'd heard Aunt Runa had done some consulting after Rodney passed, apparently making enough money to keep her in crystals.

I just hoped their competitive squabbling didn't interfere with the running of the inn—or turn into a scene from *What Ever Happened to Baby Jane*. As long as they kept their sharp repartee behind closed doors and not in front of the guests, I could live with it. I hoped.

"Mornin'," came a low voice behind me. I turned around to see Noah standing in the kitchen doorway, one hand holding a hammer, the other one tucked casually into a leather toolbelt. He was dressed in his usual well-worn, tight-fitting jeans, with a black T-shirt stretched across his chest. But this shirt included the words "Blackwood Bed and Breakfast Inn" embroidered in white lettering, with a black bird outlined in white on his right shoulder. He nodded at me, his dark eyes lingering on mine. I felt myself blush like a schoolgirl.

What was wrong with me?

I turned around to hide my reddening face and tried to concentrate on my growing to-do list.

"A cup of tea, Noah?" Aunt Hazel said, raising the cat-shaped teapot.

"No, thank you, ma'am," Noah said. "Just wanted to let you know I'm finished with the sign. I doubt anyone can knock it down now."

I looked up from my notes. "What sign? What happened?"

Aunt Runa shook her head. "Oh, some vandals took a baseball bat or something to our Blackwood Bed and Breakfast Inn sign last night."

"That's awful! Why would someone do that?" I wondered how I could have slept through that racket when the slightest creak in the house usually woke me up.

Murder at Blackwood Inn

Aunt Hazel's cheery smile drooped. "I guess not everyone in town is glad we're opening up the inn."

"Well," Noah said, "if you have any more trouble, let me know. They'll have to answer to me next time." He slapped the side of the hammer into his palm to make his point.

Whoa.

"Thank you, Noah," Aunt Hazel said, her face brightening.

I was beginning to love the way the handyman took such good care of my aunts. I smiled at him. He gave me a half smile back, then excused himself and vanished from the room so suddenly, I stared at the space he'd vacated as if expecting him to magically return.

"Carissa?" Aunt Hazel said.

I'd been so focused on Noah's disappearance, I hadn't noticed that my aunts were staring at me. Both had silly grins on their faces.

"What?" I asked, confronting them. I could feel my face fill with color.

"He *is* kind of dreamy, isn't he," Aunt Hazel said, peering at me over the edge of her teacup.

"I think he likes you," Aunt Runa added matter of factly.

I made a face. "What? No, he doesn't! That's crazy talk."

"We're sensitive to these things, dear, remember?" Aunt Hazel said, joining Aunt Runa and me at the table.

I'd once overheard them arguing about who had stronger "powers"—Aunt Hazel with her "weeds" or Aunt Runa with her "rocks." If they kept this up, they'd both end up in a mental institution. Or I would.

"Well, you're wrong about Noah," I argued. "I'm not interested. Not after my ex broke my heart, ran off with my best friend, and took most of my money. So if you'll excuse me, I have to prepare for tonight's preview party for the locals." I got up and set my teacup in the sink. "By the way, that was delicious tea. What else was in it besides pomegranate?"

Aunt Hazel held her cup up to inhale the spicy fragrance. "Oh, just a little of this, a little of that."

Top secret, eh? Yeah, I had a feeling there were a lot of secrets in this house.

Chapter Four
Epic Party Fail

The witching hour for the preview party finally arrived at six o'clock. The Blackwood Bed and Breakfast Inn was as ready to welcome the guests as it would ever be. My aunts had the brilliant idea of inviting some of the townspeople to visit the inn the night before opening day, so they would get a sense of the place and hopefully recommend it to tourists and visitors. Aunt Runa and Aunt Hazel might have been a little off center, but they weren't stupid. Not only was it a gesture of good will, but free food and drink never hurt a good promo opp.

The aromas coming from the kitchen made my mouth water as they wafted over to the rolltop desk where I was working in the foyer. My aunts and Marnie had been concocting fragrant goodies all day, and I couldn't wait to taste them. The table was set with a white tablecloth, black napkins, and the family heirloom china, white with gold trim. Aunt Hazel had arranged a floral centerpiece using a combination of yellow chrysanthemums from the garden placed among a spray of autumn ferns she'd purchased from the flower shop downtown. And Aunt Runa had placed one of her golden yellow, rusty brown, and black crystals called a tiger's eye in the middle of the display, and it shifted colors depending on the light. "For protection from negative energies," she said.

I just hoped Marnie's treats were potent enough to bring grins—and good reviews—from the guests. I had a feeling the success of the inn depended on this evening.

Unfortunately, I hadn't had the heart to tell my aunts that the expected turnout would probably be dismally low. Only a handful of the invitees had responded positively to my e-vite. It was as if there was some kind of underground boycott going on. I wondered if the ones who planned to show up had ulterior motives. Of course, that was ridiculous, and I wrote off my misgivings to lack of sleep, spooky surroundings, and ghostwriting too many mysteries.

At ten after six, the doorbell rang, interrupting my morose suspicions that the event would be a disaster. As my aunts tittered in the kitchen, excited by the arrival of their first local guests, I opened the front door, hoping to get this party started.

A woman on the far side of middle age stood on the porch holding a slightly wilted bouquet of mixed flowers. Her face was painted with brightly hued makeup and she wore a flowery top and long skirt to match. The red crocheted cape would hardly have kept the foggy air from chilling her, and the silk scarf wrapped around her neck was overkill. She was a riot of color.

"Patty Fay! So nice to see you again," Aunt Hazel called as she entered from the kitchen. My aunt was all dressed up—at least, for her—in khaki slacks, a red-and-white-checked shirt, and red Converse high tops. I took the proffered bouquet from the real estate agent, which allowed Aunt Hazel to give Patty Fay Johnstone a warm hug.

Murder at Blackwood Inn

"Hazel, dear, so good to see you." Patty Fay lightly patted her on the back.

Aunt Runa approached them, wearing black slacks, a black linen top, and a long white tunic, and gave Patty Fay more of an "air hug." I'd met Patty Fay when she stopped in a few days ago to see how things were coming along with the inn. I'd learned she'd also helped my aunts with Grandfather's will after the local attorney, Andrew Jeffers, had some health issues. At the moment, she didn't seem to remember me.

"My dears," Patty Fay said to my aunts, "tell me. After all this work and expense and everything that comes with opening an inn, are you finally ready to sell this old monstrosity and find a nice new condo overlooking the water? I have just the place. It's perfect for watching the pelicans, the whales in the spring, and the sunsets while sipping those teas you like."

Aunt Runa had mentioned that the realtor tried to encourage them to sell the house soon after they inherited it, calling it a "termite-ridden money pit with a questionable history," but my aunts had refused. They'd had their hearts set on turning their father's home into an inn, and nothing could convince them otherwise: not termites, the cost of renovation, or rumors that the place was haunted. No doubt Patty Fay hoped to make a hefty commission if my aunts decided to sell, but that didn't appear to be in her astrological forecast.

"Oh, no!" Aunt Hazel said. "We just *love* being back here in the family home. Our guest rooms are fully booked and we officially open tomorrow afternoon!"

"Well, you have my number if you change your minds," Patty Fay said, her eyes darting around the entryway and foyer. I wondered if she was looking for something, or just taking stock of the renovations and decor. She whipped off her scarf and shawl and gave them to me as if I were her maid. I barely had time to hang them in the walk-in closet under the stairs before the next guests arrived. For a few moments, I thought maybe more folks had changed their minds and decided to come after all. But at final count, there were only five attendees, in addition to Marnie, my aunts, and myself. Disappointing, to say the least, but I tried not to let it show.

The guests gathered in the parlor and looked over the "unusual" decor. My aunts had filled the room with four cozy antique chairs and two matching sofas covered in dark blue velveteen, all arranged in a circle around a square coffee table. Aunt Hazel had set the fresh flowers she's arranged in the center of the table, and Aunt Runa had added small decorative bowls filled with "positive energy" crystals on the four end tables that flanked the couches. The walls featured flocked wallpaper with light blue fleur-de-lis designs against a light green background. They had hung portraits of their seven cats on the walls, outlined in black oval frames, their names printed underneath. The guests appeared wide-eyed and speechless.

Marnie, her hair tucked back in a bun and wearing her Blackwood Bed and Breakfast apron over a plain black dress, announced wine and appetizer service in the dining room. The guests followed her in, where she poured wine for those who wanted alcohol and served herbal tea to those who didn't. The table was soon filled with artful finger foods—plates of coconut prawns, bowls of shrimp cocktail, plates of cubed sour dough bread with hot crab dip, and air fryer calamari, all local and fresh from Sam's Seafood Market in town. Everything was arranged on large lettuce leaves and garnished with herbs from my aunt's garden.

I decided I should mingle and introduce myself to the guests I hadn't met yet. One woman who looked about Patty Fay's age caught my eye. I noticed she hadn't stopped frowning from the moment she'd walked in. She was dressed in a silky beige jumpsuit, accented with too much clunky, dangling gold jewelry around her neck and wrists and fingers, that sort of matched her gold-colored heels. I headed over to say hello.

"Hi. I'm Carissa Blackwood, Hazel and Runa's niece," I said, offering my hand. She reached out reluctantly and barely touched my fingertips, then pulled them back and fluffed her poufy blond-highlighted hair.

"Annabelle Topper," she said, then stopped suddenly and stared up at the crystal that hung from the light overhead. "The light fixture—it's swaying. Are we having an earthquake?"

I feigned a laugh. "Oh, that's just one of Aunt Runa's good luck charms. They seem to catch every little draft. She has them all around the house. You know, for good luck or something like that." I took a big swallow of my wine. Mingling and small talk weren't my strong suits, but I was good at drinking wine.

"Well, she's going to need all the good luck she can conjure up," Annabelle mumbled, fondling the large gold pelican flanked by pearly seashells that hung from around her fleshy neck.

"I'm sorry—what?" I asked, taken aback by her comment. Was that some kind of veiled threat?

"Listen, Melissa—" Annabelle began.

"It's Carissa," I corrected her.

"Whatever. I own the Pelican Point Inn, the highest rated accommodation in town. I've worked very hard to build up a superior reputation and make my inn the premier destination for tourists. I really doubt this place will meet the high standards I've set for my business. I mean, look around. Who decorated the place? Alfred Hitchcock?"

Before I could haul back and smack her, I was interrupted by laughter from a man who'd sneaked up behind me. I turned to him. He was tall, thin, maybe late fifties to early sixties. He held himself erect, as if he thought of himself as lord of the manor. His silver hair was perfectly coifed and matched his trimmed goatee.

"Harper Smith," he said, extending a thin, bony hand. "I live next door." He gestured toward a side window but with the trees, there were no other houses in view. "Beyond those eucalyptus trees."

"Hi. I'm Carissa Blackwood, the Blackwoods' niece." I nodded toward my aunts, who were standing at the dining room table chatting and fussing with the placement of the food.

"I own five acres," he continued, as if he hadn't heard me. "My house was built by my great-great-grandfather, who had over a hundred acres in Pelican Point. He practically owned the town. It was a shame he sold most of his land, because the newbies brought in all kinds of traffic and transients and trash." He sighed. "And now this." He waved his hand around and shook his head. "I'm mean, what on earth have your aunts done to the place? You look like a reasonable gal. Can't you talk some sense into them before our property values take a huge dive?"

I blinked. Who *were* these people?

"Will you excuse us?" I turned to see a thirtysomething man who'd come up beside me. He took my elbow and quickly whisked me away before I could do anything requiring a 911 call. "Don't let them get to you," he whispered. "They're long-timers here in Pelican Point, set in their ways. They don't like change. Personally, I think the house looks . . ." he glanced around, "interesting. I'm sure the Blackwood Bed and Breakfast Inn is going to be a great success."

I smiled at the nice guy who'd just rescued me. He looked familiar and I tried to place him. Had I seen him at one of the shops downtown?

"Thank you," I said. "I think you saved me from an embarrassing scene and a long jail sentence."

He laughed. His light brown hair was bohemian shaggy, chin length, and he had a trimmed beard that suited his casual look. He wore glasses, a tan jacket, and jeans, with brown Sperry Topsiders. Where had I seen him before?

"I'm Aiden Quincy, by the way. I publish the *Pelican Point Press*."

"Oh my goodness! Of course," I said, recalling his picture next to the article I'd seen earlier. "I should have recognized you right away from your newspaper photo. It's so great to meet you. I read your story this morning about the inn and wanted to thank you. That was so generous of you."

"Glad you liked it," he said with a broad smile. "Hope it helps business."

I offered my hand. "I'm Carissa Blackwood. The owners are my aunts." I indicated Aunt Hazel and Aunt Runa, who were now chatting with a petite woman about their age. The three seemed to be getting along well. I wondered who she was.

Aiden's eyes narrowed, as if trying to place me. "Ah. Carissa Blackwood. Nice to meet you." He took my hand and shook it firmly. It was softer than Noah's large, strong hand. This was a writer's hand.

"You too," I said.

He nodded toward the three women. "I see your aunts are getting an earful from Gracie Galloway," he said. "She's the town librarian-slash-historian. She probably knows more about the history of Pelican Point and the Blackwood house than anyone, including the original owners."

"Really," I said. While I'd only seen my grandfather a couple of times when I was a kid, my aunts had told me a few stories about his life, and a little about my great-grandfather, as well. I wondered if Gracie had heard the "haunted house" rumors too.

"I'm sure she'd love to fill you in," Aiden said, then noticed my empty glass. "How about another glass of wine?"

"I'd love one," I said, a little too eagerly. While Aiden headed for the dining table to get refills, I studied Gracie and wondered what stories she had to tell. The woman looked unassuming, almost frumpy, dressed in baggy brown slacks, a gray knitted sweater, and loafers, with no jewelry, scarf, or frills. I guessed she was single from the lack of a wedding ring on her finger. Widowed? Divorced? Never married? Although she was probably attractive at one time, she had a sad, weathered face, framed by blunt-cut salt-and-pepper hair parted down the middle. I wondered what *her* history was.

"Here you go," Aiden said, appearing with two fresh glasses. He handed me one, then raised a spoon and clinked it against his glass. At the sound, everyone turned to him.

"Attention, please! A toast!" He looked at my aunts and hoisted his glass. "Welcome to the Blackwood Bed and Breakfast Inn. Let's wish the Blackwood sisters great success!"

Aiden and I sipped from our wine, while my aunts beamed at the attention. I studied the others in the room. Patty Fay forced a smile and downed her glass quickly. Annabelle rolled her eyes and ignored her drink. Harper mumbled something I couldn't hear, then took a generous swig. Gracie sipped her tea.

A loud thud broke the post-toast silence.

"What was that?" Annabelle asked, her eyes wide as she stared up at the ceiling. The crystal was swaying again.

"Sounded like it came from upstairs," Harper said, gesturing with his glass.

"No worries," Aunt Hazel announced cheerfully. "This house makes all kinds of noises. It's probably just our resident ghost." She giggled.

There were a few murmurs and one uncomfortable laugh.

"A ghost," Patty Fay mumbled under her breath. "That's all we need."

I turned to shoot her a look, but a movement behind her caught my eye. Noah—standing in the shadows at the back of the room. Apparently he wasn't the one who'd made the noise. *One of the cats?*

I noticed he seemed to be staring at me. And frowning. *What was that about?*

I turned to Aiden. "Would you excuse me for a minute?"

"Of course," he said.

I set my drink down on the table, maneuvered around Patty Fay, Annabelle, and Harper, all engrossed in deep but muted conversation, and headed for Noah.

Naturally, by the time I got there, he had slipped away.

Shrugging, I returned to the dining room table for my drink. As soon as I retrieved my glass, the party came to an abrupt end. Annabelle announced she had to get back to her inn and see to her guests. The others added their excuses as they retrieved their coats and wraps from the closet. After token "Goodnights" and "Thank you," they all headed out, leaving behind several uncorked bottles of wine and trays nearly full of appetizers. Except for Patty Fay, who I'd seen wrapping up a handful in a napkin and slipping them into her purse. *A little midnight snack?*

As Aiden followed the other guests out, I got the feeling he wanted to say something more, but he just shook my hand again and said his door was always open if I needed any information about the town. Then he headed down the path to his Toyota.

I closed the door and let out a sigh. If my aunts noticed the lack of attendance, not to mention the lack of enthusiasm from those who did attend, they didn't say anything as they busied themselves with cleaning up. Only Marnie seemed visibly disappointed, mumbling under her breath as she cleared the table. Still, I had a hunch my aunts were feeling discouraged after all the hard work they'd put into their party.

As for me, I wasn't just discouraged. I was angry. It was small-town thinking at its worst. I promised myself I wasn't going to let these people interfere with my aunts' dreams. Maybe Annabelle's Pelican Point Inn *was* the best inn in town, but until now it had been the *only* inn in town. I planned to help make the Blackwood Bed and Breakfast Inn the best of its kind on the entire Northern California coast.

"I'm going to talk to Aiden about placing a regular ad in the *Pelican Point Press* to get the word out," I said to my aunts. "What do you think?"

"I think he's kind of cute," Aunt Hazel said, "in a nerdy kind of way." She winked at Runa, who scoffed.

I shook my head. "Don't get your hopes up, Aunt Hazel. He's really nice, but he's not my type."

"Oh, so you go for the bad boys, like your ex—."

"No," I argued, then wondered if she was right. "And would you please stop with the matchmaking!"

While my aunts and Marnie finished tidying up, I went over the reservations one last time to make sure we hadn't double-booked a room or overlooked a cancellation. Nope. Everything appeared to be in order. I hugged my aunts goodnight, nodded to Marnie, and headed off to bed with a cup of chamomile tea, "guaranteed" to help me sleep.

I was almost to the stairs when I heard Aunt Runa's agitated voice. "It was right here, in the middle of the floral centerpiece. Now it's gone."

I glanced back to see Aunt Hazel enter the dining room from the kitchen. "Are you sure? Maybe someone just moved it."

Aunt Runa shook her head. "Why would they do that?"

Aunt Hazel shrugged. "Listen, you've got plenty more. What's one missing crystal? Besides, I'm sure it will turn up."

Hmm. One of Aunt Runa's crystals was missing from the dining table centerpiece? That was odd.

I climbed the stairs, slipped into my comfy threadbare T-shirt and boxer shorts, and sipped the tea during my nighttime routine, though I noticed an odd aftertaste. After making sure Pyewacket wasn't lurking underneath my bed, I climbed in and snuggled under the cozy covers, trying not to think about my grandfather dying in this bed. Glancing over at the moonlight coming in through the window, my thoughts went to Noah. There had been no sign of him after his strange appearance and disappearance at the party. *Was something wrong?*

Unfortunately, more questions would have to wait until tomorrow. At the moment, I needed a decent night's sleep or I'd be nothing but a ghost of myself in the morning. It would take lots of fresh energy if I wanted to help keep this place from dying a slow death. I reached over to switch off the lamp, but to my surprise, it flickered, then went out on its own.

Maybe all those ghost stories are getting to me.

Chapter Five
Who Called the Cops?

I used to sleep well at night. I could sleep just about anywhere, anyplace, anytime. I once slept through an entire horror movie at the theater, surrounded by a bunch of screaming fans who were terrified by the hideous deaths the poor camping teenagers had to endure.

Not this past week.

I don't spook easily, not even reading—or writing—murder mysteries. But I had to admit that ever since I'd arrived at the Blackwood Bed and Breakfast Inn a week ago, I had the feeling something strange was going on. I'd heard odd noises I'd written off to the settling of an old house. My bedside lamp had gone off and on, but I figured it was due to poor wiring. I'd have to ask Noah to look into that. And sometimes the place smelled like . . . garlic? Maybe my aunts were trying to keep vampires away—or was it werewolves? I needed to get my occult characters straight.

Anyway, the house was really starting to creep me out. I'd checked every inch of my bedroom and found no peepholes, trap doors, hidden microphones, or warnings written in blood on the walls. But even with the supposedly soothing teas, I tossed and turned during the night as if I were lying on a bed of rocks, and I awoke to every creak and moan the old house produced. I hadn't slept more than an hour or two at a stretch without waking up in a sweat.

The night after the party I startled awake around midnight, certain there was someone in my room. Since I was the only one staying on the second floor until the guests arrived—my aunts' rooms were on the third floor—I knew it was my imagination, but I couldn't shake the feeling I wasn't alone. After checking for hidden cats, I finally fell back asleep, but I had a fitful nightmare about my aunts. I dreamed Aunt Hazel had turned her neighbor into a cat and Aunt Runa had summoned the Ghost of Blackwood Inn with a Ouija board. I woke up in the morning to find the covers kicked off—in spite of the room being deathly cold—and felt more tired than when I had gone to bed.

Would I ever get used to sleeping in a house—in a room—where my eccentric grandfather had suddenly—and mysteriously—died? I couldn't ask my aunts for a different room, not after all the trouble they'd gone to, making it special for me. Besides, I was sure it would be fine. After all, there's no such thing as ghosts.

I heard what I thought was pounding in my fuzzy head that turned out to be rapping on my bedroom door. I got up, pushed myself out of bed, staggered over, and yanked open the door, wondering what my aunts could possibly want at this ungodly hour of seven o'clock in the morning.

Noah stood in the hallway. He wore clean black jeans and his Blackwood Bed & Breakfast Inn shirt. If only I looked as good as he did in the morning.

He checked me out as I stood there in my well-worn college T-shirt and boxers. Suddenly self-conscious, sure my nipples were at full attention, I grabbed Nancy Drew's blue chenille robe from the coat rack, slipped it on over my skimpy sleepwear, and crossed my arms to keep it together.

"What is it, Noah?" I asked, stifling a yawn. I ran my fingers through my bed head in an attempt to tame it. I must have looked a fright. What was it about this man, always appearing and disappearing at odd times, always looking great, and always making me feel uncomfortable?

"Sorry to wake you, but your aunts need you."

I checked the Nancy Drew clock on the wall and frowned. "Noah, it's the crack of dawn! The first guests won't be arriving until this afternoon. Can't it wait?"

"Afraid not."

I shrugged. "Okay. Tell them I'll be right down. I just need to change—"

"Better come now," he said.

I hesitated. I hadn't seen this assertive side of Noah. Normally quiet, he'd barely said two words to me since I'd arrived, but I had a weird sense he watched me when I wasn't paying attention. I wondered if he'd noticed me doing the same.

"But Noah—" I began to complain.

"Carissa," he interrupted me. It was the first time I'd heard him use my name. "There's a problem."

Instantly alarmed, I asked, "What is it? What happened?" I searched his face for a clue. Had we had a sudden rush of cancellations? Had someone knocked down the sign again? What could be so important that my aunts had to send Noah to get me so early? And why hadn't my aunts come themselves?

A chill ran through me. "Oh my God, are my aunts okay?"

He frowned. "They're in the kitchen . . . with the sheriff."

"Sheriff?" I repeated. "Why? What happened?"

Before he could answer, I rushed past him and was down the stairs faster than a witch on a broomstick. I don't believe in premonitions, but I was sure something terrible had happened to one of my aunts. Taken a fall? Had a heart attack? Cut off a finger? Lost a cat?

I glanced out the front window as I dashed toward the kitchen. No sign of fire trucks or an ambulance. No sirens or lights. Only a lone law enforcement vehicle parked in the driveway.

I dashed into the kitchen to find my aunts sitting at the small table in their robes, teacups in front of them. Marnie, wearing a long denim dress covered by a black apron embroidered with "Blackwood Bed & Breakfast Inn," stood at the stove, stirring up something that was bubbling in her cauldron . . . er, pot. The smell of cinnamon wafted from the teakettle, filling the room with its spicy scent.

But it was the man in a khaki uniform standing in the middle of the room that caught my attention. He had one thumb tucked into a belt that was laden with weapons—a gun, a knife, a billy club, handcuffs, and a flashlight clipped to leather loops. In the other hand he held his hat.

"What's happened? What's wrong?" The words rushed out more like a demand, not a question. I looked at my aunts. "Are you all right?"

Marnie glanced over, frowning. Under her breath, she said, "I knew I should have put the lid back on the teapot. You know what they say about bad luck."

I shook my head, completely baffled.

"We're fine, dear," Aunt Hazel said, although her response wasn't as chipper as it usually was in the morning. She patted the chair next to her. "Come sit."

I remained standing, staring at the uniformed officer for an answer. "What's going on?"

"Ms. Blackwood?" the sheriff said.

I nodded and sized him up, while he appeared to do the same to me. Football-player big, he stood with the "I'm in charge" attitude common to many police officers. Clean-shaven, with dark brown eyes, he wore his black hair slicked back. The few lines on his forehead suggested he was in his late thirties, early forties. He offered a well-manicured hand that didn't look as if it had seen much police action.

I shook it reluctantly. It was warm, and strong. What had I expected—a cold, dead hand? "What's this all about? Has something happened?"

"I'm Sheriff Wil Lokey from the Sonoma County Sheriff's Department. I understand you're the Blackwood sisters' niece, Carissa Blackwood. New in town?"

I nodded.

"I'd like to ask you a few questions, if you don't mind."

My heart was pounding. A sentence like that never boded well.

"Please sit down, Carissa," Aunt Runa gently ordered, indicating an empty chair. Aunt Hazel pulled out another chair for the sheriff. I plopped next to Aunt Hazel while he sat by Aunt Runa, carefully arranging his belted equipment as he lowered himself onto the seat.

Noah suddenly appeared in the back doorway. *Odd.* I'd assumed he'd followed me down the front stairs, but he must have used the staircase at the rear of the house—the one my aunts told me Bram Blackwood had built for his servants. Nancy Drew would have called it a "hidden staircase," I'm sure.

I glanced at my aunts. "Noah said it was urgent. I thought one of you . . ."

Aunt Hazel patted my hand. "We're fine, dear. Honestly. Marnie, would you get Carissa and Wil some tea, please?"

Marnie nodded, then touched the necklace she wore under her top and mumbled something I couldn't make out.

What's up with her? And why are my aunts on a first-name basis with the local law enforcement?

"Sorry to alarm you, Ms. Blackwood—" Sheriff Lokey began.

"Call her Carissa," Aunt Hazel said. For a moment, I thought this might be a social visit with matchmaking in mind. I wouldn't have put it past my aunts. But while the sheriff was certainly attractive in his uniform, I hadn't come to Pelican Point to hook up, especially at seven in the morning. I really needed to set my aunts straight.

"Carissa," he began solemnly, "there's been a . . . death." He watched me with narrowed eyes.

"What?" I frowned at my aunts, then over at Noah, who stood listening in the doorway. In the corner of my eye, I saw Marnie stiffen at the stove.

My aunts nodded, confirming the sheriff's words, but Noah's blank expression told me nothing. "Who? What happened?"

"One of the townspeople died sometime last night or early this morning," the sheriff answered.

"Oh. Goodness. I'm sorry," I said. "But what does that have to do with us?" I took the proffered cup of tea from Marnie and inhaled the intoxicating smell of cinnamon. I wondered if it would cure the anxiety that had crept into my psyche.

Over the rim of the teacup, I saw my aunts look knowingly at each other, then quickly turn their attention to the insides of their own teacups. Noah continued to lean against the doorjamb, his arms crossed at his chest. I wondered what he was thinking.

"This is just routine," the sheriff said. "I'm checking with everyone who might have seen the victim last night."

I frowned. "The victim? Last night? Who was it?" I looked at my aunts for an answer. Aunt Runa continued to stare down at her cup. Aunt Hazel sipped her tea.

"One of your party guests," Sheriff Lokey said.

"What? Who?" Stunned at the news, I quickly ran through the guest list in my mind. That obnoxious Annabelle, owner of the Pelican Point Inn? The jerk who lived next door—Harper something? Gracie—the quiet, unassuming librarian/historian? Surely not Aiden, the newspaperman who rescued me from the others. Who was I missing?

"Tell me!" I demanded, when no one volunteered the information.

The sheriff leveled his eyes at me. "Patty Fay Johnstone."

"Oh my God," I said. I'd almost forgotten she was there. "My aunts' realtor? She's . . . dead? But we just saw her last night."

"That's why I'm here," the sheriff said. "Did you notice anything unusual about her at your party? Did she seem upset about anything? Did she look ill?"

"No. She seemed perfectly fine. She was all dressed up. She brought flowers. She mingled with the other guests, drank some wine, had some of the pastries. Even took some home, I think. What happened to her?"

The sheriff made a note in his small notebook, then said, "We're not sure yet. The coroner is doing an autopsy this morning."

"An autopsy?" I repeated. "Was it a suspicious death?" Even in real life, I couldn't stop my mystery-writing mind from wondering.

"An autopsy is routine for someone her age, especially since she didn't seem to have any serious medical conditions."

Noah spoke up from the back of the kitchen. "She lived alone, didn't she, Sheriff?"

The sheriff nodded.

"Who found her?" Noah asked.

"Yes," Aunt Hazel added. "Who discovered her . . . body?"

"We're not sure," the sheriff replied. "We got an anonymous text."

Noah frowned. "You couldn't trace the source?"

Why the sudden interest in all this? I wondered. *Does he know something about Patty Fay that we don't?*

"Whoever it was used a burner phone," the sheriff explained.

"That's odd," I said. My mystery-writing mind kicked in again. "Why would someone have a phone like that unless they knew ahead of time they'd be tossing it?"

"My thoughts exactly," the sheriff said. "That's why I'm looking at all the possibilities and questioning folks who were with her last night." He stood up, rearranged his police belt, and patted his stomach. "Thanks for the tea, ladies. If you remember anything, give me a call, would you?" He handed me his card. It read: "Sheriff Wilu 'Wil' Lokey. Sonoma County Sheriff's Department, Pelican Point Branch." There was an office number and a cell number.

My aunts stood to escort him out. Aunt Hazel gave him something wrapped in a napkin, no doubt some pastries leftover from last night. I was wrong.

"Here, Wil," she said. "A couple of Marnie's oatmeal muffins with a hint of peppermint. She baked them fresh this morning. They'll help with your IBS."

Sheriff Lokey looked at Aunt Hazel oddly, as if she'd somehow read his mind—or stomach. "Thanks." As he reached the kitchen door that led to the dining room, he turned around. "Oh, one more thing," he added, Columbo style. "We found something under Patty Fay's bed."

We waited silently as he reached into his pocket and pulled out a plastic bag. He held it up for us to see.

Aunt Runa gasped.

Aunt Hazel's eyes went wide.

Marnie began rubbing her necklace through the fabric of her top.

Inside the bag was a spectacular bicolored stone in rich striped shades of golden yellow, rusty brown, and black.

Tiger's eye.

"That's my gemstone!" Aunt Runa said. "It went missing last night. How on earth did it end up under Patty Fay's bed?"

"Good question," the sheriff said.

"Maybe she took it?" Aunt Hazel suggested. "You know. For good luck."

I immediately thought of the napkin Patty Fay held in her hand just before she left the party. Had the gem been inside that napkin?

But why would she steal something like that?

Chapter Six
The Ghost of Blackwood Inn

"Remind me," I said. "What's the significance of a tiger's eye crystal?" I wondered if maybe its so-called power had something to do with Patty Fay lifting it—if she did.

Runa sighed. "It's actually a member of the quartz group called chatoyancy."

I looked at her blankly. There was a word I'd never remember.

She caught my look. "Basically, quartz is made up of intergrown fibers called chatoyancy that weave through it. That's what gives the gem its unusual yellow and brown coloring, and causes the stripey, shimmering wave that's so mesmerizing."

"So what are its superpowers?" I asked.

Aunt Hazel rolled her eyes as her sister began to explain.

Aunt Runa ignored her. "A tiger's eye is supposed to give protection, confidence, and courage to the wearer. It's also considered a good-luck piece."

Not such good luck for Patty Fay, I thought, but I kept that to myself.

"I wonder why it was under Patty Fay's bed?" I pondered aloud. "The sheriff wouldn't have mentioned it if it hadn't been some sort of clue."

My aunts remained silent.

"So how long have you known the sheriff?" I asked, curious about their familiarity with the local law enforcement.

"A few years," Aunt Runa said.

Aunt Hazel broke into a grin.

I frowned at her, thinking that wasn't really an appropriate reaction under the circumstances. "Aunt Hazel? What's going on?"

She sipped her tea, then said, "He's kind of delicious, don't you think? He's part Miwok, by the way. His ancestors have been here longer than our own."

I stared at her, open-mouthed and dumbfounded. "Are you serious? The sheriff? Oh my god, he's way too old for me! And I'm not interested!"

"Dear, watch your language, please," Aunt Hazel said. "It's not becoming. Especially to men."

Seriously? A woman was found dead the morning after our party with what looked like one of Aunt Runa's gemstones under her bed, and Aunt Hazel was worried about my love life and unladylike language? Would they never stop playing matchmaker?

I looked around for Noah, wondering if he'd heard all of this. Gone.

I sighed. I had a feeling my aunts weren't taking this seriously enough. "Aunt Runa, how do you think Patty Fay ended up with one of your crystals under her bed?"

"I have no idea," Aunt Runa said, calmly brushing nonexistent crumbs from her skirt. "As you know, I have them all over the house. Like Hazel said, she probably stole it and hid it there."

I shook my head. "But why? Why would she take something like that?"

Aunt Runa shrugged. "I don't know. Maybe she needed protection. Maybe she was afraid of something."

"Like what?"

Aunt Runa shrugged again.

I pressed on. "It doesn't make sense."

"Oh, Carissa," Aunt Hazel said. "You'd be surprised how many people around here are into alternative medicine and the occult. It's not just us. Remember, Father made a little extra money holding magic shows, hosting theatrical séances, and reading tarot cards and whatnot after Mama died. I heard Patty Fay was one of his most devoted clients."

How devoted? I wondered. "But that doesn't explain how the gem ended up in Patty Fay's room."

Aunt Runa scoffed. "Well, I certainly didn't give it to her—or put it under her bed, if that's what you think."

"No, no," I said quickly. "I'm just trying to make sense of things."

Aunt Hazel nodded. "It's the mystery writer in her."

"Even so," Aunt Runa said, leveling her voice. "I still can't tell you how it got there. But if you're implying I'm responsible for Patty Fay's death—"

"No, no, of course, you're not," I said. But by the way Aunt Runa was working her jaw, I had a feeling there was more to the story than she let on. "What if someone else took it and put it under Patty Fay's bed to make it look like she stole it?"

Aunt Hazel gasped. "And then that person . . . murdered her!"

Murder at Blackwood Inn

The timer on the oven rang. Saved from jumping to conclusions by the bell, so to speak. In fact, I'd been so caught up in questions, I hadn't noticed the sweet smell of fudgy brownies baking in the oven.

Marnie entered from the back door, pulled out the brownies, and set them on the cooling rack. There was nothing like fresh, chewy brownies to distract us from a recent death. I just hoped Aunt Hazel hadn't added any psychotropic "herbs" to the mix for our guests.

Our guests! They would be arriving in just a few hours. There was still so much to do before we greeted the folks who would soon fill the themed rooms upstairs. My aunts began buzzing about the kitchen, starting their preparations to welcome their first customers at the inn.

Apparently they were finished talking about Patty Fay's death. *Not so fast*, I thought.

"Aunt Runa," I said, interrupting her as she got out fresh linens. "You might want to check the house to see if any of your other crystals are missing. How many do you have?"

"Thirteen," Aunt Runa said.

Of course. "Are any of them missing besides the tiger's eye?"

Her eyebrows pinched in thought. "I'm not sure, but I'll look—as soon as I have a moment."

I turned to Aunt Hazel, who was busy cutting the cooled brownies into tempting squares. "Aunt Hazel, are you going into town this afternoon?"

The smell of the brownies overtook me and I snatched one and popped it in my mouth. Moments later I let out a guttural sound of pure pleasure, then promised myself to steal a couple more on my way to bed later. That is, if there were any left.

"Good, aren't they," Aunt Hazel said, grinning. She was obviously pleased at my reaction to the yummy treat.

I moaned again.

"Why? Do you need something from the store?" she asked.

"No, but I thought if you have any shopping to do, maybe you could see if there's any gossip about Patty Fay's death. In a small town like this, I'll bet there's some talk."

"Good idea," Aunt Hazel said. "I'll do my best."

Pushing thoughts of the dead woman aside, I started for my desk to make sure the registry was ready and everything was in place, then paused at the doorway. "Do either of you know where Noah is?"

"I asked him to repair the broken lock on my greenhouse," Aunt Hazel said. "I want to make sure none of our guests go wandering around my special garden. You might check there."

Special garden, eh? "Thanks," I said.

Aunt Hazel raised an eyebrow. "Why do you want to talk to Noah?"

"Uh . . . ," I stammered, not ready to share my motive yet. "The light in my room keeps flickering on and off. I thought maybe he could take a look at it."

Aunt Hazel shot Aunt Runa one of her looks. I hoped they couldn't read my mind. They wouldn't like knowing why I really wanted to see the handyman.

I headed out the back door and traveled the stone path past the flower garden and the herb garden to the greenhouse where Aunt Hazel grew her special "medicinal" plants. Over the past week I'd seen her pamper the plants in all her gardens as if they were her pets. She kept records of their food, water, sunlight, and growth, and I'd caught her singing to them when she didn't know I was around. When I asked her why she grew "those" particular plants, she'd simply said, "They have curative properties, so I use them for special remedies."

"But aren't they poisonous?" I asked.

"Dear, all plants are poisonous," she'd answered. "It just depends on the quantity used. Like most anything, a little bit can cure you, but a little more can kill you."

I guessed that was true. Still, I was glad she kept her poisonous plants locked up in the greenhouse.

I spotted Noah standing by the greenhouse and waved. Brushing back a forelock of his dark hair, he stopped tinkering and waited for me, almost as if he'd been expecting me. I suddenly felt self-conscious and flashed on the once-over he'd given me earlier when I was dressed in nothing but my threadbare sleepwear.

"Uh, Noah?" I said, trying to sound casual when I caught up with him. I hoped my cheeks weren't as red as the nearby roses.

"Hey, Carissa. Everything okay with your aunts?"

"That's what I wanted to talk to you about. I'm worried about Aunt Runa."

"The missing gem," he said simply.

"Yes! Doesn't it concern you that her tiger's eye was found in Patty Fay's bedroom, under her bed? I mean, what if Patty Fay's death wasn't . . . natural?"

Noah frowned. "Where did that come from?"

"I guess I have a suspicious mind," I answered, trying to shrug off the implication. "Probably from ghostwriting all those mystery novels."

"You're a ghostwriter?" he asked, giving a half grin.

I shrugged. "I was, until recently. Work has slowed down, so now I'm thinking of writing my own book."

"One of those romantasies?"

He knew about romantasies? Another surprise. "No, no, still a mystery."

He nodded. "Well, if you think Patty Fay's death is a mystery to solve, I doubt we'll learn anything more until we hear from the sheriff."

Or any gossip Aunt Hazel managed to get from the locals.

"Sure, but isn't he going to wonder why that particular gemstone was under Patty Fay's bed—on the same night she happened to drop dead—after attending our party?"

"That sounds like the mystery writer in you," Noah said, grinning. "Look, Carissa. You know and I know that your aunts had nothing to do with Patty Fay's death, but if there's something you want me to do, I'd be happy to—"

I cut him off. "Yes, there is. You've lived here a while, right? I'm guessing you know a lot of people in town."

He shrugged.

"Could you ask around, do a little investigating, find out any information you can about Patty Fay? See if there's anything to connect her to the tiger's eye? I'd like to be proactive about this for my aunts' sake, just in case."

"You mean, in case Patty Fay *didn't* die of natural causes?"

I felt a shiver run down my back. "Well, the timing of her death does seem odd."

"All right," Noah said. "I think you're worried about nothing, but I'll see what I can dig up. For your aunts' sake."

I let out a sigh of relief. While I thought Aunt Hazel might learn a few things, I was afraid she'd find the townspeople a little tight-lipped. Maybe Noah could fill in the gaps.

"Thank you, Noah. I really appreciate it. I'll pay you for your time."

"Don't be silly." He pulled a screwdriver from his leather work belt and prepared to get back to fixing the lock.

"Oh, I insist," I said.

He paused, then said, "All right. How about dinner?"

"What?" I said, stunned.

"Dinner. You know. Third meal of the day. Usually in the evening. A good time to share information over a glass of wine."

I saw mischief sparkling in those dark brown eyes. *Uh-oh. What was this about?*

"Um . . . well . . . tonight's going to be hectic with all the guests arriving," I stammered.

A small smile played at the corners of his mouth. "How about after you've tucked everybody in. Say eight o'clock? If there's any dirt out there, I should have something by then."

"Uh, okay," I managed to say. "I'll have Marnie whip something up—"

He held up a hand. "Not at the house. I know a place."

I felt my skin turn hot. This was sounding more and more like a date. I hadn't been on a real date since my divorce. Nor was I ready.

Noah must have read my expression. "Look, it's just dinner."

I let out a sigh. "Okay, sure. Listen, I have to get back. Still a million things to do." I turned to go, then remembered my excuse for needing to find him. "One more thing. The light in my room keeps flickering on and off. Any chance you can fix that?"

"I'll check on it after I'm finished here. But I'll warn you—the lights in that room have never worked right. There's some kind of problem in there, like a loose connection or crossed wires or something."

"Thanks," I said, then thought, *Wait—was the problem just in my room?*

Noah read my thoughts again. "Of course, your aunts might not want the lights fixed. They say it's your grandfather trying to communicate with them from the beyond." He winked.

I shook my head as I made my way back to the house. Great. It was opening day at the inn and one of our party guests from last night was dead. The sheriff had found one of Aunt Runa's gemstones under the deceased's bed. The mysterious handyman wanted to have dinner with me. And my bedroom was supposedly haunted by the ghost of my grandfather.

What was this? The *Ghost of Blackwood Hall*? If only I could channel the Girl Sleuth.

And by the way, what had happened to the nice, peaceful new life I'd envisioned in picturesque Pelican Point?

Chapter Seven
Animal Magnetism?

Okay. I'd accepted a dinner date with a man who was practically a stranger.

What was wrong with me? What was up with him?

I'll find out soon enough, I thought, as I made my way back to the house.

I spent most of the morning double- and triple-checking everything to make sure the Blackwood Bed and Breakfast Inn would be ready for the inaugural guests. When I had a little down time, I went over the checklist at a site that had helped called "How to Run a Bed and Breakfast Inn." I wanted to make sure I hadn't missed anything.

So far I'd learned about financing (my aunts had been lucky since they'd inherited their inn), renovation costs (their father had left them a sizable inheritance as well), best locations (Pelican Point was a popular tourist destination), signage (which had oddly become an issue), staff (Marnie and Noah seemed to have come with the house), and additional amenities. The Blackwood Bed and Breakfast Inn cleverly offered scary movie-themed bedrooms, a delicious pastry-filled brunch and wine-tasting happy hour, and a beautiful outdoor setting with benches, ponds, and gardens in which to ponder nature. Now all we needed were the guests and a smooth opening to nail it. Hopefully there wouldn't be too many mishaps.

But I had to admit, thoughts of Noah kept interrupting me. *Why had I agreed to that dinner with him? And why did it bother me so much?*

I managed to keep my thoughts at bay between three and five o'clock as we had a steady stream of check-ins that kept my aunts and me hopping. While Marnie stayed busy in the kitchen, I handled the registration and fees. Aunt Runa welcomed each guest with a salted caramel brownie while sharing info about sights and attractions in the surrounding area. And Aunt Hazel showed them around the inn before leading them upstairs to their assigned rooms. Apparently Noah was busy with outdoor tasks because I didn't see him the rest of the afternoon.

We'd put Lindsay and Jonathan Duke, a newlywed couple, in the Sleepy Hollow Room (it was the most romantic), the McLaughlin family—Staci and Mike and their two boys, Luke and Jake, in the Scooby Doo Room, (fun and not too scary), Partners Javier Cruz and Malik Wilson, screenwriter and actor, in Hitchcock's The Birds Room (figuring they were fans of the local movie sites), and a traveling salesman named Henry Hill in the Ghostbusters Room (the only room left when he'd called at the last minute).

The newlywed couple came down to enjoy happy hour before heading out for dinner. Most of the others went out soon after checking in, apparently eager to explore the town and find a place to eat. As far as I knew, the traveling salesman never left his room.

By the time we were finished with cleanup and everyone had settled in for the evening, I was exhausted and ready to curl up in my Nancy Drew room, certain I'd sleep like the dead after such a hectic day. As much as I wanted whatever information Noah might have learned, I was just too tired to meet him—or was it something else? At any rate, I got out his card and sent him a text asking for a raincheck. Since we'd heard nothing more from the sheriff regarding Patty Fay's death, I figured that was a good sign.

"Goodnight, Aunties," I called to my aunts, who were sitting at the kitchen table with their cups of tea. I grabbed a last brownie and mouthed "Thanks" to Marnie, who was wrapping up leftovers.

"Bedtime so soon?" Aunt Hazel asked.

I yawned audibly in response.

"Okay, well, sleep tight," she said cheerily.

"See you bright and early, dear," Aunt Runa added in her husky voice.

Where did they get their energy? Something in their crystals and tea?

I trudged up the stairs, feeling as if I were wearing leaden shoes. I unlocked my door at the end of the hall, entered, and switched on the stained glass Tiffany lamp on my bedside table. It flickered several times, then stayed on for a few minutes before flickering out again. Apparently Noah hadn't found the time to fix the light yet. Surely the lock on Aunt Hazel's greenhouse door hadn't kept him busy the entire day. Had he forgotten? Or had he been busy looking into Patty Fay's death for me? I felt a surge of regret at canceling our dinner, but I knew I wouldn't be great company. With no more news from the sheriff, I figured tomorrow would be soon enough to hear what he'd learned—if anything.

I turned on the overheard light, then I dragged myself into the tiny adjoining bathroom, filled the tub with warm, soothing water, and ate my brownie before the water turned cool. I toweled off and changed into my soft, worn T-shirt and boxer shorts. Feeling the room was a bit stuffy, I opened the window to let in some fresh air, then climbed into bed and switched on the Tiffany lamp, hoping it would stay on this time. I noticed a copy of *The Secret of the Old Clock* on the bedside table and wondered if one of my aunts had left it there for me.

I ran my hand over the tattered cover that featured a picture of an old-fashioned Nancy Drew wearing a blue ankle-length suit and matching cloche hat, and carrying a large clock. I checked the date inside: Copyright 1930. An original. The book brought back fond memories. If I hadn't been ill with mono for two months in the fourth grade, I might not have discovered the Girl Sleuth. A neighbor girl had lent me a few of her Nancy Drew books to read while I recuperated, and those cliff-hanger stories had kept me company until I recovered. I even penned a fan letter to Carolyn Keene and was devastated to learn that the so-called author of the series didn't really exist. The books were ghostwritten by writers who belonged to a syndicate. And now I was a ghostwriter. Go figure.

I was about to begin the first chapter, but as soon as my head hit the puffy pillow, my eyes closed and I felt the book slip from my hand. I reached over and pulled the chain on the bedside lamp. The light went out.

Just as I closed my eyes again, the lamp flickered back on.

By itself.

Okay. Maybe I'd been so tired, I hadn't turned the light all the way off.

Then again, living in a house that my aunts liked to call "haunted" was probably causing me to spook myself. I seemed to startle at every little noise and light. I reminded myself about the earplugs and sleep mask I planned to buy and hoped they would help. If not, I might be going a little woo-woo soon myself.

* * *

I don't know how long I was out before I heard a noise. I sat upright, dripping with sweat, and switched on the table lamp. It flickered again, giving an eerie, shadowy cast to the dark room. Out of the corner of my eye, I caught a glimpse of Pyewacket as he leaped onto the window seat and fled out the open window.

Where had he come from? The window? Had he been inside my room all this time?

Hmm. I could explain the lamp—there was obviously a loose connection. I could explain the noises—all old houses had them. But when had the cat gotten in? *After* I opened the window? Or some time *before*?

I got up, rubbing the goosebumps on my arms, and knelt down to look under the bed for more lurking cats. I didn't see any glowing eyes, but I noticed one of the bedframe slats lay on the floor. Maybe that was causing my sleeplessness—a lumpy bed. I reached for it but couldn't quite grasp it, so I rolled over onto my back and scooted underneath, then spotted something odd tucked in the small space between two of the bed slats. I reached up and felt it—a book?

Odd place for a book, I thought. Obviously someone had hidden it there. With a little pushing and tugging, I managed to release it from its secret spot. I replaced the slat, scooted out, and dusted myself off. In the flickering light, I read the book's title: *Mesmerism: The Study of Animal Magnetism*, by Franz Anton Mesmer.

That was weird. Why would a book on animal magnetism—whatever *that* was—be hidden in the bedframe?

Naturally curious, I opened the cover. To my surprise, the pages had been cut out to create a secret compartment. Talk about a scene right out of a Nancy Drew mystery. Inside was a small notebook with the initials "A.B." handwritten on the outside cover. *Abraham Blackwood?* Next to the letters was a symbol—a triangle with an eye in the middle. *Something occult?*

I withdrew the notebook and opened it to the first page. The letters "**MTNGS**" were written in an old-fashioned flourish in black ink that matched the two letters on the cover. I turned the page.

This one was filled with columns, all written in the same scrawl. Each column was topped by more letters: **DT**, **PLC**, **CLNT**, **GSTS**, **CNTCT**, and **CNJRD**.

Some kind of code?

I scanned down the first column made up of numbers—two in each set. The latest one read: **04/15**. A date? From six months ago? That would have been around the time my grandfather died.

I read over the remaining column entries:

"**PLC**: *Snc Rm.*"

No clue what that meant.

"**CLNT**: *P.F.J.*"

My breath caught when I read the letters and the little hairs on my arms tingled. PFJ? Did that mean what I thought I meant? Patty Fay Johnstone's initials? If so, what was the deceased real estate woman's name doing in this old notebook?

I read on.

"**GSTS**: *A.T., G.G., M.C. . . .*"

More initials? I wondered, scanning a half-dozen more.

Under "**CNTCT**" were the letters "*Cptn Vktr Vsl.*"

I was pretty sure those were not initials.

The column beneath **"CNJRD"** was blank. *What did it mean?*

Before I could flip to another page, the bedside lamp went completely out, leaving me in darkness. I pulled on the ball chain several times, but the lamp refused to cooperate. The moon coming through the window was just enough to light my way to the desk where my cellphone lay charging. I picked it up, tapped the flashlight app, and shined the beam toward the bed where I'd left the old book on animal magnetism.

Then a chill passed through me like a spirit. The book was closed.

I could have sworn I left it open.

* * *

The first thing I did when I woke up the next morning was check the nightstand where I'd placed the animal magnetism book before going to sleep. It was still there, the cover still closed. I really needed to get a grip. This lack of sleep was getting to me.

I stretched and climbed out of bed, planning to ask my aunts about the secret notebook I found inside the book and why it was hidden under my bed. Maybe they'd know something about it. As soon as I was showered, I dressed in black jeans and the black B and B logo T-shirt my aunts had given me, picked up the book, tucked it under my arm, and opened the door.

I nearly bumped into Noah, who was standing right outside. Startled, I dropped the book. I started to kneel down, but he beat me to it.

"I'll get it," he said.

When he stood up, book in hand, I realized we looked like twins in our black outfits. But that's where the resemblance ended. He filled out his shirt quite differently from me.

He turned the book over and frowned. "What's this? You into hypnosis?"

I frowned back. "What? No! Where did you get that idea?"

He tapped the book. "You're reading Mesmer."

"No, I'm not," I said, taking the book from him. "I just found it. In my room. Under the bed, actually."

"Let me guess," he said. "Was it hidden between the bed slats?"

My mouth dropped open. "How did you know? Wait, did you put it there? Was that some kind of princess and the pea test?"

He grinned and shook his head. "No. Mr. Blackwood must have hidden it there. He was like that."

I wondered if Noah knew about the hidden compartment—or the secret notebook—inside. I thought about asking him. Instead, I asked about the book itself.

"So, who's this Mesmer guy and why would my grandfather have a book like this?"

Noah gave his wide, disarming smile.

"You never heard of Anton Mesmer?"

"Should I have?" I answered. "I don't remember being assigned anything on animal magnetism in my biology class. And I fell asleep in my zoology class."

"More likely you would have heard about it in your pseudo-psychology class. "Animal magnetism" was a term made up by a German doctor named Franz Anton Mesmer back in the eighteenth century. He believed animals had special powers, which led him to the theory of hypnosis. His idea of alternative medicine was never proved, but his followers began using hypnosis to put people in a trance and cure them of ailments through the power of suggestion. He also believed he had power over women. It became quite a secretive practice, until it was proved to be theatrical quackery."

"So you think my grandfather was studying animal magnetism? Or hypnosis?" *Hopefully not to gain power over women*, I thought.

Noah laughed. "I think he used elements of hypnosis during the séances he was rumored to have."

I didn't know what to think about my grandfather and his strange occult practices. I'd heard he'd gotten into this stuff after my grandmother died. Maybe I'd do some research on hypnosis and see how much validity it carried today. All I knew was it was supposed to help some people stop smoking or lose weight.

"Well, thanks for the insight. Sounds like my grandfather was quite a character. By the way, sorry about canceling last night. I was wiped out."

"No problem."

"Um, by the way, my light is still flickering."

"Really? I fixed it yesterday while you were helping the guests. It's not working?"

I shook my head. "It still keeps going off and on."

"Okay, I'll check it again in a few minutes. I came up here to tell you your aunts would like to see you. Don't worry. No sheriff this time."

"Thank goodness," I said, letting out a breath. "Actually, I was on my way down to see them." I tucked the book under my arm, started to shut the door, then left it open for Noah, even though I knew he had a key. As I walked away, I felt him watching me, but I refused to turn around and check.

Just as I reached the first stairstep, I thought I heard him call out my name. I whirled around, but he was gone and my door was closed.

I might as well have been talking to a ghost.

I was halfway down the stairs when I heard the siren outside. A chill ran down my back and I quickened my pace, reaching the entryway in time to hear a knock at the door. A very loud, insistent knock.

Aunt Hazel and Aunt Runa came scurrying from the kitchen, teacups still in their hands.

I shot them a concerned look, then opened the front door.

Sheriff Lokey stood in the doorway. Behind him was a uniformed female officer, hands on her hips, a serious look on her makeup-free face. Her nametag read: "Dep. Santos."

"Wil?" Aunt Hazel said. "You're back again? Have you learned something more about Patty Fay?"

"May I come in?" he asked, sounding more formal than yesterday.

"Of course," Aunt Hazel said. "Would you like some tea?"

"I'm afraid not," the sheriff said, removing his hat. "I have some news."

"You found out what happened?" Aunt Runa asked.

He glanced back at Deputy Santos, standing mutely and stone-faced behind him, her dark hair pulled back into a knot.

"Sorry to have to tell you this," he said solemnly, "but yes, I have news about Patty Fay. It appears she didn't die of natural causes. We believe it was a homicide."

"Murdered?" I cried. "What? How?"

I looked at my aunts. Aunt Runa was white as a ghost. Aunt Hazel stood frozen, staring wide-eyed at the sheriff.

"How do you know?" I asked the sheriff.

He took a deep breath, sighing as he let it out. "The coroner did some tests. She found evidence of poison in her system. She suspects it was belladonna."

"Deadly nightshade," Aunt Hazel whispered. Aunt Runa took her hand.

"Hazel," the sheriff said, "I understand you have a poison garden in your backyard. Is this true?"

"Well, yes," Hazel muttered. "But—"

He nodded. My heart dropped into my stomach. Surely he wasn't thinking that she—

"Do you mind if I have a look?" he asked.

"Of course not—" Aunt Hazel started to say.

"No way," came a voice from behind us. Noah stepped forward from the shadows. "Not without a search warrant, Sheriff."

The sheriff sighed. "All right, then, we'll be back with a warrant to search your property."

"A search warrant!" I cried. "You can't be serious! There's no way my aunt—"

The sheriff held up a hand to stop me from blathering on. "Ms. Blackwood, you might want to get your aunt a lawyer, just in case."

Chapter Eight
The Not-So-Secret Garden

The sheriff headed out the door to his patrol car, followed by his silent partner. It was clear from Aunt Hazel's teacup clattering against the saucer that she was scared. Aunt Runa closed the door, then wrapped an arm around her sister. It wasn't often I'd seen Aunt Runa show any open affection toward Aunt Hazel.

Marnie appeared from the kitchen, wiping her hands on a small towel. "I have freshly made tea. Come," she said, taking Aunt Hazel's cup.

I had a feeling Marnie had heard everything the sheriff said and she'd immediately gone into action—action meaning making tea, the apparent cure-all for everything at the Blackwood Inn. I realized I still had my grandfather's book tucked under my arm. Since it wasn't a good time to ask about it, I set it on the desk in the foyer and followed the others into the kitchen.

"Oh my goodness," Aunt Hazel said as she sat down at the table where steaming cups were already waiting. She looked stunned, gazing into space.

Aunt Runa picked up her spoon and started to stir her sister's tea when Marnie quickly reached out a hand and stopped her. She shook her head, then handed Aunt Hazel her own spoon. *What was that about? Did Marnie have some rituals of her own? Or was it some superstition about tea?*

As for me, I was too upset at the sheriff's implication to drink tea. Although a bottle of wine would have been nice.

"I can't believe the sheriff thinks Patty Fay was poisoned," Aunt Hazel finally said. "With belladonna. Who would do that? And why?"

"I think the sheriff is right," Noah said as he entered from the far side of the kitchen. "We need to get you a lawyer."

"I agree," I said. "Just in case. Do any of you know if there's a good one in town?" *Any that might not already be prejudicial toward my aunts?* Maybe Aiden the newspaper man would know someone. He seemed to care about them.

"A lawyer?" Aunt Hazel said. "I don't need a lawyer. Lawyers are only for guilty people. I didn't poison Patty Fay." She tapped her fingers on the table.

"We know you didn't." Aunt Runa patted her shoulder. "And I didn't put that tiger's eye under her bed. The idea is ludicrous."

Then who did? I wondered.

Marnie turned to the group at the table. "Does the sheriff think one of me pastries from last night had poison in it? Because that's nae possible," she said in her still lingering Scottish accent. She pulled off the dish towel that was hanging over her shoulder, wadded it up, and threw it in the sink.

I looked over at her. "He hasn't said anything like that."

Marnie harrumphed, her face pinched. "I knew we shouldn't have opened the inn on Friday the thirteenth." She toyed with the necklace tucked under the top of her dress as she spoke. It seemed to give her some kind of comfort.

"Okay," I said, grabbing paper and pen from a kitchen drawer. "Let's focus on the facts and try to come up with some possibilities. When I ghostwrite a mystery, I usually have the sleuth begin with 'MOM—Motive, Opportunity, Means.' If Patty Fay was murdered, what was the method? The sheriff suggested it was poison, apparently belladonna, which you grow in your poison garden, right, Aunt Hazel?"

"Yes, but I never really use it," Aunt Hazel answered.

"Never? Then why do you grow it?" I asked.

She shrugged. "I've always been interested in various kinds of herbals. The plant itself is quite beautiful, with bell-shaped purple and yellowish flowers and shiny black berries. It's not easy to grow, but I use a little gibberellic acid to help the plants along."

"But isn't it lethal?" I asked. "I mean, it's powerful enough to kill someone." I wanted to say, "like Patty Fay," but I didn't.

"Only if you use too much," Aunt Hazel said. "Or if you're careless."

"Well," Aunt Runa said to her sister, "I've told you before, it's crazy to grow something that dangerous. Everyone knows that. After all, it's called deadly nightshade."

"I'll admit, it can be toxic," Aunt Hazel conceded, "if you don't know how to use it. But I've studied it for years. Did you know it belongs to the same family as tomatoes, potatoes, eggplant, and chili peppers?"

"Only those aren't poisonous," Aunt Runa said. "They don't kill you."

Aunt Hazel sighed. "I told you, I've done my research. The berries, leaves, and roots contain tropane alkaloids. You've heard of atropine, scopolamine, right? Anesthetics.

Murder at Blackwood Inn

They use those all the time in medicine. Belladonna has been around for centuries for treatment of wounds, gout, insomnia. Back in the day it was used as eyedrops to dilate the pupils and make a woman's eyes appear more seductive." She batted her eyelashes. "You might call it one of the original love potions. After all, 'belladonna' means *beautiful woman*. It's just that too much can cause blindness, hallucinations, and delirium."

"And death," I added.

Aunt Hazel shrugged.

"So how would someone know they've ingested belladonna?" I asked.

"Well," Aunt Hazel began, "it invades the nervous system very quickly. At first you'd feel flushed, develop a rash, have a dry mouth, get a headache. Then comes loss of balance, increased heart rate, slurred speech, confusion, hallucinations, and finally convulsions. And yes, death."

"Good God! What a horrible way to die!" I said. "I hope you can't just buy it on the street corner, like pot."

"Actually," Aunt Hazel said, "it's legal in parts of Europe, Pakistan, Germany, and South America. But here in the United States, there's only one approved prescription drug containing belladonna—atropine—which is used to treat antispasmodic conditions. Anything else is illegal, although there's a small amount of atropine in some OTC cold medicines. I use a little dab for my . . . ahem . . ." She pointed behind her.

"Your back?" I asked, puzzled.

"Lower." She raised an eyebrow.

"She uses it for her hemorrhoids," Aunt Runa said, matter of factly.

I winced. Again, TMI. Too much information.

"And by the way," Aunt Runa continued, "it is *not* approved for that by the FDA, due to its side effects. Am I right, Hazel?"

Aunt Hazel scoffed. "You should talk." She turned to me. "Why don't you ask your aunt about her flying ointment?"

"Fly ointment?" I asked.

"Fly*ing*," Aunt Hazel corrected me.

Aunt Runa shook her head. "Ridiculous rumor."

"So tell her, then," Aunt Hazel urged.

"All right, all right," Aunt Runa snapped. "Back in the day—way back, I should say, when there were witches—it was believed that if a witch applied a mixture of belladonna, opium, monkshood, and hemlock they could fly. Turns out they just had hallucinatory dreams—waking states—you know, sort of like zombies on acid."

No, I didn't know. How would I?

"Listen," I said, hoping to bring us back to the urgent topic at hand. "The sheriff will be back with a warrant to search your poison garden, and if he finds anything suspicious—"

"He won't," Aunt Hazel said, cutting me off.

"You're sure you didn't clip off a piece of belladonna, say, by accident?"

Aunt Hazel scoffed. "I told you I didn't. I'm careful, not stupid, you know."

"Arguably," Aunt Runa mumbled under her breath.

Time to break this up before it turned into another untimely death. We'd get to Opportunity and Method later. "I think we'd better go check on the garden before the sheriff comes back and make sure your plants are intact and undisturbed." I got up and glanced around for Noah. He was gone. *Now where to?*

Murder at Blackwood Inn

Aunt Hazel led the way out the back door, with Aunt Runa taking up the rear. We walked along the winding path past the two "normal" gardens to the poison garden located in the greenhouse. Located at the back of the property, it was almost hidden among the trees. I noticed it wasn't far from an Airstream parked a few yards farther.

Aunt Hazel pulled out her key ring, but as she reached for the lock, she stopped.

"What's wrong?" I asked.

"It's unlocked!" she whispered.

The door to the greenhouse opened. "It's just me," Noah said, stepping out. "Sorry if I scared you."

"What are you doing in there?" I asked him. It seemed awfully suspicious, finding him inside the supposedly locked entrance with the sheriff on the way.

"Thought I'd do some checking," he said, casually swiping a lock of hair off his forehead. "If the sheriff thinks Patty Fay was poisoned with belladonna and brings that warrant . . ." He didn't finish his sentence.

"Well? Did you find anything . . . suspicious inside?" I asked him.

He shrugged. "I can't tell for sure. Hazel, you should take a look." He stepped aside to let my aunt pass by. I followed her in as she headed for what I assumed was the belladonna plant. She stopped beside a delicate looking plant with small purple-yellow leaves and tiny shiny berries.

How could something so beautiful be so deadly?

Aunt Hazel pulled out her gloves from her pocket and put them on, then donned her reading glasses that were propped on her head. She bent over to get a closer look. After a few moments, she said, "Uh-oh."

"What?" I asked, my skin tingling at the ominous phrase.

She pointed. "Right there." She indicated the jagged end of a stem that had obviously been broken off. "There were more berries there yesterday—or was it the day before? Anyway, I'm sure there were more." She took off her glasses and looked at Noah, who'd come up behind us. "Noah! I thought you fixed the lock. Someone must have gotten in."

Noah raised his hands as if in surrender. "I did fix it, as soon as you told me about it." He glanced at me for verification.

I nodded. "So, the door to the greenhouse was supposedly locked, right? And only Aunt Hazel—and Noah—have keys. I assume few people even know about this garden, only Aunt Runa. Marnie. Me. Anyone else?"

"No one else," Aunt Hazel said. "Besides, how many people would recognize belladonna, let alone know about its lethal properties?"

"So what do we do?" Aunt Runa asked, her hands clenched together in front of her. "What about the sheriff? He'll be here soon."

"Like I said," Noah said, "Hazel needs a lawyer, ASAP."

And maybe Aunt Runa, too, I thought, remembering the gemstone under Patty Fay's bed. "Noah, do you know any attorneys?" I asked.

He shook his head. "There's only one attorney in Pelican Point—Andrew Jeffers. And I heard he had a stroke or something. I know a few lawyers from the city have vacation houses here, but they don't come often or stay long. But I'll ask around."

We headed out of the greenhouse to find Marnie running toward us, waving her arms.

Uh-oh, I thought. *Is Sheriff Lokey back already?* If so, I was sure he'd brought a warrant this time.

Murder at Blackwood Inn

Marnie arrived out of breath and tapped her watch. "It's almost time!" she puffed.

"Oh, goodness!" Aunt Hazel exclaimed. "With all this talk of murder and whatnot, I nearly forgot about our guests. Breakfast is supposed to be in half an hour!"

As Aunt Hazel started to dash off, I reminded her, "Don't forget to lock up the poison garden!" She stopped abruptly, pulled out her keys, and locked the greenhouse door.

"Silly me," she said. "I'd lose my head if it wasn't attached."

Hmm. A little scatterbrained, but a wealth of trivia about poisons. Go figure.

Chapter Nine
Suddenly Seymour?

Noah took off, God knows where. Once I returned downstairs, I found my aunts and Marnie buzzing about the kitchen in a frenzy. Marnie, sporting a floral peasant dress covered by her Blackwood Bed and Breakfast apron, was pulling raspberry scones from the oven, while Aunt Runa, now wearing a long dark blue dress and apron, kept checking on the table settings to make sure everything was perfect. Aunt Hazel, apronless and wearing her usual plaid shirt and jeans, seemed dazed as she flitted around, talking to herself. She finally settled on filling small serving bowls with lemon glaze, while intermittently glancing at the teapot-shaped wall clock.

Everything came to a standstill when Aunt Hazel whispered, "I hear footsteps."

"They're coming," Aunt Runa whispered back.

Marnie, her face pinched, mumbled something I couldn't hear as she focused on her plated presentation. Each scone was circled with a swirl of lemon glaze, making it look like a work of art.

After giving the ladies a thumbs-up, I pushed through the swinging door into the dining room to greet the first guests.

"Good morning," I said to the Dukes, the newlywed couple who had come to the inn for a short honeymoon before returning to work in the city.

Lindsay Duke was dressed casually in khaki slacks and a tan-colored fuzzy sweater, her hair swept up in a messy twist held in place by a toothy comb. Jonathan wore jeans and a light blue collared polo shirt. He looked like he hadn't shaved.

I gestured toward the table. "Please, take a seat. The other guests should be here soon."

"How did you sleep?" came a voice from behind me. I turned to see Aunt Runa, her hands folded in front of her, a tight smile on her mostly serious face.

The couple looked tired. I figured they probably hadn't slept much, being newlyweds. At least I hoped that might be the reason and not, well, ghostly creaks and spirited squeaks.

Lindsay glanced at Jonathan. "Fine," she said noncommittally.

Jonathan turned and looked out the double glass doors that led to the gardens.

Aunt Runa didn't seem to notice their lack of enthusiasm. "May we start you off with some of my sister's special breakfast tea?"

I cringed at the word "special," now aware of it's possible double meaning.

On cue, Aunt Hazel entered with her cat teapot, which was wrapped in a quilted cat-covered cozy.

"Good morning, everyone," she said in a singsong voice. "This tea is my special blend of ginger, turmeric, lemongrass, and orange essential oils."

Marnie appeared behind her with two plates of scones and set them in front of Lindsay and Jonathan.

The bride smiled. "I love homemade scones."

"They're me special raspberry scones," Marnie said. "The berries are from the garden. They're served with lemon glaze made from lemons from our tree."

Lindsay broke off a piece and slid it around in the glaze, then ate it. The look on her face was sheer joy. "Fantastic!" she said, licking the lemon from her lips.

"I'm glad you like it," Marnie said. She almost curtsied before returning to the kitchen, followed by my aunts.

I suddenly realized I'd been abandoned. An awkward silence followed. Not one for small talk, I started to leave, too, when Lindsay said, "How long have you owned the home?"

"Oh. It actually belongs to my aunts."

"Ah," Jonathan said, reaching for a scone. "Come to help out, have you?"

I nodded. "So, I hear it's your honeymoon," I blurted, not knowing what else to say. "How did you happen to choose the Blackwood Bed and Breakfast Inn?"

"To tell you the truth, we were originally planning to go to the Pelican Point Inn in town," Lindsay said, a little sheepishly, "but it was last minute and they were full."

"Oh, did they recommend us?" I asked.

She hesitated, then glanced at her husband. When he said nothing, she explained. "No. Actually, I did a quick search and found yours was just opening and had a vacancy. When I read the rooms were themed, I was intrigued. I'm a big scary movie fan, although Jonathan, not so much." She gave him the side-eye, which he ignored. "Anyway, our room is perfect. I loved reading about Sleepy Hollow when I was a kid. It's kind of a romantic story when you think about it."

Jonathan looked down at his plate.

His body language was clear. "Not a fan of haunted houses?" I asked him.

He wiped his mouth. "No, sorry, don't believe in that stuff like my wife here. I think she'd defend the Headless Horseman if she got the chance."

I was about to ask what he meant when I heard footfalls on the staircase. Two elementary school-aged boys, identical except for their hair—one with a buzzcut, one with an asymmetrical cut, longer on one side—came bolting down the stairs in an apparent race to reach the bottom. They shouted, "Rut row" with each step, then said, "Beat ya!" at the same time they landed on the first floor.

Rut row. Apparently the boys were Scooby-Doo fans. My aunts had put the family in the Scooby Room thinking it would be fun for the kids. I had a feeling they should have created an Omen Room for these two little Damiens.

"Jakey! Lukey!" their mother called out behind them. "Stop! That behavior is not appropriate here. This is someone's home. Please be respectful."

This would be the McLaughlin family—Staci, Mike, and their two rambunctious boys. I wasn't used to kids, so I had a feeling I might have to bite my tongue when it came to dealing with these little imps.

The parents sat down at the table opposite the newlyweds, flanking the two boys, no doubt ready to strongarm them if they began a food fight. Staci smiled politely at the couple, and polite smiles were returned.

"Who are *you*?" one of the boys said to the couple.

"I'm Lindsay and this is my husband, Jonathan. What are your names?"

"Scooby," the boy answered.

"Dooby," the other said. They both laughed and gave each other fist bumps.

"Boys!" their father Mike commanded. "Are you going to behave or will I have to send you back to the room?"

"*Be*-have," they said in deadpan unison, drawing the word out.

Right, I thought.

"Uh, welcome, McLaughlin family," I said to the parents. "Let me go check on breakfast. I hope you like scones and crepes."

I caught a glimpse of yuck faces on the boys just before I disappeared into the kitchen.

"Oh my God!" I said softly, after the swinging door closed.

"What's the matter?" Aunt Hazel asked, picking up a tray of beautifully plated crepes. They were topped with strawberries, bananas, pecans, and a drizzle of Nutella.

"Did something happen?" Aunt Runa asked as she lifted the teapot off the stove.

"Uh, got anything stronger than tea?" I asked Aunt Runa. "Those kids . . ." I rolled my eyes.

Aunt Hazel laughed. Aunt Runa frowned. Marnie, sautéing maple-flavored sausage links, just shook her head.

"Here goes," Aunt Hazel said, as she pushed open the swinging door with her backside and entered the dining room with her tray of delights. I followed behind her to help serve.

"There goes my diet," Mike said, patting his stomach. I glanced at his boys. They were making yuck faces again, acting as if Aunt Hazel had just brought out a plate of worms. Actually, maybe they would have preferred that.

"Got any Lucky Charms?" one of the boys asked, tapping his spoon on his empty plate.

"Or Pop Tarts?" asked the other.

"No Lucky Charms! No Pop Tarts!" their mother said.

Aunt Hazel smiled patiently. "I'm afraid not. Would you like some sprouted whole grain toast with flax seeds? It has plant-based omega threes for cardiovascular health, not to mention it's high in fiber."

I assumed she was kidding, but her description only drew more yuck faces.

"I'm sorry," Staci said, "but they're gluten intolerant. Do you have anything that's gluten-free?"

She might as well have said, "Do you have any belladonna that's poison-free?"

"Uh . . . ," Aunt Hazel said. She held up a finger, then ducked into the kitchen. Moments later she returned holding a ceramic pitcher. "Boys, would you care for a Scooby-Dooby breakfast slushie?"

Lindsay eyed her suspiciously, while the boys nodded enthusiastically.

Surely she's kidding again, I thought. I knew all about Scooby *shots* from when I was in college. They were light green cocktails, usually made with melon liqueur, coconut rum, banana liqueur, pineapple juice, and heavy cream. Definitely not for children. Or was she planning to drug them?

Aunt Hazel began pouring what looked like green tea into their cups. From her apron pocket, she whipped out a can of whipped cream and squirted a dollop on top of each drink. She topped it off with some green sprinkles.

Talk about conjuring up some magic. My Aunt Hazel had just dazzled the boys with her sorcery. I could tell by the way they scarfed down the drinks that they loved it.

Three more guests descended the stairs. Javier Cruz, tall, thin, with dark curly hair, had mentioned he was a screenwriter when he'd made the reservation. His partner, Malik Wilson, big, bulky, shaved head, was a former football player-turned-actor. Both were wearing jeans and T-shirts with different movie logos. The couple waved good morning to the others and took their seats at the table next to the newlyweds. Aunt Runa had put them in the Birds Room, figuring they'd enjoy the tribute to Alfred Hitchcock's classic film, set in the area.

Behind them came Henry Hill, a traveling salesman who actually looked more like an overweight tourist on permanent vacation in his classic Hawaiian shirt and knee-length surfer-type pants than a snazzy-suited entrepreneur. We'd put him in the Ghostbusters Room since it was the only one left when he'd made his reservation at the last minute.

While the newcomers introduced themselves to one another and made small talk, Marnie and my aunts continued to serve them. I popped in and out from the kitchen to make sure everything was to their liking. As soon as the twin boys slurped the last of their Scooby drinks, they asked to go out back and play. Permission was granted from their mother, with a stern warning: "Don't go far, leave the cats alone, and be respectful of the yard."

They tore off like vampire bats out of hell, leaving the room in temporary peace. As I began clearing dishes, I picked up bits and pieces of conversation about the foggy weather, the cute town, the best places to eat, and where everyone was from.

"So what do you do?" I heard Henry ask the parents of the boys. He gestured with his fork as he talked with his mouth full.

"I'm in tech," Staci said, her shoulders sagging. "Long hours, so that's why we needed this getaway." She glanced at her husband.

Mike shrugged. "Me? I'm just a stay-at-home dad."

"I couldn't do it without you, honey," she said, patting his hand.

He barely nodded. Sounded like a hella job, dealing with those two hellions.

"How about you guys?" Henry asked the two men just before he took a last bite of his scone.

"I'm a screenwriter," Javier said, pointing to himself. "Malik's an actor. A great one. We met on the set of one of my films." He reached over and touched Malik's arm affectionately. I saw Henry micro-wince. *Hmmm.*

Staci leaned in. "How exciting. What was the film?"

Javier waved a dismissive hand. "Oh, it was just an indie flick about a zombie who feels bad about eating all his friends."

The wide-eyed guests nodded, saying nothing. What was there to say?

Henry turned to Lindsay and Jonathan. "And you two lovebirds? I hear you're newlyweds."

Jonathan nodded and wiped his mouth. "I'm a defense attorney. Lindsay's a prosecuting attorney."

My ears pricked up. So that's what he'd meant about defending the Headless Horseman.

"Wow," Staci said. "That must be so exciting!"

Jonathan glanced at his wife. "Sometimes."

"Seriously?" Staci asked. "All that drama in the courtroom. Is it like you see on TV?"

He sighed and put his fork down. "Not exactly. With two lawyers in one household, each one on an opposite side, let me tell you, you will constantly be 'lawyered.'"

Lindsay pursed her lips. She looked as if she'd just bitten into a poisoned apple.

"It's true," he said, defending himself. "You'll never win an argument with your spouse. In fact, you'll run out of words before the opposing counsel even gets started."

Everyone chuckled at his exaggerated description. Everyone but Lindsay.

"Plus," he continued, "you'll find all kinds of stuff written on yellow legal pads—the grocery list, your to-do list, even romantic notes."

More laughs. Lindsay cracked a smile.

"Not to mention," he continued, "you'll be using a whole new vocabulary—words like 'voir dire,' 'de facto,' and 'exculpatory'—and that's just in the bedroom."

More laughter. I thought I saw Lindsay blush.

"Don't forget 'presumed' and 'allegedly,'" she added.

"Right," Jonathan said. "But worst of all, we ruin every legal show we watch, from *Perry Mason* to *Suits*."

When the laughter died down, Lindsay turned to Henry. "And how about you, Henry?" she asked, as if to deflect from answering more questions.

"Me? I'm just a traveling salesman."

Mike frowned. "They still have those?"

Henry shrugged. "Maybe not like the old days, when my dad peddled everything from kitchenware to cleaning products for over fifty years. But not that much has changed. These days I scout the neighborhood, do some internet searches, then make a few phone calls. Still, it's basically sales."

"What kind of stuff do you sell?" Mike asked. "Vacuums? Encyclopedias? Thin Mint cookies?" He grinned widely at his attempt at humor.

I cringed.

"Whatever I can," Henry said. "Right now it's solar panels and artificial turf. Used to be fancy storage units—basically closets—but that fad died pretty quickly. Senior living is still a good bet. And luxury vacation time-shares. They always put money in your pocket." He pulled out a toothpick and began picking at his teeth.

I was puzzled by his incongruous attire and wondered if he mainly worked from home. "With the internet, why do you have to travel?" I asked.

"Like I said," Henry replied, stretching back in his chair, "I have to get out and scout the neighborhoods for roofs with no solar or yards with dying lawns. When I get back to the hotel, I use a reverse directory to find out phone numbers. Then I call folks, offer my services, and boom."

Just then the boys burst in through the French doors that led from the dining room to the yard and gardens.

"Look what we found!" one of the boys cried. He held up what appeared to be a folded green pancake edged with spikes. He ran to his mother and practically shoved it in her face.

She let out a "Yikes!" as she pushed her chair back.

"See?" the boy said. "There's a bug inside." He opened the folded leaf, revealing a still wiggling fly.

"Oh my God, Jakey!" his mother cried. "What *is* that?"

"That," came a low whisper from the doorway, "is a venus flytrap." Aunt Hazel set down the tray she was holding and rushed over to Jakey. She took the big leaf from his hand and examined it before looking him in the eye. "Where did you get this?"

The boy shrank back at Aunt Hazel's sudden stern look.

"Out . . . out there," he stammered, pointing toward the backyard.

Aunt Hazel looked at me. I knew exactly what she was thinking.

Had they been to the poison garden?

Chapter Ten
The Unlocked Room

Noah appeared at the open French doors. He didn't look happy. "We have a problem," he said to Aunt Hazel, ignoring the guests at the table.

Aunt Hazel held up the venus flytrap leaf. "I know!"

He sidled up to her and whispered, "Looks like there's been another break-in."

Staci gasped. "There was a break-in?" She wrapped an arm around her two boys.

"No, no," Noah said, raising his hands. "One of the gardens was breached, probably by a deer or raccoon looking for food. No cause for alarm."

Nice cover, I thought.

The guests let out a collective breath, reassured that the house itself had not been invaded by a thief—or worse.

Noah jerked his head, signaling for Aunt Hazel to follow him. She turned to the guests. "Please enjoy the rest of your breakfasts. Let Runa or Carissa know if you need anything." With that she headed out the French doors.

Jonathan waved me over. "So, what was that all about?" I had a feeling it was the lawyer in him asking.

"I'm sure it's nothing," I replied softly. "My Aunt Hazel is a stickler about her gardens. Noah will take care of it." I turned to the boys. "Did either of you take anything else from, uh, any of the gardens?"

They shook their heads and looked down at their shoes. One of the boys touched his pocket.

Uh-oh. If the poison garden had been breached as Noah said, had they taken something seriously poisonous? If so, I hoped they hadn't sampled it.

"Are you sure?" I asked, eyeing the guilty-looking one. "Is there something in your pocket?"

"Just this," he said, digging into his pocket. He slowly withdrew the contents and held up the sparkly item. It was one of Aunt Runa's crystals.

"We found gold!" the other boy said.

"Finders, keepers!" said the little thief.

Aunt Runa gasped. "Give me that!" She rushed over and snatched it from the boy's hand. "Where did you get this?"

The boy cowered next to his mother in fear of Aunt Runa's wrath. I didn't blame him.

"Excuse me," Staci said. "I don't appreciate you talking to my boys like that. I'm sure they didn't mean any harm. And Jakey certainly knows better than to take things that don't belong to him." She turned to her son. "Jakey, apologize to the lady for taking her rock."

He mumbled a listless, "Sorrryyyy."

His mother patted him. "I'm sure it won't happen again. Besides, I think you're overreacting. I mean, it's just a little rock."

"That is *not* a little rock. It's a crystal with very strong metaphysical powers," Aunt Runa said.

Staci chuckled. "Seriously?"

Aunt Runa's eyes narrowed. She held the crystal close to her chest. "It happens to have multiple healing properties, including protecting one from psychic attacks, helping to overcome fear, and dealing with anxiety and depression. All of my crystals have powers. They're strategically placed on purpose. If they're disturbed—"

"That's ridiculous," Staci said.

I could see Aunt Runa wanted to say more, so I gave a tiny shake of my head.

She pressed her mouth shut.

I filled in for her. "My aunt is very serious about her crystals. She mainly collects them for good luck. She's placed them all over the inn and the gardens to watch over the guests and to promote good energy."

Staci scoffed but said nothing.

Henry Hill cleared his throat. "It's not surprising you boys thought that iron pyrite was a gold nugget. It's often called fool's gold because it fools a lot of people." He winked at the boys.

"Well." Staci looked at Aunt Runa. "I'm sorry he took it. He knows better now, don't you Jakey?"

Jakey gave a single nod.

Henry smiled. "I heard pyrite is also associated with prosperity. I could use more of that!" He laughed.

"Well, we don't believe in that sort of thing," Staci said. She turned to her husband. "Right, honey?"

Mike shrugged. "I heard some crystals can be bad luck, and even cause death."

Henry shook his head. "You've been getting the wrong information, buddy. Personally, I believe they're harmless, as in, no powers at all."

Aunt Runa tucked the crystal into her apron pocket and left the room, shaking her head and mumbling to herself. It was definitely time to change the subject.

"So, what are you all planning for today?" I asked the group. "There are lots of great things to see and do in the Pelican Point area. The Pelican Point Lighthouse, the barking seals over on the dock, and of course the shops."

"Any whales?" Mike asked.

I shook my head. "Whale season runs from January to April. You'll have to come back then."

"We're going antiquing," Malik said. "I've got a list of places." He pulled out a piece of paper and read off the names of some familiar local shops: "The Time Machine, Retro Hunters, Vintage Fab, Quaint and Curious."

"Plus, we'll also be doing some thrifting," Javier added. He ticked off his fingers as he recited his memorized list. "Let's see, there's Second-Hand Savvy, Affordable Attic, and Tossed but Treasured. Can't wait to see what we find."

I smiled. "Sounds fun." I turned to Lindsay and Jonathan.

"I want to go to the lighthouse. I hear it's haunted too," Lindsay said.

Her husband sighed. "I just hope we have time to do some wine-tasting at the Grape Escape or Tangled Vines."

Lindsay nodded, but she didn't seem to have her heart in his suggestion.

The boys spoke up, apparently having forgotten all about their run-in with Aunt Runa. "We're going kayaking!" one of them shouted.

"And paddle boarding!" said the other.

It sounded exhausting. I turned to Henry, but he was frowning as he texted on his cell phone. As soon as he stopped, I said, "Henry?"

He looked up and tucked his phone into his shirt pocket.

"Any plans today? Are you taking a day off work, or do you have business here?"

"Uh, a little of both." He abruptly stood up. "Better get to it."

The other guests followed his lead and left the table, then headed upstairs. I was relieved to see them go. How had my first breakfast at the inn become so stressful?

I cleared a few dishes and took them into the kitchen, hoping to check on Aunt Runa and see how she was doing after all the drama, but she was nowhere in sight.

"Where did Aunt Runa go?" I asked Marnie, who was busy at the sink.

"She's outside with Hazel and Noah."

Ah, yes. I'd nearly forgotten about the greenhouse. I set the dishes on the counter and headed out to join them. When I arrived, Noah was standing outside the greenhouse, working on the lock again. Aunt Runa stood next to him. There was no sign of her sister.

"Where's Aunt Hazel?" I asked her.

"Inside," Aunt Runa said. "She's checking on things."

Hmm. Was she worried the boys had taken more than just the fly trap leaf and the pyrite?

Moments later Aunt Hazel appeared at the entrance. She removed her glasses and propped them on top of her head.

"Did you find anything?" I asked. "Missing, I mean?"

She shook her head. "I wonder how long the door was open this time. And how they got in."

"Was it unlocked when you got here?" I asked Noah.

Noah nodded.

"How could this have happened?" I asked him. "Aren't you and Aunt Hazel the only ones with keys?"

"Yes," Aunt Hazel answered. "That's what puzzles me. I told you, I keep mine on a ring in my pocket." She looked at Noah.

"Same with me. They're with me all the time," Noah said, tapping his pocket.

"Must be the ghost of Blackwood Bed and Breakfast Inn," Aunt Runa said under her breath.

Well, if it was a ghost, I thought, *why would they need a key?*

* * *

I decided to do some errands to get my mind off everything. The sheriff hadn't shown up yet, which was good. And since we needed a few things for happy hour that evening, I volunteered to go to town. Hopefully, there wouldn't be a disaster while I was gone—or when I returned.

I got in my Mini Cooper and thought about putting the top down for a better view of the beautiful coast, but the fog was still lingering and there was a chill in the air. Instead, I turned on the seat heater and drove toward town.

Pelican Point was a small and cozy village, like most coastal towns in California. When we'd first visited my grandparents when I was a kid, my dad gave me a short history lesson. Once a fishing village, Pelican Point still offered recreational and sport fishing, as well as swimming and surfing, if you dared enter the cold ocean waves. Miwok tribes were the first known people to populate the coast. Then came the Spanish, followed by people from Russia and Alaska, who hunted sea otters for their pelts. By the time the Mexicans arrived in the mid-1800s, the otters had been overhunted and the area became a harbor for shipping lumber. That boom ended when the railroad came, bringing in people from

Europe and Great Britain, but the already small town began to dwindle in size and population. These days Pelican Point was mostly supported by tourists who like to fish, surf, shop, eat, and whale watch.

I parked next to a pristine vintage Mustang, gold with black trim, and drooled over it for a moment before heading into Candy, Kites & Cockle Shells to pick up some saltwater taffy for gift bags. I was sidetracked when I saw the tiny *Pelican Point Press* newspaper office squeezed in between the Pelican Point Library and Historical Society building and the Best Clam Chowder in the World café.

I decided to make a detour, hoping Aiden might have a recommendation for an attorney, if it should come to that. But when I reached the door, a flip-over sign read, "Closed until," and the picture of a clock underneath indicated one o'clock. I tried the door handle, just to make sure no one was in, but it was locked. I peered through the window. No one sat at either of the two desks, which stood a few feet apart.

As I turned to head for the candy shop, the door to the library/historical society opened. Out stepped Henry Hill, the traveling salesman. He was still wearing his Hawaiian attire, in spite of the cool weather, along with flip-flops. I was surprised he hadn't added a straw beachcomber hat to his outfit.

"Henry!" I said, surprised to see him there. I hadn't pegged him as a big reader, more of a newspaper skimmer. He seemed the type to Google for information if he needed it. Plus he was empty-handed—no books. "I see you found the town's little library." I was curious why he was there, but it sounded too nosey to ask. Maybe he was doing research for one of his sales products?

"Ah, Miss Blackwood," Henry said, looking a little flushed. Was he embarrassed that I'd caught him at the library? Was it the cool air? Or was that reddened face from something else?

"I was just . . . talking to Gracie what's-her-name," he said, "the librarian . . . to get some background on the area. Seems this town has little need for solar panels, artificial lawns, or a retirement village what with all the rentals. As for time-shares, that's apparently handled by someone named Patty Fay Johnstone. Or should I say, *was*."

"So you've heard," I said quietly. I wondered what Gracie had told him about Patty Fay's death. And why.

"Yes, tragic," Henry said lightly, glancing over my shoulder as if looking for someone. "And strange. Have the police determined what caused her death?"

I shook my head. No way was I telling him about the poison in Patty Fay's system or the gemstone under her bed. "I understand it was quite sudden."

"Gracie told me that you and your aunts had a party the night before you opened the inn," Henry said. "You invited the locals as a good neighbor gesture. Nice idea. Odd that you didn't mention the woman's demise at breakfast this morning."

"I didn't think there was a need to," I said, feeling defensive. "Patty Fay's death had nothing to do with the Blackwood Inn. Since the guests don't know her, it seemed more like gossip than anything informational."

"Hmmm," Henry said, almost to himself. "Well, I won't keep you. I'm sure you have lots to do today. See you back at the inn. What time is happy hour again?"

Was he trying to blow me off?

"Five o'clock," I answered.

Murder at Blackwood Inn

He touched his forehead in the manner of a salute, then headed down the street.

What an odd man. He seemed awfully interested in Patty Fay's death. I wondered what else Gracie had told him. She'd been around Pelican Point long enough to know where all the bodies were buried. I shivered at the image of bodies everywhere.

Maybe I was worried for nothing. I entered the candy shop, deliberately bought too much taffy knowing I'd eat the leftovers—especially the coffee-flavored ones—and headed for my car. The cobblestone sidewalks were filled with people, some arm in arm, some walking their dogs, some with kids plugged into ear pods and wearing hoodies with logos like "Salt Life," "Ripcurl," and "Pipeline."

I got into my car, cautiously backed into the busy street, and started down the block toward the inn. Just as I reached the first corner, I spotted the local sheriff's station.

I stepped on the brakes and did a double take when I spotted the man entering the building.

Henry Hill.

Chapter Eleven
NIMBY

So what was Henry Hill doing at the sheriff's office? Trying to sell him a vacation home? Solar panels? Fake lawn? Not likely.

When I got back to the inn, Noah was in the front yard talking with Harper Smith, my aunts' next-door neighbor/nemesis. I hadn't seen the older man since the party. He was gesturing wildly, and not happily. Noah stood there listening—or maybe tuning him out. I pulled up the driveway, parked, and got out with my bag of goodies.

"Finally!" Harper said as he walked over to me. "Maybe you'll listen to what I have to say. Something's got to be done around here!"

I looked at Noah, but he just rolled his eyes.

"What's wrong, Mr. Smith?" I asked respectfully.

"I thought you were going to speak to your aunts."

I was clueless. "About what?"

"About selling this place. I mean, look at it. What an eyesore." He nodded toward the house.

I had to admit, it stood out from the other houses in the neighborhood.

Murder at Blackwood Inn

"It looks like Count Dracula's summer home," he continued. "Can't you see it doesn't fit with the aesthetics of Pelican Point? All that black and purple and green. Good God! It used to be such a grand place. Now that monstrosity is ruining the serenity of our little town, not to mention my view from next door."

Harper was the one ruining the serenity of the place. And as for the view, the only way he could see the Blackwood house was to come over here, since it was blocked by trees.

Aunt Runa appeared at the door holding a black cat. "What's all the commotion?" she asked, squinting in our general vicinity. "Is that you, Harper?" She came down the steps, carefully avoiding another black cat that lay in her path. "May I help you with something?"

"Yes," Harper said, nearly spitting out the word. "I've asked you nicely to either paint your house a normal color that blends with the environment or sell it and find somewhere else to practice your new-age nonsense." He wiggled his fingers at her. The cat leaped from her arms, apparently startled. "I mean, with your bizarre rooms and hints of ghosts and gremlins, you're bringing down the value of our neighborhood."

Aunt Runa bit her lip before she responded. "I'm sorry you feel that way, Harper, but there are no laws that say we can't paint our house the way we like. We're trying to be good neighbors and boost the town's economy with our bed and breakfast inn. If you can't be civil and stop all this petty poppycock, I'll have to ask you to get off our property. And stay off!" She crossed her arms.

"Petty poppycock?" Harper responded. "You and your weird sister are the ones full of poppycock. One of you is crazy and the other's a loon. Well, you haven't heard the last of me.

I'll find some way to get you all out of here. People around town are talking, you know." He jabbed his finger toward her.

"Talking about what?" I asked.

He raised an eyebrow, as if I should know.

"You mean Patty Fay's death?" Noah said, not mincing words.

Harper looked around, no doubt checking for spies before whispering, "They say she was murdered. Everybody thinks so. And it happened right after your party, I might add."

"What are you implying?" Aunt Runa asked.

"Consider the evidence," Harper suggested.

Aunt Runa eyed him. "What evidence?"

"Poison!" he exclaimed. "From your yard. Not to mention that woo-woo charm that was found clutched in her hand."

"It was a tiger's eye. And it was under the bed," I said, correcting him.

Aunt Runa narrowed her eyes at him. "Who told you about all this?"

Good question, I thought. It was amazing how quickly news—and rumors—spread in this small town. Or maybe not so amazing.

"Everyone knows Patty Fay wanted you to sell your house," Harper said. "She told me the day before she died that if you didn't budge, she knew a way to force you out."

Aunt Runa frowned. "What are you talking about?"

"Isn't it obvious?"

Aunt Runa took a deep breath. "I think it's obvious that you need to get off my property—*our* property—and stop spreading lies or I'll sue you for libel."

"Slander," I said quietly. As a writer, I couldn't help myself. "Libel is a defamatory statement in writing," I whispered, "and slander is spoken."

Aunt Runa shot me a look, then turned to Harper. "*Slander*, then!"

Harper held his hands up and shook his head as if he were dealing with a crazed maniac. Maybe he was. But she was my crazed maniac. And she was right. It was her house—hers and Aunt Hazel's—and they could do whatever they wanted with it, even if I didn't agree with their choices.

Harper turned to go, then spun back around and shook his finger at her again. "You haven't heard the last of this. I'm not the only one who thinks something evil is going on in that house of yours, same as when your father owned the place. You better watch your back."

"Harper," Noah spoke up. "You heard the lady. Stop with the threats. Leave, now, and don't come back or we'll have you arrested for trespassing."

"Oh, I won't need to come back," Harper said with a twisted grin. "Now that the sheriff is involved. You just wait."

With that, Harper stomped off the property, leaving me to wonder what the hell he was up to.

* * *

I was about to say something encouraging to Aunt Runa when I caught sight of a car parked across the street from our driveway. Unlike most of the local vehicles in Pelican Point, which were pickups, this one stood out. It was the same car I'd seen parked next to me downtown—the vintage Mustang, champagne gold with a black side stripe.

I headed down the driveway to check it out. As soon as I reached the street, the car started up. I waved, but the driver ignored me, pulled out, and drove on past. I caught a glimpse of her as she sped off.

Annabelle Topper, the woman who owned the Pelican Point Inn, the Blackwood Inn's competition. She'd also been at the pre-party.

Had she followed me from town? Why was she parked across the street from us? Had she been spying on us? Had she been talking to Harper Smith?

Seconds later I heard the squeal of tires, followed by a crunch and thud. I ran to the end of the driveway and spotted the Mustang in a ditch at the corner. With my phone in hand, ready to call 911, I raced to the car. But when I reached the scene, Annabelle was already out of the car and on her phone. Dressed in a designer suit, with a Hermès scarf around her neck and two chunky gold bracelets around her wrists, she appeared to be unhurt.

"Are you okay?" I asked, puffing, my heart racing.

"Look what you made me do!" Annabelle exclaimed, holding her hand over her phone.

"What?" I asked, baffled by her accusation. "What did *I* do?"

"You . . . you distracted me and made me drive off the road!" she shouted. "I could have been killed."

"Wait. How did I distract you, exactly?"

"I . . . you . . . you were waving like a madwoman," she sputtered.

"Annabelle, I saw you parked across the street from our inn," I said. "I was going to ask you if you needed something when you suddenly pulled away."

"Of course I don't need anything," Annabelle snapped. "Why would I?"

"Then why were you parked across from our inn?"

"I just, uh, pulled over to answer my phone." She took a breath. "I got a call. I thought it might be urgent. Frankly, it's none of your business. I don't know why I'm bothering to tell you."

I shrugged. "Well, if you're okay then, I'll head back—" I started to go.

"By the way, Melissa," she called to me.

"It's Carissa," I corrected her. Again.

"Whatever. You might as well tell your aunts that I know what they did."

"What are you talking about?" My first thought had to do with Patty Fay's death.

She surprised me by saying, "Stealing customers is frowned upon in Pelican Point. You can tell your aunts they won't get away with it."

"Stealing customers? Who did they steal?"

"Henry Hill, for one. He was supposed to be a guest at *my* inn until a room at *your* place suddenly opened up." She snapped her fingers. "Then just like that, he canceled. Coincidence? I don't think so. As soon as I found out he was at your inn, I realized you'd stolen him from me!"

"You can't be serious!" I said, totally flabbergasted. "We never even talked to him until he checked in yesterday. I have no idea why he changed his plans, but we certainly didn't 'steal' him."

"Oh, really?" Annabelle said. "That's not what Patty Fay said before she . . . died."

That caught me off guard. What did Patty Fay have to do with this? "Oh, really? What did she say, exactly?"

Annabelle shook her head. "I'm not in the habit of gossiping, but she made some pretty serious allegations."

"What, *exactly*?" I asked again.

"Oh, no. That's not for me to say. Besides, you'll find out soon enough when Wil—Sheriff Lokey—shows up at your doorstep. Meanwhile, I'd advise you to tell your aunts they won't get away with it."

"Get away with what?" I said, frustrated at her innuendos.

Annabelle ignored me and punched some numbers on her phone. "This is Annabelle Topper. I need a tow."

It was obvious she was done with me. But she'd left me with some disturbing questions, not to mention accusations. Without knowing what exactly she *thought* she knew, I was helpless to do anything about it.

As I walked back to the inn, I decided not to mention my run-in with Annabelle to my aunts. They already had enough on their plates, with the opening of the inn, seeing to the guests, and dealing with Patty Fay's death.

I headed up the pathway and surveyed the uniquely painted house that Harper had complained about. But what caught my eye wasn't the black paint job or the purple and green accents. It was the figure in the window on the top floor.

Someone was in the attic.

I went inside and called to my aunts.

"We're in here, dear," Aunt Hazel answered from the kitchen. "Come join us."

I glanced upstairs. If it wasn't my aunts, who was in the attic? Noah? What was he doing up there? I told myself I was probably overreacting, but with all the weird things going on, I needed to find out if someone might be snooping around. I knew my aunts had stored a lot of my grandfather's belongings in trunks and boxes in the attic. Instead of joining my aunts, I decided to have a look up there.

I was halfway up the staircase, watching carefully for sleeping cats, when I bumped into Henry heading down. *Back already? When had he slipped in?*

"Whoa!" he said, reeling back.

"I'm so sorry," I replied. "I wasn't watching where I was going. Are you okay?"

"Of course. We traveling salesmen have tough skin, not to mention a cast iron gut, resilient liver, and calloused feet. How about you?"

"I'm fine," I said. I didn't want to get into a conversation with him, so I squeezed past him and hurried up the rest of the stairs to the attic on the fourth floor.

Had he been the one in the attic?

The door was open.

I stepped inside and took a look around the room lit only by the sunlight coming in through the window. Not a soul—that I could see, anyway. *Had Henry come from here? Or had my eyes been playing tricks on me?* Talk about gas-lighting yourself.

But that only happened in scary movies.

When you were alone.

In the attic.

I switched on the overhead light—a bare bulb—and circled the small room crowded with boxes, chests, trunks, old furniture, and miscellaneous junk my grandfather had apparently collected over the years. I spotted a trunk labeled "Personal" against the wall and headed over. I tried to open it—I mean, who wouldn't, with a family history like the Blackwoods'. But it was locked. I noticed rust around the lock, so I looked for something to pry it open and found an old wire coat hanger lying on an antique sewing machine deck. I straightened out the hook, stuck it into the lock, and wiggled it around inside until the lock popped open. Easy peasy. Nancy Drew would have been proud.

I lifted the top and found a stack of notebooks inside, much like the one I'd discovered under my bed. I fanned through them—more coded entries dating back thirty years. Apparently my grandfather was quite the record keeper. I set the notebooks aside and noticed a wooden box underneath the pile.

I opened the lid and blinked. *A crystal ball? Seriously?* I lifted the heavy orb—about as heavy as a bowling ball—and peered at it, as if I might see my future. So did my grandfather really believe in this sort of thing? Or was he one of those charlatans, preying on naive townspeople? If so, *Tsk, tsk, Grandfather. Shame on you.*

Inside the box were more occult offerings—candles, incense, tarot cards, a book on palm-reading, a Y-shaped metal stick, and a necklace with an odd symbol like an eye, much like the one on my grandfather's hidden book I'd found under the bed. But to my surprise and delight, at the bottom of the trunk I found an early version of a Ouija board made from wood. It was scratched and somewhat faded and appeared to have been well used. The board brought back childhood memories. Aunt Runa had given me a Ouija board for my tenth birthday, and I'd had so much fun using it to scare my friends. I wondered what had my grandfather had used it for.

I replaced the items, closed the trunk, stood up, and headed for the attic door. A sound came from behind me, somewhere at the back of the attic.

I froze.

After listening for a few seconds, I called out, "Who is it?"

No answer.

I had to check it out, but I needed something to protect myself, just in case. *Like what?*

I tiptoed back to the trunk and reopened it, hoping to find something there. What was my plan? Throw tarot cards at him—or her? Bonk them with the crystal ball? Frisbee the Ouija board at them?

The Y-shaped metal stick seemed to be the only thing that might work. I shoved the Ouija board aside and pulled out the stick. It was about two feet long, made of copper, with a pointed tip sharp enough to stab someone, not that I'd actually do that if it came down to it. Still, whoever was hiding behind those boxes at the back of the attic didn't know that. Maybe it would be enough to scare them off.

I tiptoed over to the boxes, stacked wide and high enough to hide a body—er, person.

"Come out of there!" I yelled.

I held the two ends of the stick and pointed the sharp end out, ready to lunge.

No response.

I poked the top box with the tip, knocking it over.

"Rrrrowwwww!"

Pyewacket! The cat darted out, ran for the open door, and disappeared.

I took a deep breath, my heart beating rapidly. "Scaredy cat," I whispered to myself.

One mystery solved.

But what about the figure I'd seen in the attic window?

Chapter Twelve
Yes. No. Goodbye.

"What've you got there?" came a voice from the beyond. Or at least, that's what it sounded like. Then Noah appeared at the attic door.

"Noah! What are you doing up here?" I asked as he stepped inside.

"I was doing some repair work on the third floor and thought I heard something in the attic." He glanced at the box that had fallen over. Papers were strewn all around it. "Did you do that?"

"Uh, sort of," I admitted.

"With that divining rod you're holding?"

I lowered my weapon. "Diving rod?"

He walked over, took the stick from me, and examined it. "*Divining* rod, also called a dowsing rod, although I once heard Runa call it a 'water witch.' Supposed to be able to locate ground water, precious metals, gemstones, even buried gravesites with it."

"Seriously? Yikes. I hope my grandfather didn't use it to find dead people." What was I saying? Even using it to find water sounded weird. "How's it supposed to work?"

"You hold the Y ends, one in each hand, with the sharper end pointed out. Then you walk around the yard and when it automatically points toward the ground, jackpot—you've got water, or whatever. Be careful, though. Some people consider it satanic."

"But it's fake, right?" I asked.

He shrugged. "It's sort of like how a Ouija board works. The user's involuntary movements actually cause the divining rod to move, so it's no more effective than random chance."

Another pseudoscience my grandfather was apparently into. "Do you think my aunts use this thing? It was tucked away in that trunk." I pointed.

"I haven't seen them with it, only heard a reference to it. So what were you planning to do—stab someone?"

I laughed. *Only if I had to*, I thought.

"Noah, how do you know about all this stuff?"

"I've been working at the Blackwood Inn for a while. You hear things. You see things."

Hear things? See things? How long was a while? Longer than humanly possible? Maybe I didn't want to know.

Okay, I was losing it. I took the rod from Noah and went over to the trunk. After replacing it, I picked up the old Ouija board I'd found and showed it to him. "I think this was my grandfather's too."

"Yup."

"But this one doesn't look like the one I used as a kid," I added. "It's made out of wood, not cardboard, and some of the lettering has worn off."

Noah took the board from my hands and ran his fingers over it. "Yeah, this one seems more like the original Ouija boards from the eighteen hundreds than the ones made today by the toy company. They used to call them spirit boards or a talking boards." He studied it. "This one uses the same alphabet, but the letters are gothic style, arranged in a three-quarters of a circle, with the numbers completing the circle. 'Yes/No/Good Bye' are in the corners." He looked into the trunk. "Did you find the planchette?"

"The what?"

"The little gizmo you use to point to the letters and numbers."

I dug inside and pulled out what I assumed was the planchette. It was also made of wood in the shape of a heart, with a hole in the middle and a nail pierced through the center.

"Planchette, huh? Never knew it was called that. Anyway, this one also looks different from the one I had when I was a kid."

"Same idea," Noah said. "You put it in the middle of the board, place your fingers on one side, your partner does the same on the other side, then you ask a question and wait for it to spell out a message. Most people try to contact a deceased loved one."

I laughed. "My friends and I used it to find out which boy liked us."

Noah smiled. "At least you didn't use it to get money from gullible people."

I looked at Noah. "Do you think my grandfather might have used it for that?"

Noah shrugged. "No clue. Never attended one of his so-called séances. But you'd be surprised how many people believe in things like this. Even smart people, like Arthur Conan Doyle."

"Seriously? The author of *Sherlock Holmes* was into Ouija boards?"

"Yup."

I grinned at him. "Hey, want to give it a try? Is there anyone from the beyond you want to contact?"

He scoffed. "Uh, no thanks."

"You're not scared, are you?" I teased.

"Nope. Too busy." He started for the door.

"Wait! Noah, were you up here a few minutes ago? I thought I saw someone in the window."

"Wasn't me. Could have been one of your aunts. Like I said, I heard someone up here too. But that turned out to be you."

I sighed, knowing it hadn't been my aunts. "Never mind."

He nodded toward the Ouija board still in my hands. "Be careful with that thing. Remember what happened in *The Exorcist*. The girl became possessed by a demon after using one of those. Then her head turned around and she threw up."

I frowned at him. "Stop."

"So, dinner tonight? I may have some news."

He didn't give me a chance to answer. He just winked and walked out, leaving me alone in the creepy old attic. With a mysterious Ouija board.

* * *

I put the Ouija board and planchette back in the trunk, closed it, straightened up, then headed downstairs to finish my chores. By the time I was done, it was already four o'clock, time to prepare for happy hour. There had been no sign of the sheriff or a warrant, so I guessed it had taken longer than I thought. I breathed a sigh of relief, until I had a horrifying thought. *What if he showed up in the middle of happy hour?*

That remined me of the text message I'd left for Aiden to see if he'd learned anything about getting a lawyer. Since I still hadn't heard back from him, I figured he was probably super busy writing articles about cranky neighbors and delinquent children. Hopefully I'd hear soon.

I changed into simple khaki slacks, donned my Blackwood Inn T-shirt, slipped on my comfortable black Tom's, and headed downstairs. The dining room had already been set up for the evening event. A lacy white tablecloth covered the table, and a centerpiece of homegrown flowers—white daisies and yellow sunflowers—held the middle spot. But this time there wasn't a crystal in the center. In fact, if Aunt Runa had put some out, she'd done a good job of hiding them.

I surveyed the table. Sparkling wine glasses had been placed at one end of the table, next to small porcelain plates and floral cloth napkins, items that looked like they'd been in the Blackwood family for years. Various dips and sauces in tiny glass bowls semi-circled the flowers, leaving room at the other end of the table for appetizers soon to arrive. I was surprised to hear soft classical music playing in the background, thinking my aunts would have preferred themes from movies like *Halloween* or *Psycho*.

When I entered the kitchen, I found a beehive of activity. Aunt Hazel was opening bottles of local wines. Aunt Runa was arranging aromatic snacks on several platters. And Marnie had just pulled an oozing baked brie from the oven to cool on the counter.

"Carissa!" Aunt Hazel exclaimed. "You're here! Will you take these bottles of wine to the dining table for me? The guests will be down before we know it!"

I did as I was told, making several trips. As I set the last of the bottles on the table, someone touched my back. Startled, I spun around.

"Aiden!" The newspaper man was dressed in cocktail casual—black slacks, button-down shirt, sans tie, and Topsiders. "What are you doing here?"

He seemed taken aback and I realized my question and tone sounded rude. "Sorry! I mean, nice to see you."

He chuckled and pushed his glasses back against the bridge of his nose. "No worries. Your aunts invited me. I think they're buttering me up for more publicity."

"I wouldn't doubt it. Actually, I've been trying to reach you. I stopped by the newspaper office earlier, but you were out."

He nodded. "It's been one of those days. What's up?"

"Maybe we can talk later? Right now I need to help my aunts with happy hour, but make yourself at home. And help yourself to some wine."

Before I could return to the kitchen, I heard footfalls on the staircase. Time was up. Happy hour was about to begin, and it was my job to greet the guests. My aunts and Marnie would need to finish the final preparations in the kitchen on their own.

Jonathan, one of the newlyweds, was the first to arrive. He looked tired. *A busy day of sightseeing? Or perhaps an afternoon delight?*

"Welcome, Jonathan. Will Lindsay be down soon?"

He shook his head. "Uh . . . she got a call from work. Had to leave this afternoon. I figured I might as well stay and enjoy the rest of the weekend before heading home."

That was weird. He was finishing his honeymoon by himself? From his demeanor, I sensed something was off.

"I'm so sorry," I said, "but I'm glad you stayed. Please help yourself to a glass of wine."

Moments later the McLaughlin couple appeared, minus the two boys.

"Where are your kids?" I asked as they entered the dining area.

Staci sighed. "Playing video games."

Mike nodded. "Thank goodness we brought those things along."

I smiled, feeling relieved I didn't have to deal with the twins. "How was your day in Pelican Point?"

"Exhausting," they said at the same time.

"I'll bet," I said, remembering their water activity plans. "Well, enjoy happy hour. Sounds like you need it. Wine is over there, and appetizers will be out shortly."

The Hollywood couple descended next, wearing vintage shirts with matching mufflers except in two different colors. They hugged the others in greeting as if they were all old friends, then headed for the wine.

I glanced up the stairs, but there was no sign of Henry. Although he didn't look like the wine type—more of a beer or whiskey guy—I wondered if he might be having his own private happy hour. *Shame on me.*

With the guests busy chatting and drinking, I returned to the kitchen to see what I could do to help. I grabbed a couple of plates of cheesy appetizers and returned to the dining room, where the guests were engaged in lively banter. However, that suddenly stopped when they seemed to realize I was back in the room. Everyone turned and looked at me. *Was my slip showing? I don't wear a slip. Something in my teeth? A hair out of place?*

Just as suddenly, the guests turned back. *Odd.* Jonathan said something to Aiden I couldn't hear. Staci and Mike began checking their cellphones. And Javier and Malik each stuffed a shrimp in their mouths and kept silent.

Whatever they'd been talking about had come to an abrupt end because of me, I suspected. I was about to ask what was going on when Henry called down from the top of the stairs.

"Hel-lo, everybody!" he said as he started down the steps, gripping the handrail and swaying a bit. "Am I in'errupting something? What were you all talkin' about? Is there an elephant in the room?" His slurred words told me I'd been right about the pre-function in his room. Henry was clearly intoxicated.

Everyone watched as Henry staggered down, then stumbled over toward the dining table. I worried if he fell, the inn would be in big trouble. And with an attorney present, it would be an open-and-shut case.

I ran over to him and took his arm. He frowned and yanked it away. "Leggo of me. I'm fine. Let's get this party started."

No one spoke.

Henry scanned their faces, then laughed. "Y'all look like you've seen a ghost."

"Henry," I began.

"Yes, Carissa, my dear," he said. He blinked heavily.

"Would you like some tea?" I offered. "Or coffee?" *Or maybe a cold shower?*

He smiled. "No thanks, sweetheart. What I'd like are the details about what happened here the other night. Isn't that what everyone is buzzing about?"

"What do you mean?" I asked him, although I knew.

"Your aunts' realtor. What was her name—Patty Ann? Patty Sue? The one who died just after your pre-opening soiree."

The other guests looked at me. It was obvious everyone had heard about the death of Patty Fay. That's what had caused the sudden end of their quiet conversations. I wondered how they'd found out.

"Uh, yes," I said. Just then, my aunts entered through the swinging door with more plates and set them on the table. When they saw the looks on their guests' faces, their smiles drooped.

"Is something wrong?" Aunt Hazel asked.

"I dunno," Henry said, then burped. "You tell us."

"About what?" she said, blinking several times.

I sighed. "Aunt Hazel, our guests know about Patty Fay's . . . death."

Aunt Hazel's eyes went wide. "Oh, yes. So tragic! And so sudden."

"Oddly sudden," Henry said. "According to your local sheriff."

So that's what he'd been doing at the sheriff's office—getting information from Sheriff Lokey. What had he learned?

"Has the sheriff found out anything more about . . . her death?" Aunt Hazel asked.

"You mean like she was probably poisoned and one of your crystals was found under her bed?" he answered.

My stomach clenched. Could this get any worse?

"Any idea how that crystal got there?" Henry asked loudly.

Aunt Runa spoke up. "Of course not. I assume she stole it."

"Wait a minute," Henry said. "Are you accusing the woman—now deceased—of stealing from you? That's a pretty big accusation." He looked at Jonathan. "Am I right, barrister?"

"No, of course she's not," I said, stepping in for damage control before Jonathan could say anything.

Henry returned his focus to Aunt Runa. "Why do you think she would steal something like that? Was it worth a lot of money?"

Aunt Runa shook her head. "I have no idea. I would have gladly given her one if she'd asked."

"Really?" Henry asked. "So why do you think she didn't just ask?"

The room fell as silent as a graveyard.

How had Henry learned all these details? Had the sheriff really told him everything? Why would he?

Staci suddenly set down her wine glass. "You know, I think I better go check on the boys. Don't want to leave them alone too long. Thank you for the wine and snacks." I noticed she hadn't eaten a single thing.

Mike set his glass next to his wife's. "I'll go with her. She's right. No telling what those two little imps have been up to." With that they headed up the stairs.

"Actually," Javier said to Malik, "I'm wiped out from our day of shopping." He set down his glass. "Why don't we head out for a quick bite at the Shell and Claw, then turn in early."

Malik nodded. He, too, set down his glass and followed Javier out the door.

Jonathan turned to me. "Is all of this true?"

Aiden, who'd been silently witnessing the scene, set down his glass. I wondered what he thought of all this—and what he might put in his newspaper. "Listen, folks. We can't jump to any conclusions. I'm sure the sheriff will find out what happened and all of this will be settled."

Jonathan nodded. "Agreed. Carissa, ladies, let me know if I can be of any help. Meanwhile, I'd better get back to a case I'm working on."

"But you haven't eaten anything," Aunt Hazel said, gesturing toward the table of nearly untouched appetizers.

"I'll get something from Door Dash later. But thanks." He headed up the stairs.

I looked around for Aiden, but he was heading out the door behind the Hollywood couple. Damn. I'd wanted to ask him about finding an attorney.

Henry, the lone remaining guest, turned to me, and narrowed his red, rheumy eyes. "Well, I think this party's over. G'night, y'all. See you in the morning."

I turned to my aunts, who were standing by the dining table. Aunt Hazel looked completely baffled. Aunt Runa looked angry.

What next? I didn't want to know.

Chapter Thirteen
Never Drink Alone

I had nightmares. All night. And not the good kind where I'm swept away by swashbuckling pirates. Not this time. These dreams were scary. Things in the attic. Things under the bed. Things coming to life. I'd kicked off all the blankets sometime during the night and woke up freezing, even though I was dripping with sweat.

I checked the time on my phone. Only an hour until breakfast! I'd overslept! I jumped out of bed, showered, and dressed in record time. Grabbing my phone, I headed out the door and spotted Noah in the hallway.

I'd forgotten all about our dinner!

"Noah!" I exclaimed. "I'm so sorry about last night. Things were so crazy. Rain check?"

"I heard. No worries," he said, holding up a hand. "Your aunts sent me to get you. They're concerned."

"I overslept," I said, then hurried past Noah, down the stairs, through the dining room, and into the kitchen, leaving him in the dust.

"Well, look who's finally up!" Aunt Runa said, giving me a twisted smile. "Sleeping Beauty?"

"More like Sleeping Zombie," I said. "Sorry I'm late. What do you need me to do?"

Aunt Runa, Aunt Hazel, and Marnie all gave me orders. I rushed off to fill them before the first guests arrived for breakfast in the dining room. When I was done, I checked the table, made sure everything was ready, and breathed a sigh of relief just as I heard footfalls on the stairs.

"Good morning," I said, greeting the guests as they entered the room in single file. As they took their places at the table, Aunt Hazel made the rounds with pomegranate tea. Marnie brought out bowls of blueberry cobbler topped with whipped cream and chocolate espresso biscotti. Aunt Runa passed out plates of spinach, gouda, and tomato omelets with sides of thick sliced bacon, then offered the boys marshmallow/rice cereal squares.

"Oh, I should have mentioned the other day," Staci said. "They really shouldn't have any more sugar. They were bouncing off the walls after that Scooby drink you gave them."

Too late. The boys had devoured the breakfast treats before their mother could stop them. She frowned at Aunt Runa, as if it were her fault.

"Where's Henry?" Jonathan asked, after nodding at the McLaughlins and the Hollywood couple.

I glanced at the staircase. "I don't know," I said. I decided to check on him after his intoxicated appearance last night, but as I began to climb the stairs, I saw him on the second-floor landing, about to head down.

"I was just coming to look for you," I called up to him.

"No need," he said, holding onto the rail as he descended carefully. "Just had to finish a few phone calls."

"How are you feeling?" I asked when he reached the last step. I noticed his hands were trembling a little.

He rubbed his stomach. "A little gassy."

TMI. "Well, have a seat. Breakfast is being served."

Henry took his place at the end of the table just as Marnie arrived with her savory artisan quiche. The guests certainly got their money's worth for the breakfast part of the bed and breakfast. I could barely eat half a bagel in the morning.

I noticed everyone was quieter than usual and figured they were probably tired from yesterday's adventures. That or they didn't want to bring up the topic of Patty Fay's death. Even the boys were unusually sedate, even after all that sugar. Fine with me.

And then Henry broke the silence and said, "So, any news on the dead woman yet?"

Everyone except the boys stopped eating and stared at him.

"Nothing?" he answered himself, cutting into his quiche. "Hmm. Maybe that newspaper fellow who was here last night knows something. Seems a pretty big story for a small town like Pelican Point. What was his name again?"

"Aiden Quinn," I offered reluctantly. I wondered why Aiden had left last night without saying goodbye. Probably because he was embarrassed for us. "But I'm not sure he knows much more than anyone else," I added.

"Maybe," Henry said, shrugging. "Maybe not. Hey, Jonathan, where's your bride?"

Jonathan took a moment to wipe his mouth. "Uh, she had to leave. A business thing." He cleared this throat then added, "So what's your interest in all this about the woman who died, Henry? You seem quite . . . interested."

Henry waved his fork as he spoke. "Just curious. Human nature, you know. Especially when something like this happens practically under your nose." He took another jab at the quiche, then stopped with his fork in midair. I thought he was about to say something more when his head bobbed, as if he were trying to keep it upright.

"Henry?" I asked. "Are you all right?"

Henry's eyelids fluttered. The fork fell from his hand and he began to swoon. "I . . . uh . . ." He tried to talk but seemed to struggle with the words. He looked down at his quiche, mumbled something like, "No . . . no . . ." then fell forward, his face landing in his half-eaten serving.

The other guests gasped.

Marnie, standing in the doorway, screamed, nearly dropping the tea kettle. Her other hand went to her hidden necklace.

Aunt Hazel and Aunt Runa came running from the kitchen. As soon as they saw Henry bent over in his breakfast, they froze.

I ran to Henry and lifted his face from the quiche. Cheesy pieces stuck to his cheek. "Call 911! And someone help me get him on the floor!"

Jonathan jumped out of his seat and dashed over to help me. As soon as we eased Henry onto the floor, I checked his mouth for any obstruction and cleared away the remnants of quiche. I felt for his pulse, but couldn't feel anything. Maybe I wasn't doing it right.

"Did someone call 911?" I asked, trying to push away the panic.

"I did," Staci said. "They're on their way."

"Does anyone know if he has a heart condition or some other health problem? Any allergies?" I asked.

No one answered.

I couldn't wait around for an ambulance to arrive. I had to do something. I placed my hands on his chest and began pushing, giving him CPR. He was a big man and doing chest compressions wasn't easy, but I kept at it until Jonathan took over.

Finally I heard the sirens.

"The paramedics are here!" Aunt Hazel announced, heading for the door. She let the two EMTs inside and pointed to the dining room. "He's in there!"

They rushed in with their bags and headed for the still unresponsive man lying on the floor.

"Stand back," one of them commanded as the other one knelt down.

Jonathan stopped chest compressions and scooted out of the way to give the EMTs space. While one of them got out an oxygen mask, the other took Henry's pulse. No one moved. No one breathed as the EMTs did their job.

After what seemed an eternity, one of the EMTs looked at his partner. I knew that look. It wasn't going well. "We've got to get him out of here, stat. Get the stretcher."

I felt the blood rush from my head. *This can't be happening! Not here! Not now!*

The EMT who remained checked his vitals again.

I could tell by his expression that our eccentric guest, Henry Hill, was dead.

It was the second death in Pelican Point in two days.

And both were tied to the Blackwood Bed and Breakfast Inn.

* * *

Sheriff Lokey and Deputy Santos arrived moments later and entered the inn to find a group of horrified onlookers staring at what I assumed was a dead body. Staci and Mike had sent their boys upstairs, in spite of their morbid pleas to stay. Jonathan stood nearby, stroking the stubble on his chin.

Meanwhile, Javier and Malik were on their phones, texting like mad.

The sheriff made his way around the table to the spot on the floor where Henry lay silent. The corpse was already beginning to lose the rosy color in his face. One of the EMTs packed up their equipment, then helped the other place the body on the gurney. Before they lifted it up, the sheriff knelt down on one knee, briefly examined the body, then stood up.

"Everyone stay put," the sheriff announced, as the EMTs raised the gurney and prepared to leave. "This is a crime scene. Don't touch anything and don't go anywhere. I'll want to talk to everyone." He said something to one of the EMTs, while the other one made a call on his radio.

As soon as they exited, the sheriff gestured with his pen for Jonathan to follow him into the kitchen. One by one he met with the witnesses, including my aunts and Marnie. I was the last one standing other than Noah, who was, of course, nowhere in sight.

"Miss Blackwood," he said, waving his arm toward the kitchen. My turn. I followed him in.

"What happened here?" he asked, turning a page in his small notebook.

"Honestly, I have no clue," I said, shaking my head. "Henry—Mr. Hill—was sitting at the table, chatting, eating his quiche, and all of a sudden he keeled over, face first, into his food. Jonathan and I put him on the floor, and we administered CPR, but by the time the EMTs arrived, it was obvious he was gone. The whole thing was just horrible!" I shivered at the thought.

I gave Sheriff Lokey as many details as I could remember, but there wasn't anything significant to add. It seemed like a freak occurrence. A heart attack? An aneurysm? Liver failure?

"I need to see his room," the sheriff said, closing his notepad.

I nodded and led him through the dining room to the stairs. He and the deputy followed me to Henry's room. The door was closed and unlocked.

"Stay here," the sheriff said to me. I stood outside the door for as long as I could—a few seconds, at least—until curiosity overcame me. I peered around the door jamb and spotted the two law enforcement officers standing on either side of the unmade bed. The room was a mess, with clothing, papers, and fast-food wrappers strewn about. But Sheriff Lokey wasn't focused on the clutter. He was holding up an empty bottle of whiskey with a gloved hand and sniffing the contents.

"Bag this," he said to Deputy Santos. She reached for the bottle with her gloved hand and inserted it into a clear plastic bag marked "Evidence."

Hmm. Had Henry Hill actually drunk himself to death?

The sheriff rummaged through some of the papers lying on the bed, then picked up a leather wallet sitting on the bedside table, nearly buried underneath several candy wrappers. He opened it, riffled through the contents, then pulled out the man's driver's license. After looking it over, he set the ID down on the bed, then pulled out a business card from the wallet and set it next to the license. He pulled out another business card, then another, and another, and another.

"Check this out," he said to his deputy, indicating the display laid out in a row.

She leaned over and read the cards aloud: "Henry Hill, Solar Sales Consultant. Harry Holmes, Artificial Turf Sales. Hank Hawkins, Time-Share Resales Marketing." She stopped reading after the third one and picked up the ID. "Says here his name is Herman H. Hicks." She pulled out her phone and called a number. "Yeah, Jack, can you run an NCIC on a Herman H. Hicks—Hotel India Charley Kilo Sierra." She paused for several moments, then said, "Ten-four," and turned to Sheriff Lokey. "That's interesting," she said.

"What did they find?" the sheriff asked.

"Herman Hicks is a licensed private investigator in the state of California."

"He's a PI?" the sheriff said. "I should have known, what with all the questions he was asking me earlier at the station. Wonder why he didn't just tell me when he came to the office?"

I ducked back into the hallway before the sheriff caught me eavesdropping. So what *was* Henry-Herman-what's-his-name really doing in Pelican Point? Investigating something—or someone? At the Blackwood Bed and Breakfast Inn?

* * *

I tiptoed back down the stairs and checked on my aunts, who were sitting at the dining room table whispering to each other.

That ceased when I entered.

"Hey," I said softly. "Are you two okay?"

"Yes, of course, dear," Aunt Hazel said. "A little shook up, you know." She glanced at Aunt Runa.

"Where's everybody else?" I asked.

Aunt Runa sighed. "The other guests are back in their rooms, packing up. They'll be wanting to check out soon."

Oh boy.

"Can I get you some tea?" I offered, figuring they could use a cup of their go-to remedy.

They nodded listlessly.

"I'll be right back." I headed into the kitchen, expecting to see Marnie already boiling the water. There was no sign of her. I filled the kettle, set it on the stove, and was about to get out two cups and saucers when Noah entered through the back door.

"Are they still here?" he asked, nodding toward the dining room.

"If you mean the EMTs, no. If you mean Sheriff Lokey and his deputy, yes, they're upstairs," I answered. "And if you mean the guests, they're probably getting ready to check out. Where have you been?"

"What's the sheriff doing upstairs?" he asked, without answering my question.

"Checking out Henry's—or whatever his name is—bedroom. Where have you been?" I asked again.

"They need a search warrant for that," he said, still ignoring me.

"He may have probable cause," came a voice behind me. Jonathan had quietly entered the kitchen.

"We'll see about that," Noah said. He bolted from the kitchen into the dining room. I was right behind him, forgetting about the promised tea, as was Jonathan. The sheriff was already in the dining room, standing at the double doors that led to the garden.

"What's going on?" Aunt Hazel asked, looking bewildered.

"Where are you going?" Noah asked.

"To check out the garden," he said. "I think, under these circumstances—"

Noah cut him off. "Did you get that warrant?"

The sheriff glanced at his deputy. "Uh . . . still waiting on the judge. But since we've got another dead body, I didn't think I needed one. There's probable cause."

"Technically, you don't," Jonathan said, contradicting himself from earlier. I had a feeling it was the lawyer in him.

"Listen," the sheriff said. "I was just going to look around, that's all. The ladies said it was okay. By the way, are you their lawyer?" He nodded toward my aunts.

"No, but I am an attorney. You can come back when you have that warrant."

The sheriff sighed. "All right, then. We'll be back this afternoon. With your warrant."

He turned to go and gestured to his deputy to join him. With a last tip of his hat, he was out the door.

Aunt Hazel looked at Jonathan. "Do they really need a warrant?"

"They do if they want to search the place," Jonathan answered.

"But why? We didn't do anything wrong," Aunt Runa argued.

"Any law enforcement officer needs a warrant issued by a judge to search a person, residence, vehicle, and so on, if they suspect there may be evidence of illegal activity."

"And what happens when he does get a warrant?" Aunt Runa asked.

"He can confiscate any evidence he finds and use it against you," he said. "But first he has to show probable cause to the judge that a crime has been committed."

"Like what?" Aunt Hazel asked.

"Like, if he has a reasonable belief that a felony has occurred. And he doesn't know that. At least not yet, although someone just died here, under unusual circumstances. And so recently after the other death."

"Patty Fay," Aunt Runa whispered.

"Right," Jonathan said.

"Well, I'm sure Mr. Hill had some kind of medical episode and passed away from it," Aunt Runa added. "He didn't look so well."

Aunt Hazel turned to her sister. "So why would the sheriff want to see my gardens *this* time? He can't possibly think I poisoned two people."

Jonathan raised his eyebrows.

"I'm sure he's looking for belladonna," Noah said.

"Noah!" Aunt Hazel said, clearly upset at what he'd just implied.

"Sorry, Hazel," Noah said, "but you won't be able to keep your secret garden a secret much longer. Not in this town. Now with what's happened."

"Wait a minute," Jonathan said. "You grow belladonna in your garden? Why?"

Silence from my aunts.

I looked at Noah. He met my eyes. His were filled with concern. Mine were probably filled with panic.

And I didn't need a Ouija board to tell me we'd better get my aunts a good lawyer. ASAP.

Chapter Fourteen
In Need of a Mystifying Oracle

I turned to Jonathan. "I don't suppose you'd be able to represent my aunts, would you?"

"Uh," he said, obviously taken by surprise. "I'm really swamped right now. And I have some personal issues to deal with. Surely you know someone in town who could help?"

Aunt Hazel shook her head. "Andrew Jeffers, the lawyer who handled our father's will, moved away to a retirement community or something like that. We haven't really needed one, at least not until now."

"I'm waiting to hear from Aiden about finding a lawyer," I told my aunts. "Since he's the local newspaper guy, I figured he knows everyone in this town and the towns nearby."

My cell phone rang. I checked the caller ID. Speak of the devil.

"Carissa?" Aiden said. "Sorry I didn't get back to you sooner. There's a lot going on, as you can imagine, especially after what happened. Is everyone all right?"

I stepped into the parlor so I could talk freely. "Actually, no. My Aunt Hazel really needs a lawyer. Any chance you've found someone?"

"As you probably know, the only attorney in Pelican Point was Andrew Jeffers, but he's in a care facility because of health problems. Dementia, I think. I've been trying to find someone in Santa Rosa, but so far, no luck. I still have a few contacts I'm waiting to hear back from. I'll pester them a little and see if I can get a commitment. Wish I could do more."

"Well, thanks for what you're doing," I said. "I'm really worried about her."

"Why? Has something else happened?"

I hesitated to tell him too much. After all, he was a reporter and I had no idea if I could fully trust him not to put this troubling matter in his newspaper. Bad publicity was not what we needed right now. Still, I didn't have much choice if I wanted his help.

"Actually, I think both of my aunts may be in trouble, for different reasons. I don't want to go into the details now, not over the phone, but the sooner you find someone, the better. Things seem to be heating up around here."

"I'm really sorry, Carissa," he said. "I've been hearing rumors. People talk a lot in this town, so I know what you're going through. Give me a few hours. I'm sure I'll have a name for you soon."

"Thanks, Aiden." I felt a moment of relief, until I remembered he'd said he'd heard rumors. I was about to ask, "What rumors?" when Jonathan suddenly appeared in the parlor doorway. As soon as I saw the concerned look on his face, I knew it wasn't good news. I told Aiden I had to go, and hung up.

"Still no luck finding an attorney?" Jonathan asked.

I shook my head. "Aiden from the newspaper says he may have a few leads, but so far nothing. Besides, I'm sure he's busy with his own work."

Jonathan nodded. "Okay, I'll see what I can do. But I can't promise anything, all right?"

I thanked him, forced a smile, and returned to the dining room to join my aunts and Marnie at the table. Marnie got up when I entered and said, "I'll make some tea," before disappearing into the kitchen.

I looked at my moping, silent aunts. Time for a distraction to get their minds off the latest development.

"Listen, you two, I need your help while we wait for the sheriff and that warrant. Aunt Hazel, would you see if you can find any paperwork from Patty Fay? I know it's a long shot, but maybe we missed something that might give us a clue about who wanted her dead. Aunt Runa, I'd like you to dig up everything you can find from your father's former lawyer. See if there is any information about any kind of legal action. Or even something from Henry Hill, that PI. You never know. There might be a connection."

My aunts nodded, got up, and headed for the stairs.

"Wait! Where are you going?" I asked. "I didn't mean right this minute. Marnie's bringing tea."

"To the attic," Aunt Runa answered. "This can't wait."

"Is that where you keep important papers?" I asked. I hadn't found any when I'd been up there snooping around. But then, I hadn't really been looking.

"Our father's stuff is up there, all the old paperwork," Aunt Runa replied.

"What about the basement?" I asked.

"There is no basement, remember? Not in these West Coast Italianate houses," Aunt Runa said. "They're built up to look like they have a basement, but it's just a facade."

A facade? This old house was still full of surprises. I decided that when I had time, I'd have to go back to the attic and do a little more snooping. Were there any skeletons in the closet? Or just a few ghosts? At any rate, I remembered Patty Fay's initials had been in my grandfather's secret coded notebook, along with several other locals. Was there a connection between his notes and her death?

And what about a.k.a. Henry Hill, the salesman/private investigator who suddenly appeared out of nowhere? Had he been investigating one of the Pelican Point residents? It couldn't have been a coincidence that he arrived so soon after Patty Fay's death. Why was he here? And who was he working for? I tapped my fingers on the table, trying to think. If I were a private investigator, what would I be looking for?

Marnie entered with a tray of teacups, interrupting my thoughts. She blinked when she saw my aunts had left the table and asked, "Where did they go?"

I told her. She shrugged. "Well, then. I guess I'll start cleaning the rooms."

"Thanks," I said. "I think everyone has checked out except Jonathan."

She nodded, then returned to the kitchen with the tea.

I decided to go to my room—my grandfather's room when he was alive, I reminded myself—and check out the contents of the Mesmer book I'd found under the bed. Maybe there were more secrets hidden inside, like those mysterious codes. Codes I hadn't cracked. Yet.

I climbed the stairs, unlocked the door, and got out the notebook I'd hidden in the top drawer with my underwear. Grabbing a pad of paper and a pen from the desk, I sat down on the window seat and began with the letters etched on the cover. *A* and *B*. Those had to be Abraham Blackwood's initials. But what puzzled me still was the symbol that looked a lot like the triangle on the back of a dollar bill. I'd forgotten what it meant, so I Googled "eye in triangle dollar bill" and read the first entry that came up:

"The Eye of Providence, also known as the all-seeing eye, represents protection. The ancient Egyptians called it the Eye of Horus and used it as a motif on coffins that allowed the dead to see into the afterlife."

"Oookay," I said. "So did my grandfather use the Eye of Providence for protection? Or to see into the afterlife?"

While I had my phone open, I Googled "Abraham Blackwood." Seconds later I was staring at an obit for my grandfather, published in the *Pelican Point Press* six months ago. It was the first time I'd seen it.

"Abraham Blackwood the Third, a native of Pelican Point, died last night at the age of 80. Blackwood came from a long line of Blackwoods who settled in the area in the 1800s from the British Isles. He inherited the Italianate house on Heron Drive from his father, Abraham Blackwood the Second. The house had originally been built by a Russian seaman named Viktor Vasily, who died in the home soon after his wife committed suicide. Reported to be haunted, the house sat deserted for years until Abraham Blackwood the First purchased it. After the death of Catherine Blackwood a few years ago, Blackwood was rumored to have held séances, spiritual meetings, and other metaphysical events at his residence. Labeled an eccentric by some of the townspeople, many people said he considered himself a master of the mystical arts. He is survived by three children: Runa Blackwood, Hazel Blackwood, and Robert Blackwood. It was believed he died of natural causes due to old age."

I checked the byline. The obit had been written by Aiden Quincy.

Hmm. I wondered if Aiden knew even more about my grandfather's death and the history of the house. I'd have to ask him when he got back to me about finding a lawyer.

I looked at the symbol on the cover of the notebook. So Grandfather fancied himself some kind of seer or medium? Someone who could contact the dead? I turned to the first page of the notebook. The letters **S N C R C L** were written across the top of the page in what appeared to be my grandfather's old-fashioned scrawl. I said the letters aloud, almost like an incantation, hoping that would give me a clue to their meaning. They had to stand for something. I repeated the letters a few more times. When I noticed there were no vowels, I tried sounding out the consonants.

S N C. Since. Snick. Sinko . . .

Nothing. I tried the next four letters.

C R C L. Kerkel? Sersel? Serkel . . .

Circle?

I grinned. Once I saw it—and heard it—it was obvious.

Séance Circle!

I looked at the next set of letters.

M M B R S.

Easy one. Members.

Séance Circle Members. That was the heading. Here it was—a record that my grandfather actually held séances!

I worked on deciphering the rest of the coded words, assuming my grandfather used the same cipher method—using only consonants and omitting the vowels. I turned the page and scanned the letters at the top of the five columns, all written in my grandfather's scrawl.

DT   TM   CLNT GSTS CNTCT

Curious, I fanned through the pages until I came to the last completed page. The rest of the journal was blank. I read the letters for the first column out loud. "Dit?" I glanced at the entry underneath. "0313."

Dit? Dot? Dat? Date? Wait. Did those numbers in that first column represent a date? If so, that would be March thirteenth. The obituary said my grandfather died on March twenty-first. That was six days after the last journal entry.

I went on to the next column: **TM**. That had to stand for "time." The numbers fit: 1145 had to be 11:45 PM.

Then came **CLNT**. Client? I checked the letters underneath. **PFJ**. So far I'd been sounding out the consonants to form words, but this one jumped out at me. These had to be initials: *Patty Fay Johnstone.*

The little hairs on my arms tingled. If she was a client, who was she trying to reach beyond the veil?

I went on to the next heading. **GSTS**. My first thought was the word "ghosts." Nah. Too obvious. I tried a few more words and finally came up with "guests." If you had a séance, you had a client and the rest were guests. I checked the list of initials underneath:

A.T., G.G., M.C.

Annabelle? Gracie? Marnie? All women. Were there more?

All three had been present at our pre-party the night before we officially opened the inn. The night Patty Fay died.

I took a moment to process this, then went on to the next code, which was easy to decipher. "**CNTCT**" had to mean "Contact." Underneath was the name "Cptn Vktr Vsl." The name of the seaman in my grandfather's obit—and the original owner of the house—Captain Viktor Vasily. Wow.

I flipped backward through the most recent pages and recognized the same coded names of guests attending the séances. One name in particular came up again and again as a client—Patty Fay. Had she been trying to contact this Captain Vasily? What did she hope to learn?

I heard a distant siren and looked out the window. The sheriff. Uh-oh. So soon? It had only been a few hours since he'd left. I watched as the patrol car pulled up to the house. Sheriff Lokey and Deputy Santos got out and headed for the front door.

I set the notebook on the window seat, slipped into my shoes, and bolted out of the bedroom faster than Pyewacket. I slalomed down the stairs past sleeping cats before the doorbell rang. To my surprise, Noah had beat me to the door. He shot me a look of concern before opening it.

"Sheriff," Noah said.

"May I come in?" Sheriff Lokey asked, sounding even more formal than the first time. He held up some papers. "I have a warrant."

I felt my heart sink.

Noah looked over the warrant papers, then stepped back, allowing the sheriff and deputy to enter the foyer. I caught a glimpse of my aunts sitting at the dining table, surrounded by papers and open boxes. They looked up as the sheriff entered.

"Wil?" Aunt Hazel said, setting down the paper she held. "Do you have news?"

The sheriff removed his hat and held up the warrant. "Hazel. Runa," he said softly. I sensed he wasn't enjoying being here. "We have a warrant to search your yard."

Aunt Runa glanced at her sister. Something seemed to pass between them. To the sheriff she said, "Go ahead, then, if you must. We have nothing to hide."

He nodded, replaced his hat, and headed out the double doors followed by his deputy.

Aunt Hazel sighed, then mumbled, "Oh dear."

"I'll ask Marnie to get us some more tea," Aunt Runa said, ducking into the kitchen.

I joined Aunt Hazel at the table, took her hand, and patted it. "It's going to be all right." I didn't know what else to say.

She nodded absently. Moments later, Aunt Runa returned with a tray of fresh tea and set it down on the buffet. As she placed the cups in front of us, I glanced at the papers strewn about. I picked one up and asked, "Did you get these from the attic?"

Aunt Hazel nodded.

"Did you find anything?"

Aunt Hazel dug into a pile of papers and pulled out an old newspaper. "Well, we did find this," she said, handing it to me.

Aunt Runa cleared her throat, as if to admonish her sister, but Aunt Hazel looked at her and said, "I think Carissa should know."

I took the old yellowing newspaper clipping from the *Pelican Point Press*. It read: "The Blackwood House on Heron Street narrowly escaped destruction last night by firebugs who ignited the place. The Italianate mansion, built and once owned by the wealthy Russian Captain Viktor Vasily, was purchased by . . ."

Blah blah blah. I skimmed what I already knew, then read on: "Once a rambling cobwebbed structure filled with damp musty air after years of neglect, the four-story house had been renovated by the Blackwoods, and passed down to their heirs. The current owner, Abraham Blackwood, was known to have reveled in the ghostly stories surrounding it, including its creaking floors, whistling windows, and cold draughts as if from the grave. 'No one could deny that the place was brimming with atmosphere, mystery, and something else,' said Mr. Blackwood."

I stopped reading. Again, nothing really new.

"Keep reading," Aunt Hazel said.

I nodded.

"One local resident, who asked to remain anonymous, said, 'I witnessed six people from town who crowded into a hidden séance room and held hands at the circular table, waiting with anticipation for ghostly manifestations. A spiritualist and medium by the name of Madam X began telling a story of the previous owner's wife who hung herself in the house, and said the woman's spirit roams the house restlessly, appearing as a dancing shadow, a shrill cry, a strong gust of wind, an echoing creak. Suddenly, the candle in the middle of the table extinguished itself. The medium began to speak unintelligibly under her breath, moaning and swaying in a trance. When she spoke, her voice was not her own: "I see a young woman in a low-necked gown hovering over the table. She's grasping at her throat, her face a hideous purple, her eyes bulging, her tongue protruding." At that point two of the guests screamed, claiming they saw her, too, and one guest fainted.'"

"Vivid," I said. "Any idea where that woman supposedly committed suicide in the house?"

"No idea," Aunt Runa said.

"What about this hidden séance room—do you know anything about that?"

"No," Aunt Hazel said. "If there was one, we never found it."

"Who do you think Madam X was?" I asked.

They shrugged.

I wondered if it could have been my grandfather in disguise. My aunts had said he liked to wear costumes and dress up as a magician.

Before I could ask any more questions, the sheriff and his deputy entered the dining room followed by Noah, who had apparently accompanied them. The deputy was holding a clear plastic bag with a plant inside. I recognized it immediately. *Belladonna.*

Aunt Hazel stood up. "You're taking one of my plants?"

The sheriff nodded. "For testing."

Aunt Hazel's mouth gaped open. I spoke for her. "Sheriff, what will that prove? Testing that plant doesn't mean it was used to kill someone."

Deputy Santos held up her cell phone. "Maybe not. But there appear to be several pieces missing from this one. This is photographic evidence."

Aunt Hazel glanced at her sister, then at Noah, then me.

"Hazel?" the sheriff said. "Can you explain why the plant is missing some pieces?"

She shook her head, her face pale.

The sheriff sighed. "I'm sorry to do this, but Hazel Blackwood, you need to come with me down to the station. I have some questions I'd like to ask you. On the record."

Aunt Hazel's eyes filled with tears. "Wil? Are you . . . are you arresting me?"

The sheriff lowered his head. "Right now you're a person of interest. I need to ask you some questions in a more formal setting."

Aunt Hazel hands began to tremble as she stood. Aunt Runa gave her a hug before letting the sheriff lead Hazel out the front door. Once she reached the patrol car, she turned around and looked at us pleadingly, then got in the back of the car.

"Noah!" I cried. "We have to do something!"

Noah frowned.

Jonathan appeared, descending the staircase. "I saw the patrol car."

"Jonathan! Can they do this?" I asked him. "Just take her like that?"

"I'm afraid so," he answered. "They can detain her, then depending on what evidence they have—and what she says—they could end up arresting her."

"Does she have to answer their questions?" I asked. "She might incriminate herself accidentally, and she still doesn't have a lawyer."

"No," Jonathan said. "She doesn't have to answer. But she definitely needs a lawyer present."

I looked at Jonathan pleadingly. "Please. Can you help her?"

Chapter Fifteen
How to Host a Murder

Just as the sheriff's car drove off, my cell phone rang.

"Aiden?" I answered breathlessly, hoping he finally had some news.

"Hey, Carissa! I just passed Sheriff Lokey on the road. Was that your Aunt Hazel in the back seat?"

"Yes! He's taking her in for questioning."

"Has he actually arrested her?"

"Not yet," I said, "but I have a feeling it's a matter of time. I'm getting desperate. Any news about a lawyer?"

"Not yet. Everyone seems to be tied up. Listen, I'll stop by the sheriff's office and see if I can find out anything. I'll get back to you soon."

I sighed. "Okay. Thanks, Aiden."

After I hung up, I worried about what he might learn from the sheriff—and how he might use it. He was a reporter, after all. But he seemed sincere, and I had no choice but to trust him. Hopefully he'd share anything incriminating with us—and otherwise keep it to himself

"Any luck?" Jonathan asked.

I shook my head.

Jonathan sighed. "All right, listen. I can't promise anything, but if you want to catch me up on the details, maybe I can help you until you find someone."

"What about your wife? Aren't you going home soon?"

Jonathan took in a breath. "The truth is, we had a fight. I don't want to go into details, but we both felt we needed some time apart. She has these big ideas about moving here, starting our own practice. She'd even been looking at property—at least she was, until . . . well, Patty Fay was her realtor."

"Seriously?" A coincidence? Maybe not, since there weren't too many realtors in Pelican Point, according to my aunts. Still . . . "Well, if you're sure, that would be great. Uh, sorry about your fight."

He shrugged. "We'll be fine, although it's a little more complicated when lawyers fight."

I wondered.

We headed over to the dining table where I spent the next half hour filling him in on what I knew. Each time I added something, his frown grew deeper as he jotted it down on a legal pad. After I was done, I decided to share my hunch.

"I think someone is trying to frame my aunts."

"What? Why do you think that?"

I explained the possible motives and listed the possible suspects I was considering—mainly the people who attended the pre-party. "There may be others with motives I don't know about. These are just the ones who made their complaints about the inn known." The only thing I didn't mention was my grandfather's secret notebook. It didn't seem relevant.

My phone rang. It was the sheriff.

I held up a finger to Jonathan, who was about to say something. "Sheriff! Is my aunt okay? Can I come get her?"

"I'm afraid not, Carissa."

"Why not?"

"I'm holding her for forty-eight hours."

"On what grounds?"

"Suspicion of homicide," he said.

I was speechless for a moment, then whispered to Jonathan, "He's keeping her."

"Tell him I'm on my way," Jonathan said.

Feeling relieved, I did as Jonathan directed and hung up. "Thank you so much. It sounds like things aren't looking so good."

"I'll find out from the sheriff what's going on and then talk to your aunt," Jonathan said. "Don't worry. The evidence is probably circumstantial. And I doubt this small-town sheriff has dealt with many homicide cases, if any. I'll get my briefcase, then head over."

While Jonathan returned to his room, I tried to think of a way to tell Aunt Runa that her sister was being held longer than we anticipated. But as I gathered up the papers strewn over the table and put them in the boxes on the floor, I caught a glimpse of an old leather-bound book. I lifted it out of the box and read the title:

A Magician Among the Spirits by Harry Houdini.

Wondering why this particular book was in one of my grandfather's boxes, I opened the cover, half expecting another secret notebook to be hidden inside. But the book was intact and dated 1924. I turned to the introduction and read: "Sir Arthur Conan Doyle has repeatedly told the Spiritualists that I will eventually see the light and embrace

Spiritualism. But if Spiritualism is to be founded on the tricks of exposed mediums, feats of magic, resort to trickery, then I say unflinchingly I do not believe, and more, I will not believe until the Spiritualists can show any substantiated proof."

Hmm. Had the underlined part been done by my grandfather?

The book was signed "Harry Houdini." If the signature was authentic, it had to be worth a fortune. I knew a little about Houdini from Aunt Runa, who learned some magic from her father. Obviously, he was known for his magician skills, but not many people knew of his attempts to disprove spiritualism. He was often called the original "ghostbuster" because he believed his training as a magician gave him insight into how charlatans operated.

Aunt Runa had told me that Houdini had prearranged for his wife, Bess, to hold a séance every Halloween for the next ten years after this death and try to contact him. That way he could prove the chicanery even after he'd passed over to the other side. He'd set up an elaborate plan to discredit anyone who pretended to contact him. Many tried, but no one ever did.

I searched the internet on my phone for more information and was intrigued by an article called "How to Host a Séance." It read: "A séance is a meeting of people who wish to receive messages from spirits. The event grew out of the Spiritual religion in the mid-nineteenth century, and was popular among prominent members of society. The best-known series of séances was conducted in the White House for Mary Todd Lincoln, who was grieving the loss of her son. President Abraham Lincoln had been present at the event. Other followers of

Spiritualism included President Franklin D. Roosevelt and author Arthur Conan Doyle."

Noah had mentioned the author of *Sherlock Holmes*, but the rest of the information surprised me. The article went on to explain the details of hosting a séance: "A séance is conducted by a medium for a small group seated around a table in a semi-dark room. The medium enters a trance in order to communicate with a spirit. Communication may include strange voices, odd smells, automatic writing, table raps, spirit boards, and even visions. A séance often feels authentic when the guests are believers, since they're more suggestible to paranormal phenomenon, however paranormal manifestations can easily be faked by anyone with theatrical talent."

Like my grandfather? But why would he? To bilk naive, gullible, and superstitious people into giving him money? To seduce women? Or did he really believe in this stuff?

And if he hosted séances, where exactly did he hold them? He must have had a room large enough to hold a round table that seated half a dozen people. Most of the rooms in this house weren't very big, but any of them could have fit a small table and group that size.

I wondered if there might be a blueprint somewhere among his papers that would indicate where the séance room might be. I glanced at the boxes and figured I'd have to go through them when I got a chance, not to mention any others that were in the attic. But for now, I put the plan on my mental to-do list. At the moment, I had other priorities.

I checked the time. Jonathan had been gone for at least a half hour. Since I hadn't heard from him, I called his number, anxious to learn what he'd found out.

"Carissa, I was just about to call you," Jonathan said. "I'm bringing your Aunt Hazel home as we speak."

My heart fluttered with elation. "Wonderful! How? What happened?"

"I pointed out they either had to formally arrest her or let her go, and I knew they didn't have enough evidence to indict her."

"Thank goodness!"

"We should be there as soon as she's processed."

I sighed with relief as I ended the call. I knew this didn't mean Aunt Hazel was in the clear. Knowing she was the chatty type, I just hoped she hadn't said anything potentially incriminating while she was in custody.

At least this reprieve would buy us more time to find out what was really going on.

* * *

Aunt Runa, Marnie, and I were waiting eagerly at the front door for Aunt Hazel's arrival. We watched as Jonathan helped her out of his Lexus and walked her up the porch steps, where Aunt Runa and I embraced her. Marnie handed her a cup of tea and tried to stifle a grin, but I could tell she was glad my aunt was back.

We sat at the kitchen table and took turns asking Aunt Hazel about her ordeal. She seemed chipper as she explained how kind everyone at the station was, including the sheriff, and that she planned to drop off some blueberry yogurt muffins as soon as she could. I just shook my head. I had a feeling she wasn't taking this situation seriously.

"Aunt Hazel," I began, taking her hand. "This isn't over."

She patted my hand back. "Stop worrying, Carissa, dear. Everything's going to be fine. Right, Jonathan?"

I nodded at her naivety, then decided to ask her about the strange book I'd found under the bed and the mystical stuff that was hidden in a trunk in the attic.

Aunt Hazel looked at Aunt Runa with wide eyes. Aunt Runa bit her lip.

"What?" I said glancing between them. As usual, something was going on between the two of them.

"Isn't it obvious?" Aunt Hazel said, a sparkle in her eyes.

"No, it's not!" I snapped. "What? Tell me."

"It's him," Aunt Hazel said. "He's the one who put the book there for you to find."

"Him, who?" I narrowed my eyes. "Nooooo."

They nodded. "Grandfather's ghost."

* * *

Here we go again, I thought, ready to give up. I had a feeling there would be no convincing my aunts the place wasn't haunted and there were no such things as ghosts. I was on my own. Besides, why would my grandfather hide the book under the bed if he wanted me to find it?

So what would Nancy Drew do? I wondered. Well, she'd put on her best frock, summon her chums—Bess Marvin and George Fayne—and discuss the whole thing over a luncheon of watercress sandwiches. Then they'd drive in her roadster to the haunted mansion, pull on a candlestick to open a secret passageway, and get chloroformed, only waking when someone passed smelling salts under their noses.

I definitely didn't want to get chloroformed, so I set about working on the puzzle the way I did when I first started researching how to write a mystery. Since this one was for real and not one of my ghostwritten stories, I returned to my

Murder at Blackwood Inn

usual format for creating a plot called "MOM—Motive, Opportunity, Means." I began a list:

1. Motive: Who wanted to kill both Patty Fay (realtor/fan of the occult) and aka Henry Hill (traveling salesman/private investigator)? Was there a connection?

2. Opportunity:

   Victim #1: Patty Fay Johnstone. Died after the pre-party sometime in the night when she was alone. Could have eaten a poisoned dessert at the party, or consumed the handful she'd taken home afterward. Or she could have gotten it another way . . .

   Victim #2: Henry Hill. Died during breakfast two days later. Could have been poisoned by the breakfast, or earlier in his room, from his bottle of whiskey. Still waiting for the sheriff's autopsy report.

If it was Aunt Hazel's belladonna, that meant the killer had to have had access to:

a. The poison garden,
b. The desserts on the table,
c. Henry's room, and . . .
d. Henry's bottle of whiskey???

I sighed, not sure all this was going to help, but what choice did I have? I wrote down number three:

3. Means: Poison—specifixcally belladonna—which appears to have come from Hazel's poison garden.

There were other sources of poison, but this one happened to be easily accessible—if you had a key to unlock the door. So who had that key besides Aunt Hazel and Noah?

I sat back and tapped the table with the end of my pen. Just about anyone could have entered the inn through the unlocked front door during the day since my aunts left it open for guests to come and go. Then they could have gone up to Henry's room and doctored his whiskey. They could also have slipped into my room . . . maybe hidden that book, let the cat in, and fiddled with the light.

I shuddered. The thought of someone sneaking around my room creeped me out. They could have easily poisoned me. I glanced at the empty teacups on the dining table.

What if someone was trying to scare me off?

I shook the thought aside. There was no reason to scare me off. Maybe I needed to look more into the past of the Blackwood house and family. I had a feeling there were answers in both of their histories. Time for a visit to the town's library/historical society. I remembered seeing the PI there. Maybe Gracie Galloway, the librarian/historian, could lead me to more articles about my ancestors and this house. Having lived in this town seemingly forever, Gracie might even have some stories to tell that weren't published—or publicized.

I grabbed my "handbag," ran down to my waiting "roadster," and "motored" off to the town of Pelican Point, a place Nancy might call a "hotbed of criminal activity."

I only hoped I didn't get forced off the road, knocked unconscious, or kidnapped before solving this "baffling mystery."

Chapter Sixteen
The Unusual Suspects

The Pelican Point Library/Historical Society was located in an older building in the middle of town, sandwiched between the Second Wind kite store and the *Pelican Point Press* office. When I entered, the musty smell of old books, magazines, newspapers, and other paper relics made my nose tingle. I sneezed, announcing my visit and causing Gracie Galloway to look up from her cluttered desk. She set down the book she was reading and removed her glasses.

"Goodness!" she said. "You startled me. That was quite a sneeze."

"You should hear my dad sneeze," I said. "You could lose your hearing. I'm just glad I didn't get the Blackwood nose."

Gracie smiled. "Ah, yes. You're the Blackwoods' niece from the party the other night. Carissa, is it?"

I nodded. I was about to say, "Guilty as charged," but at the moment, it hit too close to home.

Gracie placed her glasses on top of her head. "May I help you with something?"

"I hope so," I said, glancing around at the crowded rows of shelves packed with books. "I'm looking for some information about my grandfather, Abraham Blackwood. I'd like to know more about him."

I saw Gracie's face stiffen the tiniest bit, but her smile remained. *Had I hit some kind of nerve?* I knew she'd been around Pelican Point for a long time and had even attended some of my grandfather's séances, according to his secret journal. Was there more to it than just that?

"Did you know him? My grandfather?" I asked innocently.

Gracie folded her hands in front of her. "Oh, yes. Everybody in town knew him. He was quite the character, and very charismatic. Those eyes. He had a way of looking at you . . ." She paused, glancing off into space. I wondered what she was thinking.

When she didn't continue, I said, "I heard he hosted séances for the local folks, claiming the house was haunted."

She looked down at her folded hands. "Yes, I heard that too."

Did she just say she'd "heard that"? She was listed as a frequent guest at the séances. Why would she keep that little detail to herself? Was she embarrassed for me to know she dabbled in the dark arts too?

I let it go and asked, "So, do you think the Blackwood house is really haunted?"

She hesitated before saying, "I don't know. All I can say is, folks reported weird things going on there."

"Did you ever go to the Blackwood home to visit my grandparents?"

She looked down at her hands again. "Not often. Maybe once or twice."

"Did you see weird things there?"

She grinned as if amused. "Oh, I heard some odd noises, felt gusts of wind, saw a few shadows—that sort of thing. Stuff you'd expect from an old house. Nothing unusual—or haunted—if that's what you mean. But frankly, I was never comfortable there."

"Why not?"

She shrugged. "I don't know. I just wasn't."

"Did you ever attend any of his séances?" I asked bluntly.

She shook her head. "Oh, no. I'm not into that kind of thing. But there are a lot of superstitious people in this town. Some of them think Pelican Point is cursed, what with the drownings, the hangings, and the murders back in the day."

"Sounds like it was quite a violent place back then."

"Oh, yes," Gracie said. "When the town was first established in the late 1700s, early 1800s, the Spaniards invaded the land and ran off the Coastal Miwoks. Then the Russians came over, hunting sea otters for their pelts and took over from the Spaniards. When the otters were depleted, Europeans claimed the area and forced the Russians to leave. Believe me, there were plenty of battles in this quaint little town. But by the mid-1800s, Pelican Point became a US territory. The people who remained worked together to build the wharf, warehouses, and barracks for the seamen. That's when Pelican Point became a thriving harbor for shipping lumber and put us on the map."

"Amazing! You know so much about the area," I said, impressed, although I'd heard this from my father and read about it as well.

"As the town's historian, it's my job," Gracie said with a hint of pride.

"So, what do you know about the history of my aunts' house?"

She replaced her glasses, turned to her computer, and began typing. "As I recall, the Blackwood house was once owned by a Russian seaman named Vasily . . ." She paused, then read from her screen. "Ah, yes. Here it is. A twenty-year-old sea captain by the name of Viktor Vasily built the house around 1815." She read on silently, then added, "Uh . . . not much was known about him, only that he disappeared sometime later, after his wife apparently hung herself."

I'd heard this, too, but I wondered if Gracie knew more. "Goodness. Does it say anything about why she killed herself?"

Gracie took her glasses off and looked at me. "Well, you won't find this on Wikipedia, but the story goes she was having an affair with a local fisherman while her husband was out at sea. When he discovered the dalliance, he tried to throw her out of the house, but she hung herself in the parlor."

"How awful." I shuddered at the image of the woman hanging from the ceiling in my aunts' house.

"The local sheriff found her there the next day and ruled it a suicide. At least, that's the story."

Hmm, I thought. "How sad," I said. "I heard my great-grandfather Abraham Blackwood bought the house around that time."

"That would be your great-great-grandfather, Abraham Blackwood the First," she said. "I think he bought it as an estate sale soon after Vasily disappeared. Some say he had a shady reputation for buying up land, building houses, then selling them at a huge profit. Rumor was he didn't pay his workers what they were owed."

There seem to be a lot of rumors in this town, I thought. "What happened to him?"

"Well, after his first wife committed suicide, he married his second wife, Abigail. But she died a few years after they were married, leaving behind a one-year-old child—Abraham the Second."

"Another suicide? How odd." I felt a chill run down my spine.

"I think that's where the haunted house rumors started."

"So that would be my great-grandfather," I said, trying to keep track. "Do you know how Abigail died?" *Hopefully not another suicide*, I thought.

"There's no record of that, just a headstone in the old church graveyard. Folks just assume it was consumption or one of the many diseases of the time."

"And the house stayed in the family."

"There almost wasn't a house," Gracie said. "Soon after Abigail's death, there was a mysterious fire that burned down half the place and several other buildings his company had built. Back then, most of the structures were made of wood and fire was a constant threat. But the son, your great-grandfather, had the house rebuilt, this time in the sturdier Italianate style out of bricks and cast iron, probably to make sure that didn't happen again. After that, Abraham the first remarried—" she peered at her computer screen "—around 1870, to a woman named Bessie, but she died within the year."

"Good heavens!" I said. "What happened to her?"

"She drowned—accidentally, they say. Fell off the wharf and was swept away to sea."

I just shook my head at the deaths of so many women. Blackwood women.

"There's more," she said, nodding toward her screen and replacing her glasses. "Around 1895, forty-year-old Abraham the Second—your great-grandfather—married Constance, who gave birth to a boy—Abraham the Third. That would be your grandfather, who sometimes called himself Bram. As you know, he died six months ago at the age of eighty, so that brings us pretty much up-to-date. His wife, Mary—your grandmother—had three children—your Aunt Runa, your Aunt Hazel, and your father, Robert."

I was going to need a chart of the family tree to keep track of all these Abrahams and their wives. I wondered why my dad hadn't gotten the Abraham name like his forefathers.

"I heard my grandmother died from the flu," I said, "about ten years ago when she was seventy."

Gracie nodded.

I sat back in my chair, trying to take in all the dates, names, and details. "I had quite the eclectic string of ancestors, didn't I?"

Gracie closed her laptop. "If you want to know more, you can use that computer over there to access newspaper articles and such." She gestured to a desktop computer sitting at a table across the room.

"Thanks," I said. I headed over, switched on the old-school computer, and spent the next hour searching for more information on the Blackwood name. I soon realized I'd learned more from Gracie than anything else that came up, although I did find one tidbit that surprised me. While the name Blackwood supposedly came from Scotland, there was a derivative—Blakvod—that was Russian. So were my ancestors from Scotland or Russia? My father had never mentioned this. I wondered if my aunts knew.

I was about to shut down the computer when my eyes caught on an interesting subject heading: "Concerned Citizens vs. Runa Blackwood and Hazel Blackwood." It had appeared in the op-ed section of the *Pelican Point Press*, one month ago:

"To whom it may concern: We are a group of Concerned Citizens who are worried about the monstrosity located on

Heron Street in Pelican Point. Once a beautiful Italianate home, the house has been turned into a tacky bed and breakfast inn by the current owners. The exterior walls and trim have been painted a bizarre collection of black, green, and purple. There are numerous reports of 'spooky' rooms decorated to represent horror films, 'magic crystals' hidden throughout the house, and even toxic plants on the premises. We implore Sheriff Wil Lokey, to evict the owners, close the transient hotel business, convert the house to its previous majesty, and sell the valuable property that has become an eyesore and an embarrassment in our community.—Signed, Concerned Citizens."

I suspected who those "concerned citizens" might be. Maybe I'd been headed in the wrong direction, searching for information about the Blackwoods when I should have been focusing on my suspect list. I decided to check out the two recent victims while I was there.

Patty Fay's name came up several times in my search, mostly for her real estate sales. Her Facebook page featured her headshot with dozens of pictures of houses in the background and lots of quotes from "satisfied buyers." Everyone apparently liked her, even my aunts, in spite of her wanting them to sell their place. So, what would be the motive for murdering her? An unhappy buyer?

As for Henry Hill a.k.a. Herman Hicks and his other aliases, there weren't many hits on the web, and nothing about his private investigation business. He didn't have a website, and wasn't connected to LinkedIn, or any other professional site I could find. So how did he get his clients? By referral? Either he didn't care much about his business, or he was doing so well he didn't need the publicity. Or was it something else? Talk about a mystery guy.

The bigger question was: Why was he murdered? Because he found out something related to Patty Fay's death? He must have kept a notebook or log that might give me a clue, but I was sure the sheriff had confiscated all his belongings.

That made me wonder if Patty Fay kept some kind of diary or journal. And if so, had the sheriff located it?

I went on to research my suspect list—the party guests. They were the most obvious ones who would want to frame my aunts so the inn would fail. I began with Annabelle Topper, the other innkeeper who wasn't happy competing with my aunts' inn. But after a search, only reviews of her inn came up—mostly positive and nothing suspicious.

I tried Harper Smith, the next-door neighbor who didn't approve of my aunts' house or their B and B business. But no hits came up.

I tried Gracie, too, but her name also turned up nothing, other than an occasional article that mentioned the historical society. I typed in Marnie, knowing it was a long shot since she'd worked for my grandfather for years and seemed to be a faithful employee. But sometimes it was the quiet background player that had the biggest secret—or least, that's what often happened in a Nancy Drew mystery.

Nothing there either.

Who else was at the party?

Noah.

I typed in Noah's name, but like Henry Hill/Herman Hicks, it was as if he didn't exist. Then I remembered Aiden had been there too. I found multiple articles he'd penned over the years. None of them seemed relevant to the circumstances.

I turned off the computer and got up. Gracie was nowhere in sight. I called out her name.

"Back here!" she said in a muffled voice. I followed the sound to a recessed bookshelf at the rear of the building.

"Where?" I said, glancing around. All I saw were bookshelves.

Then one of the recessed bookshelves moved.

"In here," she said, peering out from a small opening between the wall and the bookcase. She pushed the shelf, and it opened wide.

"Oh my God!" I cried. "You have a fake bookcase door! With a hidden room! How awesome!"

Gracie grinned. "Come on in." I followed her through the opening and into a tiny room that held a comfy chair, a small table with a lamp, and books piled on shelves and around the floor.

"Your own secret reading room! I love it!" And then I sneezed. "Sorry about that."

"It's the dust," she explained. "Got a lot of that in here."

I glanced around. "Is this where you keep first editions and other valuable books?"

She nodded. "You wouldn't believe what some of these books are worth."

Hmm, I thought, *was anyone tempted to find out? Is that why they were hidden out of sight? And did that have anything to do with the recent deaths?*

"So, did you find what you were looking for?" she asked, breaking into my suspicious thoughts.

I shrugged. "Not really. I wondered if you could tell me anything about Patty Fay? Like, did she have any enemies? Or some sort of secret life? Maybe she knew my grandfather and—"

Gracie looked at her watch and interrupted. "I'm sorry, Carissa. I wish I knew more. But I just remembered I have an appointment. I need to close the library and scoot. Can you see yourself out?"

I blinked. *That was abrupt.* "Uh, sure. Thanks for your help. You've been a wealth of information."

"You're welcome," she said. She watched from the secret doorway as I walked back through the main library. I turned to wave, but by then the bookshelf door had closed.

When I stepped outside, I wondered what had caused her sudden change. What had I asked just before she remembered she had an "appointment"?

Did Patty Fay have any enemies? A secret life? Did she know my grandfather?

I had a feeling Gracie knew a lot more than she was telling me. After all, she was the town historian/librarian. And those people knew everything.

Chapter Seventeen
Three's a Crowd

I stood on the sidewalk for a few minutes, contemplating my next move. The *Pelican Point Press* office was right next door. If Aiden was there, maybe he could fill in a few gaps in my research. Meanwhile, I hadn't seen Gracie leave the library for her appointment. Maybe she'd slipped out a secret back door?

Just as I opened the door to the newspaper office, Harper, my aunts' neighbor, stepped out, nearly bumping into me. He muttered something, which I doubted was an apology. His breath smelled strongly of alcohol. He walked away briskly without looking back. I wasn't even sure he knew he'd bumped into me.

Jerk.

I found Aiden in the office at a desk piled high with papers, seemingly engrossed in his work. Across the way was an unmanned desk that looked even more cluttered, but there was no sign of an assistant. He looked up, obviously surprised to see me.

"Carissa! I didn't hear you come in. I was about to call you." He smiled and gestured for me to take a seat opposite him.

I sat in the scarred wooden chair and pulled it up close to his desk. "Sorry to just drop by, but I was in the neighborhood, literally."

He set down his red pencil and folded his hands, dropping the smile. "No problem at all. Listen, I've called everyone I know up and can't find a reputable attorney who is free to take your case until next week. I'm sorry, but I'm out of ideas. Maybe you could get a public defender?"

"Actually, it's okay," I said. "I just stopped by to tell you that one of our guests is a lawyer—Jonathan Duke? You probably met him. Anyway, he's agreed to help Aunt Hazel. At least for now."

"Phew," he said, leaning back in his chair. "That's a relief. I hated letting you down. Have there been any new developments?"

"Actually, I was going to ask you the same thing, figuring you're in the news business and all."

He shook his head. "All I've heard is second-hand gossip, which I don't repeat. Besides, everyone is being tight-lipped—at least with me. No one trusts a reporter." He grinned.

I sighed. "Well, I thought I'd ask, since you've lived her awhile and probably know most of the people. I was wondering if you could tell me what you know about a few of the locals who were at the pre-party the other night."

"I'll try." He checked the time on his cell phone lying on his desk. "Listen. Give me about ten minutes to finish up here. Why don't we meet at the café across the street and I'll take a lunch break. You can ask me all the questions you want, I just can't promise to have all the answers."

I was torn. I wanted to get back to the inn and see if there were any new developments, but I was dying to find out what he had to say. "Uh, okay. That works."

"Great! It's called The Birds Café, named after the Hitchcock movie that was filmed over in Bodega Bay. If you can get an outdoor table, the view of Pelican Bay is incredible, now that the fog has lifted."

"Sounds nice," I said, and stood up, ready to leave, then remembered bumping into Harper on my way into the office. I started to ask what he was doing there, but Aiden had already turned back to his work. I decided it could wait until lunch.

It was nearly one o'clock and the streets were filled with people, mostly tourists wearing Pelican Point or other T-shirts with similar logos, their phones in hand, often taking pictures, as they munched on saltwater taffy and carried shopping bags from the local stores.

I crossed the street when I got the chance and headed over to The Birds Café, which was perched on the edge of the coast and overlooked the sparkling bay. Realizing I was starving, I ordered some deep-fried artichoke fritters, something I'd never get at my aunts' house, along with a double latte. While I sat at an outdoor table waiting for my order, I caught a glimpse of Marnie, standing at the door to the library/historical society across the street. Even at that distance, her frown was easy to see. I wondered what she was doing there.

I watched as she tried the door, but it appeared to be locked. She knocked, glancing behind her several times as if she was worried someone might see her. To my surprise, the door opened. A bigger surprise—Gracie peered out. She looked up and down the street, then waved Marnie inside and closed the door.

Really? What was going on with those two? Gracie had said she had an appointment, but she didn't say with who, and she implied she would be leaving the library. Maybe it was with Marnie, but then, why all the cloak-and-dagger looks?

I was dying to go over there and find out, but Aiden would be arriving any minute. For now, I'd keep an eye on the library door for comings and goings.

"Carissa?" I heard a voice call from the café window. "Order up!" I headed over to retrieve my decadent snack and energy drink. I didn't see Aiden come up behind me.

"I see you like artichoke fritters," he said, grinning. "Next time, you'll have to try the fish tacos—best in the county. Not to mention the clam chowder."

"Sounds delicious," I said. While Aiden put in his order, I returned to the table to admire the boats, the birds, and the bay. Moments later, he joined me.

"Beautiful, isn't it," he said, nodding toward the sparkling view.

"It is," I said, staring out at the shimmering water and bobbing sailboats. Now that the fog had lifted, I could see the cormorants dive-bomb into the water and coming up with fish in their beaks. "You're lucky to have grown up here. I only visited a couple of times when I was a kid. Back then, I didn't much care about views. Now I feel like I really missed something. But I'm a little surprised at some of the people here—their reactions to my aunts' inn."

"The townsfolk don't always accept newcomers gracefully," Aiden said. "They don't like change. Even though your aunts lived here as kids, they moved away as adults, which makes them more like outsiders."

I nodded, but now that the feeling of being unwelcome had turned to hostility from a few of those people, the situation was more serious.

"Aiden? Food's up!" the voice called from the café window.

"I'll be right back." He headed for the takeout window, then returned with his fish tacos and clam chowder. The tacos looked delicious and the chowder smelled divine. He must have caught me mentally drooling because he said, "Want a taste?"

I shook my head. "I'm getting really full from these yummy artichoke fritters, but thanks. Next time I'll try a healthier—" I stopped as I caught a glimpse of a familiar couple across the street.

Aiden looked up from his meal. "What's wrong?"

I nodded toward the opposite side of the street. Harper and Annabelle appeared to be in a serious conversation, right in front of the library. Annabelle was punctuating her words with a pointing finger, while Harper was scowling and shaking his head. I wished I could overhear their conversation, but we were too far away. I studied them as they talked, trying to interpret from their body language—until Annabelle suddenly turned and looked directly at me. Then Harper did the same.

"Uh-oh," I whispered to Aiden. I glanced away, but I knew it was too late. They had caught me staring. I pretended to gaze at the water while I sipped my latte.

"Are you okay?" Aiden asked.

"Are they still looking this way?" I whispered.

"Who?"

"Harper and Annabelle. Across the street by the library."

Aiden turned to look. "They're not there now. Maybe they went inside the library."

"You're probably right," I said, thinking maybe they were meeting up with Marnie and Gracie. But why? What was up with these people?

"Do you think they might know something that would help?" Aiden asked.

I shrugged. "What do you know about them? I bumped into Harper as he was on his way out of your office earlier.

Why was he there?" I decided not to mention the smell of alcohol on his breath.

"He came in to place a personal ad," Aiden said.

"A personal ad? What kind?"

He looked down at his espresso. "I probably shouldn't say—"

I cut him off. "You mean, like a *personal*, personal ad?" I prodded.

He nodded.

"Interesting. I wonder why he doesn't just go on a dating app? There are some for people his age."

"I think he's very old school, like most of the long-timers around here. Every now and then he places one of these ads, then I don't hear from him for a while. I figure he's met someone, but when it doesn't work out, he's back. He must be quite the player." Aiden chuckled.

"Goodness. He sounds kind of sad."

Aiden shrugged. "I don't know. He seems happy enough. He's dated several women from town, including Annabelle, after she became widowed, but apparently that didn't last long."

"Annabelle? Really? Any idea why they broke up?" *Did their meeting a few minutes ago mean they were getting back together?* I wondered.

"No clue. All I know is, after that he took up with Patty Fay, which seemed to cause bad blood between Annabelle and her. That relationship didn't last long either."

"Hmm." I wondered if any of this had something to do with Patty Fay's murder.

"Wait," Aiden said. "You don't think Harper was involved in Patty Fay's death, do you?"

So, my aunts weren't the only mind-readers in this town.

"Or that Annabelle attacked Patty Fay in a fit of passionate jealousy over . . . *Harper*?"

I shook my head. "Honestly, I don't know what to think. But I do know one thing—this town and the people in it seem to be full of secrets. The more I learn, the more I feel like I'm missing something. There's got to be some other connection between Patty Fay, Annabelle, and Harper. And then there's Gracie."

Aiden frowned. "Our librarian? What about her?"

"When I went to see her, she was full of information about my grandfather. But when I started asking questions about Patty Fay, she suddenly said she had an appointment and needed to close the library."

His frown relaxed. "Ah. Maybe she really did have an appointment," he said, before finishing the last spoonful of chowder.

"Maybe, but she never left the library. Then Marnie showed up, gave some kind of secret knock, and Gracie let her in."

"Hmm. So maybe her appointment was with Marnie."

"But why would Marnie secretly want to meet with Gracie? And why close the library?"

"Honestly, I have no idea. I know they're friends. I heard they attended some of your grandfather's séances together. The time I was there, he really had them spooked."

"I saw your article," I said. "I'm surprised *you* attended one of his séances."

He nodded. "It was a while back. When I heard rumors about them, I thought it would make a great story. But Bram found out why I was there and said he'd sue me if I wrote anything that exposed him in some way."

"Wow," I said, intrigued. I tried to remember the details of the article. "So what happened during the séance?"

"It was pretty cool, actually," Aiden said. "First, we gathered around midnight in the parlor. Then Marnie blindfolded us and led us to the séance room—a hidden room somewhere in the house, upstairs, but I couldn't tell exactly where."

"Who was at the séance?"

"Five people plus me—Patty Fay, Annabelle, Harper, Marnie, and Gracie—and one empty chair, all crowded around a small round table. The room was filled with scented candles—cinnamon I think, which is supposed to attract the spirits."

"Was it a round table?" I asked. "I've never seen one at the house. Not even in the attic."

"Yeah. And there was a Ouija board in the middle of the table—one of those old wooden types that looked like an antique and had been used a lot. Your grandfather called it a spirit board. The planchette was also carved out of wood, with a nail in the center circle."

I recognized the description of the board and planchette in the attic. They had to be the same ones I'd found in my grandfather's trunk.

"No wonder you're a writer," I said. "You have an eye for detail."

He smiled. "Anyway, your grandfather came in through another hidden door—I'm pretty sure it was him. He was wearing a black mask and long black robe. He sat down in the empty chair and in a low voice asked everyone to join hands. I know that's standard séance stuff, but I thought we'd be using the Ouija board, and you need your hands free for that. Instead, he asked if anyone had a question. Patty Fay said she wanted to contact her dead husband, James. Bram—your grandfather—let out a deep breath from behind the mask, then mumbled something I couldn't make out."

Hmm. Did my grandfather know another language? I'd have to ask my aunts later.

"All of a sudden," Aiden continued, "his voice boomed. Scared the crap out of me, to be honest. Marnie and Gracie both squeezed my hands. Then he started talking in a high, shaky voice, stretching out the words and saying something like, 'Tonight we are here to contact the spirit of James Johnstone, beloved husband of Patty Fay Johnstone. Are you here, Spirit?' I heard a single tap on the table and everyone gasped. I assumed one tap meant yes."

I felt a chill run down my spine and wondered how I would have reacted at the séance.

"After a few seconds, he asked, 'Spirit, are you in any pain?' Two raps on the table, meaning no. 'Do you have a message for your wife, Patty Fay?' he asked. "One rap. Yes. So now I'm totally hooked. I mean, I knew it wasn't real, but I couldn't figure out how he was tapping the table while holding hands. And if there was an accomplice, who was it?"

"Whoa," I said. "I would have loved to have been there."

"It gets better," Aiden said. "A gust of wind came up, the candle flames started flickering, then one of the candles blew over and went out."

"Seriously?"

He chuckled. "I know. It was weird. Then the planchette started moving, all on its *own*. I looked for strings or magnets, but saw nothing."

"Did the Ouija board spell out anything?"

Aiden took a breath. "Believe it or not—and remember, this was probably a while ago—it spelled out D E A T H."

"Death?" I frowned. "That's it? Anything else?"

"Nope. Patty Fay jumped up from the table and said she wanted to leave. Marnie got up and turned on the lights.

Annabelle and Harper looked like they'd seen a ghost. The party was over. We were blindfolded again and led down some stairs."

"Death. What do you think that meant?"

"Honestly, I don't know, but it sure upset Patty Fay. After the lights went on, I looked all over for signs of trickery, but your grandfather was clever. He made everything look real. No wonder his clients kept coming back."

My phone rang. "Sorry," I said, pulling it out of my purse. "Hello? . . . Oh, hi, Noah. You do? . . . Great! . . . Whoops! I almost forgot about dinner again . . . Yes, I'll be ready. Thanks."

I turned to Aiden. "Sorry about the interruption." I gathered up my purse. "Listen, I have to run, and I know you have to get back to work. Thanks for the information. I'm not sure how it ties in with Patty Fay's death, but it's something to think about."

"Happy to help," he said, although he suddenly sounded subdued. "Wish I could do more."

We said our goodbyes. He headed back to his office and I hurried to my car, anxious to see if my aunts had learned anything more. I thought about Aiden's description of the séance as I drove home. Creepy, for sure. And where was that séance room?

Just as I pulled into the driveway, my phone dinged. A text had come in. Aiden? Had he remembered something? I read the message.

"Carrie, I miss u. can I come see u?"

Oh, God. My ex-! Sergio! What was he doing, texting me? He *missed* me? He wanted to *see* me? I felt my stomach clench at the memories of his deception. Why was he contacting me now?

Murder at Blackwood Inn

Never mind. I didn't want to go there.

As I got out of the car at the inn, I saw Marnie arrive in her little Volt. After seeing her duck into the library earlier, I thought I might need to keep an eye on my grandfather's long-time trusted housekeeper. Maybe she had secrets of her own?

Maybe it was time for a little chat.

Chapter Eighteen
Secret in the Old Attic

I entered the house thinking my aunts might still be going through boxes of papers, but they were nowhere in sight. The house seemed unusually quiet—no moans or creaks or whispers. Or meows.

I pushed through the swinging door to the kitchen and found Marnie facing the sink, reading a note. Her other hand played with the necklace she wore under her blouse. Two canvas bags full of groceries sat on the counter, waiting to be emptied.

"Marnie?"

She gasped, startled, and quickly stuffed the note into her apron pocket and dropped her hand from her chest. "Crivvins, Carissa!" she cried. "You scared the bejabbers out of me! Don't creepin' up on a person like that. You'll likely end up with a kitchen knife in your gut."

I chuckled at her Scottish outburst, but also hoped she was kidding about the knife. I hadn't crept up on her, but instead of arguing, I apologized. "Sorry, Marnie. Didn't mean to scare you. Need help with those groceries?"

She shook her head and removed a baguette. "Nae. I know where everything goes and I like things just so. Did you want something, Carissa? A cuppa?"

"No tea, thanks. Actually, I wanted to talk to you. Got a minute?"

She glanced at the bags and sighed. I took that to mean she didn't have a minute, but she'd give me one anyway. She leaned back against the counter and crossed her arms. "What's on your mind?"

Wasn't it obvious? The murders, of course. Where to start? "I was downtown today, doing some research at the library, and I thought I saw you there too."

She frowned as if trying to think, then turned back to the counter and started to unload a bag. "A'course I was in town, like I am every day, buying groceries and whatnot for your aunts. I didn't see you. Where did you say you were again?"

"Well, I was at the library, until Gracie said she had to close up because she had an appointment. I saw you after I went across the street to The Birds Café. You were standing in front of the library and then you seemed to disappear. Did you go inside?"

Marnie scoffed. "I don't have time for reading. Must have been someone else."

I was sure it was her. And I was sure Gracie had let her inside right after she knocked. Why was she lying? Maybe I needed to be more direct.

"My mistake. So, my aunts said you've been with the Blackwood family for a long time. You must know a lot about them. What was my grandfather like?"

I couldn't see her face with her back to me, but her shoulders tensed. "I only worked for him. Didn't know much about his personal life." She pulled out some eggs and cheese and set them on the counter. I wondered if she was planning to make another quiche—so soon, after a face plant in the last one? Hopefully not.

"I heard he held secret séances in a hidden room somewhere in the house. Any idea where it might be?"

"Ha! I wouldn't know anything about séances or hidden rooms or any of that mumbo jumbo nonsense. Your grandfather kept me busy with the day-to-day caretaking of this old house."

Another lie. Her initials were listed in my grandfather's secret journal as being one of the guests at several séances. Rather than pursue the point, I decided to move on.

"It's weird, you know, how Patty Fay died so suddenly—supposedly poisoned. And the next day one of our guests—that traveling salesman—also died. Odd coincidence. Do you know if Patty Fay knew Henry Hill?"

She stopped unloading the bag and turned to me, crossing her arms again. "A'course not. Why would I?"

"Well, you knew Patty Fay, right? She was a longtime resident of Pelican Point."

Marnie frowned. "Carissa, what are you getting at?"

"Nothing!" I held up my hands as if surrendering. "I'm just looking for anything that could explain the deaths. I figured you and Patty Fay were friends and you might have some insight into what happened to her. The sheriff doesn't think the two deaths are a coincidence. He seems to believe Aunt Hazel is involved. I'm worried about her."

Her face tightened. "So why ask me? I know nothing about those deaths. Patty Fay and I were only acquaintances. So if you're implying—"

"No, no! I'm not implying anything."

Marnie scoffed. "Well, it certainly sounds like you are, what with all your questions."

"Again, I'm just looking for clues about what happened so I can help my aunts. I think they're in real trouble, so if there's anything you know about Patty Fay that could help me figure this out, I'd appreciate it."

Marnie took a breath and seemed to relax a bit. "Like what?"

"Like, she seemed really eager for my aunts to put the house on the market after they inherited it."

"True, but then she was a realtor, wasn't she. That's what they do. Listen, Carissa, I won't speak ill of the dead. I assume, if you were at the library, you talked to Gracie. She knows everything about this town and the people in it."

She turned back around and started emptying the second bag. That was my signal. The conversation was over, leaving me with even more questions than I'd come with.

"One more thing. Do you know if there are any blueprints of the original house?"

"Nae, why would I? That's none o' my business. Now if that's all, I have work to do."

I knew asking about the blueprints was a long shot, but it was worth a chance. Had the hidden room been in the basement before it was sealed up? Or was it somewhere else in this old house?

I headed upstairs to the attic to do some more snooping and was surprised to find my aunts sitting in a couple of old rocking chairs up there, going through boxes and trunks. Papers were scattered everywhere. It would be a miracle if they discovered anything in this mess.

"Carissa!" Aunt Hazel said, grinning when I entered. "Glad you're here. Look what I found!" She held up something made of black fabric. "My father's robe! I remember seeing him wear it one evening when I sneaked downstairs for a drink of water—probably for one of his magic shows. I didn't want to get in trouble, so I ran back to my room. Now I wish I'd asked him about it because I never saw it again. Until now."

The black robe that Aiden had described!

"Cool," I said. "I heard he wore that to his séances."

My aunts looked at each other. "Oh, that's just a rumor," Aunt Runa said.

"So it's not true? There were no séances?"

Were they fibbing, or were they really not aware of his secret activities? I looked around for the trunk that contained the Ouija board, but there were two boxes stacked on top of it. I let the question drop—for now.

"Did you find anything interesting up here?" I asked.

"Not yet," Aunt Runa said. "There are a lot of boxes to go through."

"Sorry, dear. We're not much help, are we?" Aunt Hazel added.

"Any chance you found a blueprint of the house?" I asked, glancing around at the strewn papers.

"Why, yes," Aunt Hazel said. "I did come across a blueprint. Now where did I put that?" She shuffled through the papers closest to her, then pulled out a folded blue sheet from the bottom of the pile.

"Great!" I exclaimed. I sat down on the floor, unfolded the tattered paper, and spread it out.

"What are you looking for, dear?" Aunt Runa asked, eyeing me.

I pored over the blueprint, then pointed to a rectangular room that looked to be underneath the house. "This! Is this a basement?" And was it the séance room?

Aunt Hazel shrugged. "I don't think so. Like I said, I was told this house didn't have one. Maybe it did before the original house burned down. But this one was rebuilt using brick and stone, and set on a raised foundation to provide height—a characteristic of the Italianate architecture."

I nodded, remembering the description she'd given me earlier. "Hmm. Then maybe it was covered over and sealed off?"

"It's possible," Aunt Runa said. She shot a look at Aunt Hazel.

"What about a door that's been boarded up? Or another hidden staircase? Anything like that?"

Aunt Hazel smiled and shook her head. "But if there is, you know who might know . . ."

"Noah," Aunt Runa finished her sentence. "He knows every nook and cranny. You could ask him."

Oh, I would for sure. Tonight when we went to dinner. It would be one of many questions I had for the Blackwoods' longtime handyman.

* * *

I took the tattered blueprint and headed downstairs, leaving my aunts sifting through the mess of old dusty papers. I didn't have to prepare for happy hour now that most of the guests were gone, although a glass of wine wouldn't have hurt. But I still had lots to do before meeting up with Noah. The thought of seeing him alone made me nervous. I wasn't sure how to behave or what was expected of me, so I kept telling myself to focus on *my* reasons for seeing him—getting information.

After my chores, I hopped in the bath and cleaned up, then chose some skinny black leggings and a silky white shirt for our "meeting." I fluffed my hair, put on a little lip gloss and mascara, and had just slipped into my ballet flats when I heard a knock at my door. I checked the time. If it was Noah, he was early.

I opened the door to find the devil himself standing just outside. Without preamble, he said, "Ready?"

I felt myself blush. I had expected to meet him downstairs on neutral ground. It seemed a little too intimate having him call for me at my bedroom door.

"Yup," I said, trying to sound casual. I stepped out, then closed and locked the door behind me.

"You look nice," he said.

"Thanks," I said. "Uh, you do too." *Lame.* I'd said it out of habit. Truth was, he was dressed in his usual black jeans but had exchanged his Blackwood T-shirt for a blue polo shirt.

He gestured for me to lead the way. I walked down the hall to the stairs and down to the main floor.

"I'm leaving!" I called out when I reached the door to whoever was around. I'd told my aunts I was going out for dinner. I just hadn't mentioned with whom. Probably a bad idea if I ended up at the bottom of Pelican Bay . . .

Stop it! I told myself. What was I thinking!

I expected to see a car in the driveway, although I'd never actually seen Noah's car. I assumed he parked it by his work trailer and had probably walked the short distance to the house from there.

"This way," he said, nodding toward the side of the house. I frowned, confused. He took a few steps, then waited for me to catch up. We walked together in silence along the stone path that was lit up by solar-powered garden lights. After passing two gardens, a pond, the greenhouse, and some rose bushes, we arrived at the trailer. Still confused, I looked around and spotted a vehicle parked in the driveway. A silver Jeep pickup truck. Every man's dream.

I started toward the Jeep, figuring that was our ride. When I turned around, I saw that Noah had stopped at the door to the Airstream.

"Where are you going?" he asked, sticking his key in the lock.

"Uh, to your Jeep?"

He waved me over.

I frowned. "I thought this was your work trailer. Do you live here?"

"Yup," he said.

I blinked several times, then followed him as he went up the steps and inside the Airstream. He switched on a light, illuminating the small but cozy interior. I glanced around and surveyed the wood-paneled walls, the shiny steel appliances, and the red-and-black plaid decor.

"Did you do all this?"

He grinned. "Bought the Airstream cheap from your aunts, who said it had been on the property for a few years. I gutted it and replaced everything." He opened the small refrigerator.

I sat down at the booth-style table and continued to admire the details that had gone into refurbishing this tiny home—the red Formica table, the black leather-covered booth seats, the wall clock made from driftwood. He'd hung up a few picture postcards taken around Pelican Point, including the lighthouse, the harbor, the bay, and a view of downtown. What little wall space was left he'd filled with hooks where he'd hung his jacket, a hat, and even a few tools.

"Amazing! It must have taken a long time. Not to mention how much it must have cost."

He looked up from the fridge. "Wine or beer?"

"Wine, please."

He took out a bottle of each and set them on the table. After he uncorked the wine and poured me a glass, he opened his beer and took a swig. I sniffed the air. "Something smells good. Did you cook?"

He nodded as he opened the oven door to check on whatever smelled so delicious. Cheesy, a hint of basil. Something Italian, I guessed. Then he set a small platter of cheese and crackers on the table and joined me on the opposite side of the booth.

"A man of many talents," I said, surprised at his culinary skills in addition to everything else he seemed able to do. An awkward silence fell over us and I took a sip of wine. I hoped it would help loosen my tongue and relax the tension in my body. "So, how long have you lived in the Airstream?"

"Pretty much since I got here."

"Have you always been a handyman?"

He shook his head. "I got a tech job right after college, had a condo in San Jose, but practically lived at the office. I hated every minute of it, so I quit after a few years, came out here, and answered an ad in the *Pelican Point Press* for a handyman. Your grandfather hired me, and your aunts kept me on. I stayed in the Airstream as a temporary setup. Ended up staying. Turns out I like the simple life."

"So you studied computers in college?"

"IT security."

"You mean like, security from hackers?"

"That, and deploying other protective measures, like against a breach, leak of private information, and data attacks."

"Sounds impressive. You didn't like it?"

"Bored the hell out of me. The company I worked for was trying to break into other companies' computers while protecting their own." He shook his head. "Seemed hypocritical to me. What about you? Did you manage an inn before you came here?"

I felt myself blush. "Oh, no. I learned that on the job. I'm—I was a ghostwriter for a bestselling mystery writer, but she decided to go write romantasy. I'm looking for another gig." Before he could ask me any more personal questions, I asked him, "You said you found out something about the murders?"

His cellphone alarm went off. "Dinner's ready. Let me serve it up and then we can talk."

I nibbled on cheese and crackers while he pulled a steaming pan of lasagna from the oven and set it on the stove. I watched admiringly as he tossed a green salad, scooped it into two small bowls, then used a spatula to cut and serve the lasagna onto a couple of plates. I was practically drooling by the time the food reached the table.

"This is incredible," I said, inhaling the cheesy dish. "I haven't had lasagna in forever. Is it your mother's recipe?"

He shook his head. "Epicurious.com. By the way, everything in the salad came from your aunt's garden."

I looked at him.

He grinned. "Not that garden." He poured more wine into my glass.

I took a bite of the lasagna. It melted in my mouth. "Well, this is . . . epic."

He grinned again. "Save room for dessert."

Oh my God, I thought. He was too good to be true. I gobbled up the pasta and salad like I'd just seen food for the first time. Before I fell into a culinary coma, I had to remind myself what I'd come for—information. I took another sip of wine to wash done the last bite, then checked the label.

Pelican Point Pinot. I'd have to buy some for our next happy house at the inn.

"Okay, so what did you learn?" I asked, setting down the bottle. I looked up to find him staring at me. In the dim light, his dark eyes were mesmerizing. When he spoke, his voice was low and smooth.

"Well, I managed to track down a website," he answered, "called Pelican Point Privates."

I sat up. "Sounds intriguing. What was on it?"

"I had to do a little back-end sleuthing, but I found out the person running it went by the alias of Peace Fairness Justice. Obviously a fake name. After a little more digging, I discovered the person's real name."

"What was it?"

"Peace. Fairness. Justice. P. F. J."

"Patty Fay Johnstone! Wow. What was on the site?"

He sat back and took a deep breath. "You sure you want to know?"

"If it can help my aunts, of course!"

"Okay. The site is filled with gossip and innuendo about people in town. No actual names are mentioned, but the references to several embarrassing activities and possible crimes are detailed, and it didn't take me long to find out which ones she was referencing."

Noah got up and retrieved his laptop from the bedroom, which was just a few feet down the narrow hallway. After moving our empty plates to the counter, he sat down next to me and opened the computer. I felt the warmth of his body as he typed something and shifted in my seat.

"You okay?" he asked, looking at me.

"Yes!" I answered, too loudly. *Focus*, I told myself. I looked at the screen and saw the silhouette of a person holding a finger up to her lips. Underneath the silhouette were questions with enticing click bait links:

Who's the man who can't hold his liquor?
Who's the woman who spent time in jail?
Who's the man fooling around on his wife with her best friend?
Who's the woman who stole jewelry from a local store?
Who's the teenager selling dangerous drugs to schoolkids?

The list of questions went on. I glanced at Noah, wide-eyed.

"Go ahead," he said. "Click one of the links."

I clicked the one about the man who couldn't hold his liquor and read the teaser that appeared: *You all know him. He thinks he's a bigshot in this town. But what you don't know is what happened the day he got a DUI.*

Underneath that was another link called *PAY-2-KNOW*.

"Oh my God," I said to Noah. "She's charging people if they want to know more?"

He nodded. "But even then, you only get so much."

"You clicked the link?"

"Not exactly," he said, implying he hacked his way in. I smiled.

"It's all anonymous," he explained. "At first you agree to pay a hundred dollars for information. Then she sends a teaser for more information—and more money—five hundred dollars. It's quite the hook. The more you click, the more you learn, and the more you go down the financial rabbit hole. Then, at some point, she suddenly stops."

"Why?"

"Good question," Noah said. "I started thinking, why not blackmail the person directly instead of trying to get money this other way? Well, that's probably what she did initially. She set up the link, sent the vic a teaser, and waited for them to contact her. Then she asked them to pay to keep their name off the site, and they did. But each time she'd add another clue and increase the fee. She's making money on both ends."

"And you think Patty Fay is—was behind all this?"

Noah nodded.

"Diabolical!" I said, then took a big gulp of wine. "So, did you figure out who the drunk guy was?"

"Several people in this town have gotten DUIs over the past few years. Could be any one of them. But one in particular meets the criteria. Harper Smith."

"Our neighbor! The guy who wants us gone."

"That's my guess."

I thought a moment. "And that would give him a reason to kill Patty Fay—if she's the one behind the site, blackmailing him?"

"Yeah, but there are several others who were being blackmailed by her too. The list of possible killers could be fairly long."

"Did you check out any more of them?"

"This one." He typed something, then pointed to the screen. It read: *Who's the woman who spent time in jail?* Apparently she went to prison for tax evasion and embezzlement, and when she got out, she took on whole new identity—and life."

"Amazing. Did you figure out who it was?"

"After I saw a reference to the woman taking money from tourists, plus a few more details related to the hospitality business, I had a hunch."

"Who?"

"Annabelle."

Murder at Blackwood Inn

"Oh my God! So, both Harper and Anabelle had motives to kill Patty Fay. Was Patty Fay blackmailing anyone else who was at the party? Gracie? Marnie?"

"That will take a bit more research," Noah said. "But one piece of the puzzle doesn't fit. There was someone who *wasn't* at the party, someone who seemingly had *no* links to Pelican Point, yet was also murdered."

"Henry Hill," I whispered. "The private detective."

Chapter Nineteen
The Ghost of a Scent

I glanced up at the clock and was surprised at the time. The evening had flown by.

I'd made a few notes from Patty Fay's secret website, mainly the questions she'd posed to her viewers, so I could think about them later. I wouldn't have the same kind of access Noah had, but maybe I could figure out who was who on my own.

"I better be going," I said to Noah. He had me blocked in the booth and I wouldn't be able to get out until he moved. Just as he started to get up, I remembered the blueprint in my jacket pocket. "Wait. Take a look at this." I unfolded it and spread it out on the table.

He sat back down and frowned. "Where did you find this?"

"My aunts found it in the attic with a bunch of my grandfather's stuff. They've been going through old boxes and trunks looking for papers that might, I don't know, give us a clue."

"To what?"

"To anything!"

Noah pointed to the edges of the blueprint. "It's in pretty bad shape, and torn here." He indicated a section at the bottom.

"I know. Any idea what part is missing? You know the house so well."

He shrugged. "Like what?"

"Like a secret room."

Noah grinned. "If you mean the basement, I can tell you, if there was one, it's been sealed up for years. I've never seen it. And I've been all over that house." He closed his laptop, set it on the counter, then backed up so I could slide out of the booth. I bumped into him as soon as I stood.

We were face-to-face.

"Sorry," I said automatically, feeling a little jolt of electricity at his proximity.

"Tight quarters," he said, half smiling, his dark eyes on me.

"Cozy," I countered.

He reached over for the door to let me out, then followed me down the short steps. "I'll walk you back."

I was about to say, "No need," since it was a short distance to the house, but in light of the recent murders, I accepted. Plus, the fog had come in, making it a challenge to see much in the dark. I pulled my jacket around me, but it did little to keep out the cold. We walked in silence along the stone path to the back door, where a dim porchlight shone weakly in the darkness.

I turned to thank him and was startled by how close he was to me. When he slowly began to lean in, I pulled back, not ready for what I guessed was coming. But to my surprise, he wiped the side of my mouth with his finger, then held it up.

At first, I thought it was blood.

"Tomato sauce," he said. "Hope you weren't saving it for later."

I laughed, too loudly, and felt my face grow warm at the possibility I'd worn that streak of sauce for nearly the entire evening. I rubbed the side of my mouth to make sure it was gone. "Why didn't you tell me?"

"Wait," he said, eyeing me. "Did you think I was going to kiss you just then?"

"I . . . yes . . . I mean, no . . . uh . . ."

He pulled me into his arms and kissed me—a kiss so powerful it surged through me like a ghost had passed through me. When he finally let go, he said simply, "Goodnight, Carissa," and walked off, leaving me standing on the doorstep unable to move.

Wow.

I shook my head. This was not the distraction I needed right now. *Get it together*, I told myself, as I inserted my key into the doorknob. I took a last look back, but he had vanished into the coastal fog.

A line from a song suddenly came to mind: *"A kiss is just a kiss . . ."*

I sighed, entered through the back of the kitchen, and switched on the overhead light to get some water. As usual, the place was spotless, thanks to Marnie and her work ethic. I got a bottled water from the fridge, took a few sips, then decided to bring it to my room. As I approached the swinging door between the kitchen and the dining room, I was about to switch off the light when I spotted something out of the corner of my eye.

Marnie's apron.

It was hanging on a hook next to several others that sported the Blackwood Bed and Breakfast Inn logo, each one embroidered with our names. But it was the sight of Marnie's apron that reminded me of the note she'd been reading before she slipped it into one of the pockets.

I listened for a moment to make sure no one was about, then stepped over to the rack of aprons. I started to reach for Marnie's, then stopped.

What was I doing? Snooping through the housekeeper's pockets? Reading a private note that was none of my business?

Yep.

I took the apron down and felt the pockets. *Bingo.* I pulled out the paper and unfolded it. Inside was a typed message and a computer-printed photo of a heart-shaped necklace. The note read: "I know what you did. It's time to pay up."

Oh my God. Was Marnie being blackmailed by Patty Fay too? What did the necklace have to do with the note? Then I remembered one of Patty Fays' blackmail clickbaits: *Who's the woman who stole from a local jewelry store?*

Could that be—

I thought I heard a sound.

Quickly, I slipped the note back into the pocket, switched off the light, then peered into the dining room to see if anyone was there. The room appeared empty. So what had I heard? Just the noises that emanated from this old house? While the coast was clear, I made my way to the stairs, taking them two steps at a time.

I unlocked my bedroom door and switched on the bedside lamp. Nothing happened. No light. Not even a flicker. I quietly cursed Noah for saying he'd fixed the light when he obviously hadn't. I tried the overhead light. No response. I turned on my cellphone light and shined it at the shelf where two tapered candles waited for just this occasion. My aunts must have known this might happen in an old house like the Blackwood Inn. I mentally thanked them.

I set down the water bottle and found a box of matches nearby. I lit one, held it to the wick of one candle, then the other. The flickering candlelight didn't do much to illuminate the room, but it was enough to see if there was anything I might trip over. I brought one of the candles to my bedside table and set the other one on the desk.

I sat down and opened my laptop. The screen lit up the room, almost more than the candlelight. At least the power wasn't out. I wrote the latest info I'd learned from Noah into my notebook along with the message I'd found in Marnie's apron, then sat back and pondered these new developments.

It was looking more and more like Patty Fay Johnstone was a multiple blackmailer—and that her many victims had embarrassing secrets she'd discovered and used against them. But as for this latest note I'd found in Marnie's pocket regarding the necklace—how long had it been there? Certainly before Patty Fay died. If it had been handwritten, I could have taken a picture and studied the handwriting, but it had been typed. Too bad.

I had a thought. Was this why the private detective had arrived in Pelican Point at such an opportune time? To help Patty Fay with her blackmail scheme? Or did someone hire him to find out the identity of the blackmailer?

Then again, maybe a.k.a. Henry Hill knew about her scheme and blackmailed *her*.

Before I could consider this new twist, I heard a low, mournful, almost growling noise coming from my bed. I glanced over to see Pyewacket lying on my pillow, staring at me. Funny. I hadn't noticed him when I'd come in. I wondered if he'd been hiding under the bed. I also wondered how he had gotten in.

I went over to see if there was something wrong with Pye when he bolted off the bed and dashed underneath it, nearly giving me a heart attack. *What was up with that cat?* I opened my bedroom door to let him out—no way was he spending the night in my room—when I saw a shadow moving in the hallway.

I froze, listening. A creak. *A door opening?*

A dim light bounced in the recesses of the hallway. *A flashlight?*

The light neared the staircase at the far end of the hall.

I stayed still. Listening. Another creak.

At that moment Pyewacket darted out of the room and toward the staircase. *Damn cat*, I thought, gasping. When my heart stopped racing, I looked down the hallway and heard the creak of footsteps on the stairs leading to the third floor.

One of my aunts?

I decide to check. I retrieved my phone, turned on the flashlight, and tiptoed toward the staircase that led to the upper floors. Shining my light up the stairs, I saw no one—not even a cat. I took a step, then another, moving slowly and praying the old floors wouldn't squeak as I walked. I paused at the third-floor landing, checking for a sign of my aunts. The hallway was deserted.

Another creak. This time on the dark staircase leading to the attic.

I glanced up. No light bouncing off the walls. It was pitch black.

I continued up, slowly, step by step. When I reached the top, I found the door to the attic was closed. No light peeked out from under it.

In the darkness, I turned the knob, opened the door an inch, and peered in.

More darkness.

Then a creak. Coming from across the room.

"Hello?" I called out. "Aunt Hazel? Aunt Runa?"

I waited. No response.

I shined my cell phone light around the room. The attic seemed especially creepy at night. *What if something happened to me?* No one would know I was up here. I shivered.

I was about to leave, when I heard a thud from across the room.

I froze. *Maybe it was a cat like last time?*

"Kitty, kitty?" I called.

Nothing. *So maybe not a kitty, kitty?*

"Who's there?" I cried. I took a step in and scanned the area for any sign of movement. "I know you're in here, so just come out."

Nothing. I took another step in. My heart pounding, I felt for the light switch and flipped it on. No light. A dead bulb?

Something streaked past my feet and out the open door.

The orange cat!

At least, I hoped it had been a cat and not a large rat. *How had he gotten in?*

I walked over to where the noise had come from. One of my grandfather's many boxes had fallen over. That's what must have made the thud. I started to right it when I noticed the trunk next to it was open. By the cat? Not likely. Probably by my aunts when they were looking for clues. They must have forgotten to close it.

But then, what caused the box to overturn?

I shined my light at the papers that had fallen out of the box and wondered if my aunts had been through them. I glanced at the open trunk and noticed a bunch of old embroidered handkerchiefs, all folded neatly. Underneath were tea towels, antimacassars, doilies, and some sachets. *Hmm.* Why had my grandfather saved all these delicate linens? Had they belonged to my grandmother? I pulled out the top handkerchief. The initials "A.B." were sewn into one corner in a fancy flourish. I lifted it to my nose and inhaled a musty scent.

I rifled through the linens and things until I reached the bottom of the trunk. Something struck me as odd. The linens hadn't taken up much room—not enough to fill a large trunk like this—yet it I'd already reached the bottom.

I shined my light on it. The bottom of the trunk appeared to be slanted. At first I thought it might be a cheaply made trunk, but the wood outside had been lavishly carved and, like the other trunks and boxes, included my grandfather's initials.

I pushed on the end that was slightly raised. It felt spongey. *Hmm.* Could it be a hidden compartment, like in a Nancy Drew mystery? I searched for something to wedge it up and found an old wire coat hanger lying on the antique sewing machine. I unbent the wire and inserted one end into the lower side, then began easing it up.

Moments later I had the false bottom in my hands!

Cool, I thought.

I set it aside and looked into the small remaining space, which was about three inches deep. I saw eight cigar boxes, all tied closed with twine.

Cigar boxes? I didn't recall my grandfather ever smoking cigars, although a lot of men did back in those days. Why were they hidden in the bottom of this trunk? I wondered if my aunts knew about them.

I sat on the floor and began working on one of the cigar box knots. I guessed it was one of those fancy maritime knots, the kind we learned about in Girl Scouts but never really needed. Using my fingernails, then my teeth, I finally got the knot out. The string fell away and I opened the lid.

I expected to smell the lingering scent of cigars, but perfume wafted up from the inside instead. I realized the smell came from the tidy stack of letters all tied together in a crisscross pattern like a wrapped gift.

Letters!

The handwritten name on the top envelope was adorned with lots of curvy swirls and decorative flourishes: "Bram." It must have been written by a woman.

I started to untie the first packet when I heard a noise. A creak, coming from the stairs outside the attic. I glanced around for a place to hide, then shut off my light. If someone was there, they had me trapped. I could only hope it was one of my aunts.

I decided not to take a chance.

I got up, made my way to the attic door I'd left open, and hid behind it. Holding my breath, I heard faint footsteps just outside the attic.

Someone was there.

I listened as the intruder took a step inside. The floor groaned underneath their weight. I could tell this was not one of my aunts.

Another pause. Silence. I tried not to breathe.

Stupid! I mentally scolded myself. I should have grabbed some kind of weapon before I tucked myself again the wall—like that coat hanger so I could shish kebob whoever it was. I was completely vulnerable. My only hope might be to escape out the open door before I was caught.

Hidden behind the attic door, I saw the giant shadow of a man entering the room.

I pulled back as far as I could, trying to press myself into the wall.

And then my phone chimed.

A text had come in, not only alerting me, but alerting the intruder to my presence as well.

The door swung away from me.

"Carissa?" A bright light shined in my face. "What are you doing?"

"Noah?" I almost collapsed in relief when I heard his voice. "I should ask you the same thing. You scared me half to death."

"Same here."

"Why are you up here?"

"Probably for the same reason you are."

"Really?" I asked suspiciously. "And what would that be?"

"Snooping. Isn't that why you're here?"

"Actually, I heard someone go up the stairs. I thought they went into the attic. But when I got here, there was no one around, except one of those darn cats. By the way, the attic light is out. But seriously. What are you doing here?"

He shrugged. "After you left, I got to thinking about something you'd said at dinner."

"What?" I asked, not recalling anything of significance. Except that kiss after dinner.

"You said you were looking for the other part of a blueprint."

I nodded. That made sense.

"Did you find it?" he asked.

"No, but found something else." I walked back to the trunk and picked up the packet of letters I'd dropped in my race to hide behind the door.

Noah frowned. "What are they?"

"I think they're love letters."

Chapter Twenty
The Scarlet Letters

"Love letters?" Noah asked.

I sat on the floor and Noah joined me. Picking up another packet of letters, I noticed the handwriting was different. I checked the others—each one from a different hand. All addressed to Bram Blackwood. A total of eight packets. Were there more?

How many lovers had my grandfather had?

"Did you read them?" Noah asked as I handed him one of the packets.

"Not yet." I took the top letter from the stack I'd already untied and carefully opened the envelope. Whoever had written this one must have added extra perfume because the scent was even stronger as I pulled out the letter. Printed on the outside were the simple words, "My Love."

"Whew!" Noah said, waving his hand by his nose. He sniffed the packet he held and pulled back.

"I know," I said. I unfolded the thin pink-tinted paper and began to read the letter out loud. But when I got to the part that said, "It has been so long since I held your massive manhood in my eager hand and . . . ," I stopped.

This was no teenage crush put on paper. More like erotic porn. I looked up at Noah and felt my face burning hot.

"Why did you stop?" he asked, grinning. "You were just getting to the good part."

"Massive manhood?" I said, cringing. "I'll let you read the rest yourself."

He chuckled. "Well, it's obvious the writer was having an affair with your grandfather. Who's it from? What's the signature at the bottom?"

I turned the letter over and looked for the name. "It's just signed, 'Your Maiden by the Sea.' Underneath there's a date. Seems this was written quite a few years ago, not long after my grandmother died. Who do you suppose Maiden by the Sea is?"

"Wife of a sea captain?" Noah guessed.

"Maiden by the Sea." As I repeated the signatory, I felt like I'd heard the reference before. But where?

I set down the letter and picked up two more packets written in different hands. I set one down and untied the knot on the next one, then opened the top letter and scanned it for the signature. This one read: "Patience-Faith-Joy."

That name, too, seemed to ring a distant bell. Joy. Not Justice?

"Sound like Amish names," Noah said. "Maybe he was into triplets."

I scoffed. "Yeah, right. It has to be an alias too." I checked the next packet. The letter inside was signed: "Your Scottish Mariner." Not much to go on.

The last packet puzzled me the most. It was dated thirty years ago and was simply signed, "Amen."

"What do you make of this one?" I asked Noah, showing him the signatory.

"Amen?" he frowned. "Someone who's religious? A cult follower? A play on the name Abraham?"

None of those possibilities sounded right. Especially not a religious person, after scanning the contents. Although a little less steamy and scandalous than the first letter I'd read, it was still full of flowery adoration and longings for the future. But the last line really caught my attention. It read: "P.S. I'm late, Darling." Did that mean back then what it means now?

I heard a thud at the far end of the attic and jumped. "What was that?" I whispered to Noah.

He sat still, listening. Silence. He stood up and walked over. I stuffed the last letter in my pocket, then followed him. Like much of the attic walls, the far wall was nearly covered by boxes and trunks that looked like they'd been untouched for years, judging by the dust and cobwebs. Apparently my aunts hadn't gotten to all of them yet.

"Probably rats," Noah said.

I shivered. Rats. Then I noticed one of the trunks wasn't as dusty as the others. It was one of those large old-fashioned steamer trunks popular in the 1800s that doubled as a portable wardrobe. This one was upended, with the opening on the side, secured with a padlock. It was made of canvas and wood, covered in ornamental patterned paper, with leather latches to keep it closed.

I remembered seeing one like it when we visited my grandfather years ago. Could this be the same one? My dad said they were not only used as wardrobes, but even as caskets, and some had hidden compartments for storing keepsakes, heirlooms, and treasures. Obviously when I heard that, I sneaked up to the attic and tried to open the lock with a bobby pin, something I'd learned from reading Nancy Drew mysteries.

But my grandfather caught me before I could get it open. To my surprise, that was the first time he'd ever gotten mad at me. I vividly remembered him saying, "You could have smothered in there and we might never have found you!" I didn't go near the thing again.

Had the noise we'd heard come from inside? Were there really rats in there?

I turned to Noah, the jack-of-all-trades. "Can you open it?"

He pulled at the padlock that kept the leather belts together, but it held, firmly secured. It appeared to be rusted shut. I didn't think a bobby pin would do the trick.

"What do you think is inside?" I asked him. "More secrets?"

"I need some tools. Give me a minute," Noah said. "I'll be right back."

With that he left me alone . . . in the creepy attic . . . in the middle of the night . . . where we'd just heard a strange noise. And maybe rats.

Not cool.

As soon as he was gone, I heard the noise again. It was definitely coming from inside the trunk.

It must be rats. That's why the cat was here. Rats were probably crawling all over the attic.

I shuddered and wrapped my arms around myself as if that would protect me.

What was taking Noah so long?

I heard a noise coming from outside the attic. I walked over to the door and peered out.

Voices. Loud ones. Coming from downstairs. *At this time of night?*

Shining my cellphone light, I rushed down all three flights of stairs to find my aunts standing in their robes at the front door.

"What's going on?" I asked as I joined them. "Who's at the door at this time of night?" To my surprise, Sheriff Lokey and his deputy stood on the porch. Noah had inserted himself between them and my aunts.

"But we've been through this! I didn't do anything!" Aunt Hazel cried, clutching her hands together.

Aunt Runa had her hand on her sister's shoulder.

"Sheriff," Noah said, "you know this is crazy, right? There's no way—"

The sheriff cut him off. "Noah, ladies. Sorry about this, but I'm here because there's been a break in the case."

"What are you talking about?" I asked, glancing at my aunts, then Noah, then the sheriff.

"Carissa," the sheriff said, acknowledging me. "I'm afraid I have to take Hazel in again."

"What for?" I cried.

"I'm placing her under arrest for the murders of Patty Fay Johnstone and Herman Hicks."

My mouth dropped open. "What? You can't be serious!" I looked at Aunt Hazel. There were tears in her eye and her hands were shaking. "Sheriff! You know her. You know she'd never do anything like . . . like that."

He nodded. "But as I said, there's been a development."

"What kind of development?" came a voice from the stairs. Jonathan appeared, wearing a long velour robe and slippers.

"An anonymous message," the sheriff replied, "implicating her in both deaths."

I scoffed. "You know anonymous messages aren't reliable. You need proof, right? Evidence. Rumors, innuendos, mysterious unsigned messages—those aren't evidence."

"I wasn't finished," the sheriff said. "The message indicated that the private investigator who was found dead in your inn happened to be working on a case involving your aunts."

"What case? For who?" I asked.

"Patty Fay Johnstone."

"No way." I shook my head. "This makes no sense at all. You're saying Patty Fay hired a detective, then got herself killed, and the next day the detective gets himself killed? And you're blaming all of this on my aunt? Listen, someone has been out to get my aunts ever since they opened the bed and breakfast. You should be looking for that person. And if you really think my aunt is guilty of something, where's your proof?"

The sheriff nodded patiently. "We found a receipt from Patty Fay in Hill's wallet. He wrote in his notebook that Patty Fay suspected someone was going to try to kill her. That's why she hired him. After she died, he snooped around and found a small bag of belladonna hidden in your Aunt Hazel's bedroom."

"That's ridiculous!" I looked at my aunt. "Aunt Hazel, tell him. This isn't true, is it?"

"I . . . I don't know," she said, sounding flustered.

"Don't say anything," Jonathan told her. He turned to the sheriff. "You said the private investigator found belladonna in Hazel's bedroom. Anyone could have put it there."

The sheriff glanced at Aunt Hazel, then Aunt Runa. "Actually, the bag also contained one of Runa's crystals."

"That's ridiculous!" Aunt Runa cried.

"I'm afraid that's all supposition, Sheriff," Jonathan said. "You have no proof that poisonous plant was used to killed Patty Fay or that Hazel was connected to her death."

"We will when the final tests come back from the lab and we find the poison was from Hazel's plant."

"Well, until then, you have no right to arrest her," Jonathan added.

The sheriff sighed. "Actually, there's more."

The room went quiet waiting for him to drop the other leaden shoe.

"It seems Herman Hicks wrote in his notebook that he suspected someone might want him out of the way."

"Why would he think that?" I asked.

"We found a note. Typed. In his wallet."

"What did it say?" Noah asked.

"Something like: 'Who's the broken-down lush who knows too much about the people in this town?'"

Noah and I looked at each other. It sounded just like one of Patty Fay's threatening posts on her secret website. I was about to tell the sheriff when he said, "Hill wrote that he wasn't feeling too well that night—the night before he died. Said it might be the start of a hangover and that Hazel gave him something for his upset stomach. But now it appears there was belladonna in his bottle of whiskey."

"But you have no motive!" I said. "Why on earth would my aunts poison anyone? They didn't have any reason to murder Patty Fay or the detective. In fact—" I started to say, but the sheriff cut me off.

"Listen, Carissa, before you say too much, did you know your aunts were being blackmailed?"

I gasped.

My aunts gripped each other's hands.

"What? How? By who?" I stammered. Although the second I said it, I knew.

"Patty Fay," the sheriff and I said at the same time.

Did he know about the website? Maybe it wouldn't be a good idea to mention it before Noah could take a look. I turned to my aunts. Their faces told me everything. Patty Fay *did* have something on them. But what?

"Is this true?" I asked them for confirmation.

After sharing a look, they both nodded.

"But why?" I asked them. "What could she possibly blackmail you for?"

"Don't say anything," Jonathan said to my aunts.

Aunt Runa ignored him. "It wasn't exactly us she was blackmailing—at first, anyway. We were trying to protect the person she was trying to extort."

"And besides," Aunt Hazel added, "we didn't know who the blackmailer was either."

"So who were you protecting?" I asked.

Jonathan held up a "Don't answer" hand.

Once again, Runa ignored him. "Marnie."

The note I'd found in Marnie's apron! The picture of the necklace! They'd been trying to protect her.

"When we figured out it was Patty Fay," Aunt Hazel said, "we told her to stop, but she threatened to tell everyone we were harboring a criminal! I mean, we couldn't let our Marnie go to jail, could we?"

"Please, Hazel! Don't say anything more," Jonathan insisted.

"Come along, now, Hazel," the sheriff said. "I'll try to make this as painless as possible. You have the right to remain silent—"

I cut him off. "You can't arrest her!" I turned to Jonathan.

Jonathan shook his head. "I'm afraid he can."

"What about a warrant?" I cried. "She has rights, right?"

Jonathan shrugged. "He doesn't need one this time. Like he said, he's got probable cause that she committed a crime. That could be anything from an informant, including method, motive, opportunity, evidence, and reasonable suspicion based on the facts."

Murder at Blackwood Inn

I was speechless as the deputy got out handcuffs. With tears welling in her eyes, Aunt Hazel held out her hands to be cuffed.

I was aghast. I glared at the sheriff.

He glanced at the deputy, then shook his head. "That's okay, Deputy. We don't need to bother with those."

With that, he led my dear old aunt out the door of the Blackwood Bed and Breakfast Inn to his waiting patrol car, leaving the rest of us in a silent stupor.

Chapter Twenty-One
The Hidden Room

This was all too much. My aunts were being blackmailed, just like a bunch of other people in this town. Aunt Hazel had been arrested for murdering Patty Fay and Henry Hill. And from the letters I'd found in my grandfather's trunk, it appeared he'd been quite the lothario.

Were any of these events connected? If so, how?

After telling Aunt Runa we'd deal with all this in the morning, Noah and I sent her off to bed then sat at the dining room table. Jonathan had returned to his room, promising to do what he could to help Aunt Hazel. As for me, there was no way I would be getting any sleep.

"I can't believe it," I said to Noah. "What just happened?"

Noah said nothing. What could he say?

"I don't know what else to do. I just hope Jonathan can help."

"Maybe we should show him or the sheriff the letters," Noah suggested.

The letters! I reached into my pocket and brought out the one I'd stuffed there before coming downstairs. I pulled it out, opened it, and showed him the P.S. that Amen had added at the bottom. "Noah, what do you make of this?"

"'I'm late?'" He raised an eyebrow. "It's obvious. Whoever wrote the letter was pregnant."

That was a game changer. If one of Bram's paramours had gotten pregnant, who was she? How old would the child be now? Did my aunts know? And what would my grandfather have done about it?

"We've got to figure out the aliases for these letter-writers." I went to the front desk in the foyer and returned with a pad and pen. "What were the names—er, aliases—again?"

Noah raised a finger. "Amen." He raised another finger. "Maiden by the Sea." He added a third finger. "Your Scottish Mariner."

"Yes! And don't forget Patience-Faith-Joy," I said. That was a weird signature. A thought flashed across my brain . . . *initials?*

"Patty Fay Johnstone!" Noah and I said at the same time.

"It has to be," I added. "But I can't believe Patty Fay had an affair with my grandfather all those years ago."

"Why not? He was a pretty good-looking guy. Had a lot of charisma."

I hadn't thought of my grandfather as necessarily good looking.

"So who's 'Maiden by the Sea'?" Noah asked.

"That one has been haunting me. I've heard that reference before." I typed the line into my cell phone. "I knew it! Here it is:

*It was many and many a year ago,
In a kingdom by the sea,
That a maiden there lived whom you may know
By the name of Annabel Lee!*

"Oh my God, it's got to be Annabelle Topper!"

"As I recall, things didn't end well for Poe's lover," Noah said.

I took in a sharp breath. "Wait a minute! You don't suppose Annabelle is the next victim?"

Noah shrugged. "No way of telling. At least, not yet. What about 'Your Scottish Mariner'?"

There were quite a few Scots in Pelican Point. Aunt Runa told me that families had come over from Scotland in search of a better life and more bounty from the sea—including Marnie's parents. She still used some of the Scottish words and phrases now and then.

"It can't be Marnie," I whispered. "And my *grandfather*?" I shivered at the thought.

"Apparently, he was quite the chick magnet," Noah said.

I glared at him. "Not funny."

Noah made a frowny face, then added, "One more to go."

"'Amen,'" I said, aware there could be a double meaning. "Maybe it's someone we don't know. I mean, there are a lot of women in this town. Who knows how many he charmed."

"Ah, but so far, three of them have one thing in common," Noah said.

"Like what?"

"They attended your grandfather's séances."

"You're right! Patty Fay, Annabelle, Marnie. So . . . Gracie?"

"Gracie," Noah repeated. "As in saying, 'Amen' at the end of grace."

Murder at Blackwood Inn

I thought for a moment. Maybe all four of them got together and . . . what? Murdered my grandfather? He supposedly died under mysterious circumstances, but I just couldn't see this playing out like *Murder on the Orient Express*. And why would they? It sounded as if they were all in love with him.

"I wonder if my aunts knew any of this? They never said anything to me. And they kept that blackmail secret from me. What else haven't they told me?"

Noah eyed me. "I think your grandfather is the key to all this."

I was about to agree when I heard a noise coming from the kitchen. I glanced at Noah. He'd obviously heard it too.

I got up as quietly as I could and tiptoed over to the swinging door between the dining room and the kitchen. Listening and hearing nothing, I pushed the door open.

Then, from the other side, a thud, followed by an "Ouch!"

Startled, I backed up. The door began to open toward me.

Marnie stood in the doorway, rubbing her forehead. I could see a red mark where the door had hit her.

"Oh, dear! Are you okay?" I asked, although that wasn't the first question that came to mind. I wanted to ask, *What were you doing in there at this hour? Spying?*

"I couldn't sleep," Marnie said, her Scottish accent a little heavier than usual. "Not with all that's 'appened around here. Came in 'ere to get a cuppa."

I glanced into the kitchen. There was no sign of tea-makings anywhere. How long had she been there? What had she heard?

"Where did you come from?"

She began playing with her hidden necklace. "The back stairs. Servants' entrance."

A.k.a. the hidden staircase.

"Sorry about bumping into you," I said. "I had no idea you were on the other side of the door. Let me get you some ice for that."

She waved me off. "I can do it meself," she said. "It's just a wee bump. I'll live."

She started to back into the kitchen when Noah said, "Marnie?"

She sighed. "Yes, Noah? You need something?"

"I didn't see you around when the sheriff came earlier. Did you know that Carissa's Aunt Hazel was taken to jail?"

"A'course. Just figured there was nothing I could do but stay out of the way."

"Marnie," I said. "I think someone might have been trying to frame both of my aunts with these murders. Any idea who?"

"Not a clue," Marnie said, shaking her head emphatically. "I mind me own business, I do."

"Did you know Carissa's aunts were being blackmailed?" Noah asked.

Marnie's face paled. She clenched the hidden necklace in her hand. "I don't know anything about that."

I pulled out the letter I'd stuffed in my pocket and held it up. "Do you know what this is?"

Marnie's eyes narrowed. "Where did you get that?" she snapped. She reached out to snatch it from me, but I pulled my hand back.

"So you *do* know what that is," Noah said.

Marnie's face tightened. "Listen, the pair of you. I dunnah 'ave to answer these silly questions. If you're implying I know something about the murders, well, you'd be wrong then."

"So what do you know about this?" I asked, tapping the letter.

She scoffed.

"Marnie, was Patty Fay blackmailing you?" Noah asked.

Marnie stiffened.

"Why did she do that?" I pressed her.

"I dunno what you're talking about," Marnie answered.

"Does it have anything to do with that note in your apron pocket I saw you reading yesterday?" I asked.

Marnie's eyes flared. "You've been snooping in my stuff! You've no right!"

"Patty Fay had something on you, Marnie," I continued. "I'm guessing it had to do with that necklace you wear under your clothes. Somehow she found out you stole it from the jewelry store downtown and then she made you pay her to keep quiet about it. Am I right?"

"She had no business stickin' her nose in my affairs!" Marnie exclaimed. "This necklace was . . . special to me. Someone nicked it a few months ago from my drawer, then sold it to that Jewels of the Sea shop downtown. I recognized it right away when I went in. Since it belonged to me, I took it." She tapped it gently through her nightgown. "No one's ever gonna to get it again 'cause I'm never takin' it off."

To my surprise, she pulled it out and showed it to us. Tears welled in her eyes as she held it out. Hanging on a delicate gold chain was a thin gold ring studded with tiny diamonds. A promise ring? A wedding ring?

"But if that's your ring, why steal it?" Noah asked. "Why not tell the owner it was yours? Or buy it back?"

"I did tell him. He didn't believe me," Marnie answered. "And I had no proof. He called it an antique, made up some story about an old sea captain giving it to his bride. He was trying to sell it at an outrageous price! So I went in one day when he wasn't there, only his employee—old Mrs. Applegate. I pretended to be interested in something else, then took the necklace and ring when her back was turned. Like I said, I did nothing wrong 'cause I'm the rightful owner."

"The sheriff might not see it that way," Noah said.

"Is that why Patty Fay blackmailed you?" I asked.

Marnie's face flashed bright red. "I've had enough of this claptrap. I'll answer no more of your questions. You'll have my resignation in the morning, Ms. Blackwood."

"Marnie! You don't have to—"

Marnie stepped back into the kitchen. The door swung closed in my face. I turned to Noah. "She wasn't serious about quitting, was she? My aunts will kill me if we lose her."

"She'll calm down," Noah said. "I've seen her blow up before. She's got quite the temper."

"I hope you're right. So who do you think gave her that ring?"

Noah smiled. I nodded. It was obvious. My grandfather!

I sighed, then yawned.

"Listen, we better get some sleep," Noah said. "We can't do much else tonight."

"You're right," I agreed. "The more I learn, the more confused I become." I checked my phone in case the sheriff or Jonathan had tried to reach me. There were two texts. One from my ex and one from Aiden. I ignored the first one. The text from Aiden appeared to have come in soon after Aunt Hazel was arrested.

I read it quickly: "Are you OK? Just heard about your aunt on the police scanner. I think I may have some news for you. Will come by tomorrow."

I smiled, feeling a sparkle of hope. I looked up from the message to see Noah staring at me.

"Good news?" he asked.

"Uh, just Aiden, checking in. He wanted to see if I was all right."

"He's up late," Noah said.

I nodded. "He heard the news on his police scanner. He said he'll stop by tomorrow with some news."

Noah nodded. "Well, good night, then."

Did I detect a hint of jealousy in his tone?

"Good night. See you in the morning?"

He nodded, stood there for a second, then headed through the swinging door to the kitchen.

No good-night kiss? I thought, feeling a little disappointed. *Not a good time, Carissa*, I told myself. But I couldn't help wondering if the text from Aiden had something to do with Noah's sudden change in behavior.

As for Aiden, he mentioned having some news. Had he learned something more from the sheriff? Or had he been doing some sleuthing of his own?

I headed up the stairs to my room, hoping tomorrow would bring answers.

* * *

I awoke to the sound of low mewing and sat up. Pyewacket was perched on my window seat, apparently asking to go out. How he had gotten in was a constant mystery. I got up, opened the window, and he leaped out onto the eaves, then disappeared.

Damn cat.

I yawned. It was not yet dawn, but there was no way I was going back to sleep, not after that short, fitful night. Besides,

Aunt Hazel was on my mind constantly. I had to come up with a way to get her out of this mess. I had a feeling she wouldn't do well in prison, trying to bribe the staff with her pastries and herbal teas.

With a sense of urgency, I quickly dressed in jeans and a Pelican Point T-shirt, planning to head back to the attic to search for anything that would help clear my aunt. Since I'd found those letters, I had a hunch there would be more to discover. Until I could figure out what else to do, all I could think of was to snoop around up there to see if I'd missed anything.

I headed down the hall and took the staircase up to the attic. I stopped and listened at the doorway, just in case, then turned the knob and entered. To my surprise, the attic light was already on. Had Noah fixed it? Had he forgotten to turn it off? I listened again. No moaning cats. No pitter-patter of rats. So far, so good.

I stepped over to the steamer trunk, still curious about what was inside. It was the only container I hadn't breached—and the most curious one because of its size. I looked at the lock, wishing I'd brought something to open it, then blinked when I realized it was unlocked. Had Noah come back and unlocked it late last night?

I pulled open the rusty metal latch, then tugged at the front of the trunk. At first it didn't budge. I tried again, giving it a good yank, and one of the double doors creaked and started to open. Dust particles swirled in the air and I coughed as I continued to pull open the front. When one side was wide enough for me to get a look inside, I waved at the dust and sneezed three times in a row.

I opened the other side, then pulled out my cellphone light to get a good look inside the trunk. It was larger than it initially appeared, and the walls were covered with frayed and faded wallpaper. I tried to imagine what the trunk must have looked like new. My grandfather had said large steamer trunks were a popular way to carry clothes and accessories for long-distance travel by ship, back in the day. I imagined it filled with glamorous outfits, shiny shoes, fancy hats, and even expensive jewelry.

But to my disappointment, there was nothing inside. It had been stripped of its contents. I leaned in and ran my hand along the inner walls where compartments used to be. Then I noticed the back wall had a tiny hole in it. I leaned in and peered through the hole.

Darkness.

I stuck my finger in, hoping there wasn't a big spider waiting for its lunch.

I felt air.

I knocked on the back wall. It sounded hollow. That was odd because the trunk rested against the attic wall. I pushed on the back of the trunk again, hoping my hand didn't plow right through from the rot, but instead, it swung forward through what should have been the solid wall of the attic.

"Oh my God," I whispered. "It's a hidden passageway!" As I peered through to the other side into darkness, I wondered why I should be so surprised. This house was full of mysterious passageways, staircases. . . . and rooms? I shined my cellphone light into the darkness.

Was that a hidden room back there?

I gasped. Inside I spotted a round table that sat in the center of the room, with six chairs circling it. Perched on top of the table was Pyewacket, the orange cat.

Seriously? How had he gotten in there?

"Hey cat," I said, "I think I just found my grandfather's séance room!"

I ducked my head and squeezed through the narrow trunk opening, then straightened up as soon as I was in the hidden room. Although the area was large enough to hold the table and chairs, there wasn't space for much else, other than the cobwebs that filled the corners. The dusty table was covered with paw prints. *Pyewacket?* I looked for another way in or out, but didn't see one. Surely there had to be some kind of secret door somewhere, no doubt camouflaged by the garish velvet-flocked wallpaper that covered the walls of this inner room.

I spotted a box under the table about the size of a microwave oven, marked "Private." It was tied up with string.

Aha! More secrets? The spirits were about to speak.

I pulled the dusty box out from underneath the table, finding it surprisingly lightweight, and set it on top of the table. I untied the string, but before I could lift the lid, I heard a sound.

Coming from back in the attic.

"Noah?" I called out. "Is that you?"

No answer.

"Aunt Runa?"

Nothing.

I held my breath, listening. The floor squeaked. I ducked and squeezed through the trunk opening between the hidden room and the attic, then pulled the connecting door closed.

"Who's there?" I called again, straightening up and waving cobwebs from my hair.

Murder at Blackwood Inn

Silence.

I glanced over at the attic door. I was certain I had closed it, but now it stood ajar.

Someone had been in here just moments ago.

But who? And where did they go?

Chapter Twenty-Two
A Secret Certificate

"Carissa?" I heard my name being called from downstairs.

"Noah?" I called back. Was he the one in the attic a few moments ago? Is so, why hadn't he answered me then?

I heard his footsteps as he climbed the stairs. When he reached the attic door, I frowned at him. "Was that you earlier?"

"When?"

"Just now. I mean, a few minutes ago. I heard someone come into the attic. I called out. Was that you?"

"Nope," he said. "Just got here. Actually, I'm surprised to see you up so early. Already snooping?"

My eyes flashed. "You won't believe what I found!" I lead the way to the steamer trunk. He followed me over and I gestured toward the opening.

"You unlocked it?" he said, looking surprised. "How'd you do that? Find a key?"

I shook my head. "It was already unlocked when I got here this morning. I thought you might have done it."

"Nope."

"That's weird. I woke up early and couldn't get back to sleep, so I came up here and found it unlocked. I guess someone else has been in here. Maybe it was Aunt Runa?"

He peered inside the open trunk. "Looks empty. You didn't find anything?"

I ducked inside, pushed open the back, and stepped through the narrow opening, into the secret room hidden behind it.

"Whoa!" Noah said, his eyes wide. He bent over and had to do some twisting and turning to get through, but when he stepped into the room, I could tell he was as amazed as I had been.

"The Séance Room," he said immediately, glancing around. "Not in the basement, but hidden up here in the attic all these years. Clever."

"This room is small, so I'm not that surprised we didn't figure it out sooner. I'll bet it's not even on the rest of that blueprint. And with all the wall-to-wall trunks and junk up here, who would have suspected?"

He nodded at the box I had placed on the table. "What's in there?"

"I don't know. I found it under the table and was just about to look inside when I got spooked by that noise in the attic."

"Well, let's have a look," he said, wiping dust off a chair before sitting down.

I did the same and sat across from him. "More love letters?" I wondered aloud.

Noah lifted the lid. A spider crawled out.

"Yikes," I said. "Any more of those in there?" I cautiously peered inside.

Apparently not afraid of spiders, Noah reached in and pulled out a handful of dusty old books. He sifted through them, then said, "Burns."

"What?" I asked.

"Robert Burns, the Scottish poet. Know him?"

I eyed him.

"What?" he said, sounding defensive. "A handyman can't be into poetry?"

I tried to stifle my grin but it persisted. "Uh, sure."

"I read him in college," he said. "Don't remember much other than he wrote 'Auld Lang Syne.'"

"I did too. I was an English major and he was part of the curriculum. All I remember is that he grew up writing poetry, which apparently attracted the ladies. He courted something like nine or ten women, including his own mother's servant. Had a dozen kids by these various women."

"Women do love poets," Noah said.

"Yes, but he suffered from manic depression and died before he was forty of a rheumatic heart condition."

"I don't remember all that," Noah said, "but I do recall that a bunch of phrenologists removed his skull and studied his brain in an attempt to measure his personality."

"Seriously?" I said, shaking my head. "Bizarre. The question is, why did my grandfather keep these books in here? Was he a fan?"

Noah opened the cover of the top book. It was signed, "To Sylvander, All my love, Clarinda."

Those weren't family names, but they sounded familiar. I pulled out my phone and typed in both names. A reference came up immediately. "Ah ha! I remember now. Those were the pseudonyms used by Burns and one of his lovers, Nancy Maclehose. I wonder if that's where my grandfather got the idea for his code names."

Noah flipped through book. A folded slip of paper fell onto the table.

I picked it up and unfolded it. "Noah! This is a photocopy of a birth certificate." I held it up for him to see.

"What's it say?"

"County of Sonoma, California, Certificate of Live Birth, male, born . . .'" I did the math. Born thirty-five years ago at Santa Rosa Hospital."

"What's the baby's name? Who are the parents?"

"Uh, the father's name is blacked out, but the mother's name is . . . Oh my god . . . Gracie Galloway!"

"And the baby?" Noah asked.

"The name is blacked out. It just says, 'Baby Galloway.'" I looked up at Noah. "I'm surprised Gracie didn't black out her own name."

"Maybe she wasn't the one who blacked out those other names," Noah said. "Maybe your grandfather did."

"Wow," I said, trying to pull this latest bit of info together. "So, Gracie had a child about thirty-five years ago. She looks to be in her sixties now, so she must have been around twenty-five or so? And the child was probably illegitimate. I wonder why my grandfather kept this copy of the birth certificate." I paused a moment. "You don't think . . ."

"Abraham Blackwood was the father?" Noah said it for me.

"He would have been around forty-five at the time." I folded the "Amen" letter and tucked it in my pocket. "I think it's time to pay another visit to the town librarian."

We sifted through the rest of the Burns books, but found nothing else hidden inside. I put the books back and slipped the birth certificate inside the last one where I'd found it. Noah lifted the box off the table. He was about to slide it underneath when I grabbed his arm to stop him.

"Look!" I said, and pointed under the table.

"What?" He glanced down.

"I thought I saw something," I whispered, staring at the spot. "A flash of light, from between the cracks."

He set the box on the table and lowered himself to one knee to examine the area. "I don't see anything." He ran his hand slowly over the wooden floor. "Wait a minute," he said, feeling again with both hands. "What do you know? I think there's a trap door."

"You're kidding!" This house was getting curiouser and curiouser. "Can you open it?"

He traced his finger around what looked like about a four-foot square ridge in the floor, almost invisible in the wood pattern. He stopped at a small indentation and stuck his fingers inside. With a grunt, he raised the trap door and laid it over flat, just missing the table legs.

I couldn't contain my excitement. "Amazing! Did you know this was here?"

He shook his head.

"I thought you knew every inch of this place."

"Apparently not."

Hmmm, really?

He turned on his cellphone light and shined it down into the shaft.

"What do you see?" I asked, trying to peer in.

"Not much, other than a wall ladder that seems to go into the abyss."

"This must be how my grandfather did some of his séance tricks!" I thought about Pyewacket. Had he used the secret entrance too?

"Probably," Noah said, still shining his light down into the darkness. "Not sure how, since I'm not a magician, but the trap door is a classic séance tool. The table was probably covered with a cloth, which would have hidden what was underneath."

"Are you going down there to check it out?" I asked.

He looked at me like I was crazy, then sighed. "I guess." With that, he turned around and began descending the ladder attached to the wall.

"Let me know what you find," I said.

"What? You aren't coming with me?" he teased, looking up at me.

"I'm not sure that old ladder will hold both of us," I answered. "Besides, if you don't come back, I'll need to alert the authorities."

"Ha. Ha," he said.

I held my phone light on him until he disappeared through another opening in the floor beneath.

"Noah?"

No answer. I got a chill.

"Noah!" I called again.

"What? I'm busy here."

I grinned. "Just checking."

"I'll let you know if I fall," he called back.

"Ha. Ha."

Then more silence. I waited, listening, hoping not to hear a loud thud, or even a distant one. All I could see were dust particles swirling in the light.

Another chill ran down my back when I suddenly remembered that flash of light I'd seen coming from the crack in the floor. *Odd.* There had only been darkness when Noah lifted the trapdoor.

My imagination?

Or had someone been there, under the floor, listening . . .

I caught a glimpse of a light shining up at me. I hoped it was Noah, on his way back up.

"Noah?"

A grunt.

With the light shining toward my face, I couldn't make out anything. If it wasn't Noah, I might need to use something to protect myself. All I had was my cellphone—and some chairs. I grabbed a chair, tipped it over, and held it like I was about to tame a lion. It was better than nothing, and I had no time to find anything else. I could leave, but I didn't want to abandon Noah.

I leaned in again. The light grew brighter, shining right in my eyes. I backed up and gripped the chair with both hands, ready to push the unexpected arrival back down into the hole. Or at least defend myself.

Noah's head popped out of the opening. He looked at me as I stood there, holding a chair sideways, ready to defend or attack.

"What are you doing?" he said, climbing out and dusting himself off.

"Nothing," I said, turning the chair upright. "I . . . never mind. Did you find anything?"

He shook his head; specks of dust flew out of his hair.

"Where does the shaft lead to?"

"All the way down to the first floor," he said. "It's basically a narrow shaft that was probably used as a dumbwaiter at one time."

A dumbwaiter! I remembered discovering one in the kitchen when I was a kid. It was big enough to climb inside, but Marnie caught me and told me how dangerous it was. Eventually they sealed it off, probably to keep nosy kids from doing what I'd tried to do.

Could it have been used as an elevator?

"So that's it?" I asked, a little disappointed. "No more hidden rooms?"

"Nope. Each floor has a little space to stand in as the dumbwaiter passes by, but not much more than that."

"Hmm. Enough room for someone to help my grandfather with the séances?"

"You mean like an assistant? A thin one, maybe."

Noah closed the trap door, then set the box on top of it. Remembering the flash of light, I wondered if someone else had been through the trapdoor lately. Although there had been a box on top of the trapdoor, it was lightweight enough to slide off if you opened the door from below.

My thoughts returned to the birth certificate. I checked the time. Almost nine thirty. "I'm going to pay a little visit to Gracie," I announced. "Want to come?"

Noah shook his head. "Naw, I've got something to do. What are you going to say to her?"

"I'm just going to ask her a few questions."

He eyed me.

"Don't worry. I'll be fine."

"Famous last words," he said, before heading through the wardrobe and into the attic.

Hmm. What was it Noah had to do instead of coming with me?

* * *

Aiden called, just as I was about to leave.

"Hi, Aiden," I said, grabbing my car keys. "Any news?"

"Yes, I talked to the sheriff a little while ago. You'll never believe this. He said that the private eye, Herman Hicks, was hired by Patty Fay!"

"I know," I said. "Weird, right?"

"You already knew?"

"Yes. Did the sheriff have any idea why?"

"He said he didn't know, but then maybe he isn't saying for a reason." I stepped onto the porch, my keys in hand, and closed the door behind me.

"Aiden, I have to go. I'm on my way to the sheriff's office to see if I can visit my aunt. I have a few comfort items for her. Some teabags, muffins Marnie made especially for her, a cozy blanket, her slippers. If I have time, I'm stopping by the library and see if I can pick Gracie's brain about a few things."

"Oh, I'll let you go, then," he said. "By the way, I finally found your aunt a lawyer. He's in Sonoma. He'll be contacting you soon."

"That's great! Thanks so much!" I had a feeling Jonathan would be relieved at this news.

I hung up, got in my Mini, then sat for a moment, thinking about my plan. Would Gracie talk to me once I told her about birth certificate? Or would she deny it, even if it was the truth? And, I wondered, did she have anything else to hide?

I started the engine and headed out. "Hang in there, Aunt Hazel," I whispered to myself, then wished I hadn't used the word "hang."

Chapter Twenty-Three
The Cat and the Crystal Ball

The sign on the library/historical society door read "Closed." *Odd.* It was half past ten and according to another sign underneath, the place was open from ten to four every day except Sunday. As far as I knew, Gracie was the only employee.

I knocked. Maybe she was inside and hadn't gotten around to unlocking the door. The blinds covering the front window moved. I saw an eyeball peering through the slats. It disappeared.

I heard a lock turn. The door swung open, revealing a very tired-looking Gracie. She appeared as if she hadn't slept in days. *Join the club*, I thought.

"Hi, Gracie," I said. "Is the library open? It's past ten."

She looked confused. "What? Oh, uh . . . I was just . . ." She stepped back to let me inside, then flipped over the "Closed" sign to "Open."

"Come in, Carissa. What can I do for you today? Are you looking for more on your family background? Because I think we've found all there is."

I followed her to her desk. She sat down and started stacking several books that were spread across the top. I caught a glimpse of a few titles, mostly genealogy books.

I sat down opposite her. "Are you researching your own ancestry?"

She frowned "What, these? No, no. Someone returned them. I was just about to reshelve them."

I leaned forward. "Gracie, I wanted to talk to you about something."

She pulled back, as if I were invading her space. "Well, like I said, I think I've told you all I know about your grandfather."

"Yes, you've been really helpful. But I've been snooping around in my grandfather's attic." I paused to watch her reaction. Her face stiffened, but when she said nothing, I continued. "I came across some letters."

"Letters?" Her lips trembled slightly.

I could tell she was trying to remain calm, but her reaction told me she knew exactly what letters I was referring to.

"I . . . I don't know about any letters," she said, avoiding my eyes. She placed another book on the stack. "If you found them in your grandfather's attic, they were probably personal letters that he wanted to keep private. Uh, where did you find these letters?"

"In one of his trunks."

She blinked several times. "Did you read them?"

I nodded.

She glanced away. "Well, like I said, I don't know anything about any letters. Especially personal ones that belonged to your grandfather."

"Actually, there were several packets of letters," I said, "each one written in a different handwriting. By different women."

Gracie's mouth dropped open. Her attention shifted back to me. "What do you mean, different women?"

"I mean, I found eight separate packets of letters obviously penned by eight different women."

"Eight women? Who were they?"

"That's just it," I said. "For some reason, the writers used pseudonyms. Actually, I'm not surprised, since the contents were pretty steamy."

The color rose in Gracie's face. "What were the pseudonyms?"

I wondered whether I should reveal the other names or not. I decided to keep all but one name to myself. "The one I remember best was signed, 'Amen.'"

Gracie stiffened. "Well, I don't know what this has to do with me. So if you'll excuse me, Carissa, I have work to do—"

"It was you, wasn't it, Gracie?" I said, my eyes focused on hers. "You were the one who wrote the love letters signed "Amen" to my grandfather. You had an affair with him years ago, didn't you?"

Gracie burst into tears. They streamed down her face. She grabbed a tissue from a drawer and used it to wipe her cheeks and dab her eyes. I reached across the desk and patted her arm. I felt for her, keeping this secret for, what, over thirty years. *But why?*

"What happened?" I asked gently.

She shook her head and sniffed. "I loved your grandfather—Bram. And I thought he loved me. The affair began awhile after his wife had passed. I thought . . . I thought we'd get married, but then something happened."

I nodded. "You got pregnant."

Her eyes widened. "How did you know?"

"You signed your last letter with the words, 'I'm late.' It could only mean one thing."

She took a deep breath and sighed. It was as if a burden had been released. "I thought when I got pregnant, he would be so happy. We would be a family. But he turned his back on me, refused to even see me again, let alone marry me and make our child legitimate. He said he wouldn't have anything to do with the baby and that I needed to get an abortion. I just couldn't. I come from a very religious background. So I worked as long as I could, but when I really started to show, I took a leave and went to my sister's place in Fort Bragg. I had the baby, then gave him up for adoption. There was no way I could care for a child being single, and certainly not on a librarian's salary. Besides, the disgrace back then . . . like I said, my family was very religious." She shook her head and looked down at the tissue in her hands.

"No one ever knew?" I asked.

"Only my sister. She handled the adoption for me. I couldn't deal with it. She passed away several years ago."

"I'm so sorry," I said. "Do you know where the child is now?"

"No," Gracie said. "It was a sealed adoption. I wish I could meet him. I just hope he's happy and had the childhood I couldn't provide." More tears sprang to her eyes.

A question sprang to my mind. I had to ask. "Any chance you hired that private investigator, Herman Hicks, to find him?"

She shook her head.

I patted her hand again, then quietly let myself out of the library so she could recover from my probing questions in peace. I felt bad making her relive the trauma, but now I knew—my grandfather had fathered a child—a boy, according to the birth certificate—about thirty-five years ago. Where was the boy—the man—now? Had Gracie told the truth about not hiring the PI to find him? Had Patty Fay been using Hicks to gather blackmail information about Gracie? Or had Hicks learned something more and was killed because of it?

In view of these recent murders, was Gracie in some kind of jeopardy?

I had a sudden thought. Was it possible Gracie was actually responsible for the two deaths? Maybe the PI learned that Patty Fay was blackmailing Gracie and when he told her, she killed Patty Fay. Then maybe she murdered Hicks because he knew too much. If so, how did she get access to the poison garden? Was my aunt just collateral damage?

But *Gracie*? Surely not the librarian/historian.

* * *

I decided to head back to the inn and put together as much evidence as I could find to take to the sheriff, including the birth certificate. I hoped that would convince him my aunt was innocent—and that someone else—Gracie?—had framed her. The librarian had practically confessed to having a grudge against Bram. Maybe she carried this grudge over to his daughters?

When I arrived back at the Blackwood Inn, I noticed Marnie's car was gone, as was Jonathan's Tesla and my aunts' minivan. *Nobody home. Good.* I could make all the noise I wanted up in the attic and not bother anyone. Only question was—where was Noah?

"Anybody here?" I called out just in case I was wrong about the house being completely empty. All I heard was a faint meow coming from who knows where. I checked the inn's landline to see if there had been any calls for reservations for the weekend and was surprised to find there were none. Had the murders deterred prospective visitors? Or had we somehow been blacklisted?

With more pressing issues to deal with, such as securing Aunt Hazel's freedom, I took the stairs up to my room and dropped off my bag. I glanced around to make sure nothing had been disturbed, but everything seemed in its place, including Pyewacket, who was asleep on my pillow. He opened one eye when he heard me come in, then closed it. Truthfully, it kind of creeped me out.

As soon as I left my room to go to the attic, I heard footsteps on the stairs.

"Noah?" I called out. "Is that you?"

I heard chuckling, then to my surprise, Aiden appeared on the second-floor landing. He was holding two to-go cups.

"Aiden!" I said.

"Hey, Carissa. I rang the bell, but no one answered. Saw your car, so I figured you were home. Hope you don't mind that I let myself in. It was unlocked."

"Of course not. We keep the door unlocked for our guests, although right now we don't have anyone staying here." I hoped that wouldn't be permanent after all that had happened at the Blackwood Inn.

He held up the coffee cups. "I brought lattes."

"How nice! I could use a jolt right now. Have you learned anything new?"

"That's why I'm here. I paid another visit to the sheriff's office."

"What did he say?" I asked. "I was planning to go over there after I got a few things from the attic."

"Did you find something that will help your Aunt Hazel?"

"I think so," I said, gesturing up the stairs. "Come on. I'll show you."

"After you," Aiden said.

As we headed up to the attic, I asked again, "So what did the sheriff say?"

"He thinks he may have found the real killer."

I stopped midstep. "Seriously? Who?"

"He wouldn't say, but I have a feeling your aunt is going to be released very soon."

"That's wonderful!" I said, relieved. I almost wanted to hug Aiden, but instead I continued to the attic. I opened the door and switched on the light, then peered in, just to make sure the coast was clear.

"You okay?" Aiden asked when I paused. He handed me one of the lattes.

I took the warm cup. "Thanks," I said. "Just checking for . . . rats." I felt a little foolish as I walked cautiously across the room to the steamer trunk. "You have to see this—" I began, then stopped midsentence. "No!" I set the drink down on a nearby trunk.

"What's the matter?" Aiden asked, coming up behind me.

"The steamer trunk! It was unlocked earlier . . . open. It looks like someone locked it up again. Only with a new lock!" I reached out and touched the shiny new padlock.

Aiden frowned. "You're sure?"

"Yes, I'm positive," I said, irritated at his question. "Someone has been here!"

"Maybe your Aunt Runa?" Aiden suggested.

I thought a moment. It was possible that Aunt Runa had relocked the trunk. But she'd never mentioned the steamer trunk when she and Aunt Hazel had been up here looking through my grandfather's things. And why would she do that, anyway?

"Was there something inside you wanted to show me?" Aiden asked.

I nodded. "The trunk—it has a false back. It's actually a passageway to another room—my grandfather's hidden séance room. There's a table inside, with a trap door underneath that leads to a shaft. Plus a box of books with a birth certificate hidden inside."

"Cool. These old houses, you know, they're full of secrets," Aiden said. "You found a birth certificate?"

"Shoot!" I said. "I should have taken it with me." Then I remembered the letters. "Wait. I do have something I was planning to show the sheriff." I walked over to the trunk that held the letters in a secret bottom compartment. Aiden followed me. I opened the trunk—and gasped. It was empty.

"What's wrong?" Aiden asked.

I shook my head in disbelief. "The letters. They're . . . gone!" I felt my pocket. Empty. I must have left behind the one I'd shown Gracie at the library.

"What letters? What's this all about?"

I sighed. "There were packets of love letters inside, written to my grandfather by several women. Very intimate letters. One in particular mentioned a pregnancy. It was signed 'Amen,' which I figured out was a code name for Gracie the librarian."

"Whoa," Aiden said. "You're sure about all this?"

I nodded. "I was going to take the letters and the birth certificate and show them to the sheriff. I figured he could send the certificate to his lab and get them to reveal the names that were blacked out."

"What names?" Aiden asked, frowning. I gathered he was trying to put all this information together. It was a lot, I had to admit.

"The father's name."

"What about the baby?"

"Only 'Baby Galloway.'"

"So," Aiden said, "Gracie was the mother of an illegitimate baby . . ." He drifted off.

"Yes. I think she may be the one who framed my aunt by poisoning Patty Fay and that PI and making it look like Aunt Hazel did it. I think she's a sad, bitter old woman who never forgave my grandfather for not marrying her when she got pregnant, and she sought revenge on our family."

Aiden scoffed. "I can't believe it was sweet old Gracie." He wandered over to where I'd set down my latte, picked it up, and brought it to me.

I sat on the closed trunk, took the lid off the cup, and downed a large sip of the still warm drink.

Aiden sat opposite me on another trunk and began drinking his own latte. "Not Gracie." He shook his head. "She's been the librarian and historian here for years. But the killer needed access to the house and to know the hiding places, like the dumbwaiter, to pull that off. Plus, access to the poison garden. Do you really think Gracie could mastermind all that?"

I took another sip of the latte. But instead of warming me, I felt a chill run down my back.

I froze, cup in hand.

I hadn't mentioned the dumbwaiter.

"How did you know there was a dumbwaiter?"

"I just assumed," Aiden said. "I mean, what else could it be, right?"

I gulped.

He'd slipped up.

I was alone in the house, in the attic, with a man who shouldn't have known anything about the dumbwaiter. But he did.

And now I wondered what was in my latte.

Chapter Twenty-Four
The Ghost of Blackwood Inn

"Carissa, are you okay?" Aiden asked. "You look like you've seen a ghost."

I couldn't speak. How much of the latte had I ingested? I was certain he'd poisoned it. After all, that was his method of operation. The question was, how much would it take to kill me?

My first thought: *Fight or flight.*

I set the cup down and glanced toward the attic door.

Aiden sat between me and the only feasible exit, blocking my path.

No flight.

Fight.

I pretended to take another sip of the latte while I glanced around the attic for something I could use to defend myself.

The boxes and trunks were closed, and other than my grandfather's séance stuff, most held only papers. There were a few pieces of furniture here and there—a rocking chair, end table, Tiffany lamp, old record player, sewing machine, dial phone, some bad paintings, plus more random stuff you might normally find in an attic.

Nothing I could really use to protect myself. Or subdue someone.

"Carissa?" Aiden said again. "Are you okay?"

"What?" I asked, holding the cup in my hands. "Oh, sorry. I was just thinking . . ."

"What about?" His eyes narrowed.

I stood up. So did he. "Uh, those letters I was going to show you and the sheriff. Now, where were they?" I eyed a few boxes and frowned, while trying to remember exactly which trunk held my grandfather's supplies. If I could find that one, I could use the divining rod I'd discovered. It wasn't much, but better than nothing.

"Oh, yes!" I said, stepping over to the trunk I hoped was the right one.

Aiden followed me over. "What are you doing?" His tone sounded lower, his words slower.

"The letters. I think it's—I mean, they're in here." I pointed to the box.

"I'll get them," he offered.

No! I thought. *He'll find the rod!*

It was now or never.

"Wait!" I cried. When he turned to me, I threw the remaining liquid in his face, hoping it was still hot enough to at least temporarily blind him. I made a run for the door. Just as I reached the doorknob, Aiden grabbed my shoulder. I spun around to see him wiping the coffee drink off his face with his other hand.

"Carissa! Stop!"

Still grasping my shoulder, I saw him slip his other hand into his jacket pocket.

"Why did you do that?" he asked.

I tried the doorknob. It wouldn't budge.

"Why did you lock this door?" I asked him. My heart was beating so rapidly, I could hear it inside my chest. "What if the sheriff is here? What if he's bringing my aunt home?"

He tightened his grip. "What's gotten into you?"

"Uh . . . I thought I heard someone," I said. "Aunt Hazel's voice coming from downstairs. Maybe the sheriff brought her home."

Aiden smiled, a patient smile. "Oh, that. No, I don't think so. I sort of made that up, about her being released. I never actually talked to the sheriff."

Sweat broke out on my forehead. I tried the doorknob again; it held tight. I turned to Aiden, hoping to stall him with words, since I couldn't do much else. "Why would you make something like that up?"

"I think you know," Aiden said, his left hand still in his pocket.

What was in there?

"What do I know?" I asked, playing dumb. "I don't understand."

"You said you talked to Gracie at the library earlier."

Not knowing how much time I had—or how much poison I'd ingested—I spun out from under his grip and made a dash for the box that I hoped held the divining rod. But Aiden was too quick. He lunged, grabbed me around the waist, and tackled me to the floor, landing on top of me. I grunted, the air knocked out of me. In a panic and unable to breathe—or was it the poison?—I tried to pull my phone out of my pocket. As soon as I had it in hand, he wrenched it away and threw it across the room.

I tried to take in a deep breath, but with Aiden pressing on my back, I couldn't get much air. "Aiden, let me up! I can't breathe!" I wheezed, feeling dizzy.

"Sorry. Not just yet," he said calmly. Too calmly.

"I'll scream!" I said as loudly as I could.

"Go ahead," he said. "Nobody's home. It's just us and the rats up here, remember?"

I tried to talk, to distract him, but his weight was too much. All I could manage was a breathy, "Aiden! Stop!"

I felt him lift up a bit and I took a big breath.

What was he doing?

I tried to roll over, but he yanked my wrists together behind my back and bound them tightly with zip ties. *That's what was in his pocket.* He forced my ankles together and bound them so tightly, I felt the plastic scrape into my skin.

"Aiden, that hurts. Why are you doing this?"

"Oh, Carissa. I was hoping not to make you a part of this, at least in the beginning. I had no grudge against you. In fact, I thought we could be friends. But then you had to go snooping around, sticking that Blackwood nose into everybody's business. I knew I couldn't let you find out my secret. That would have ruined everything. But you didn't give up."

"What secret?" I puffed, trying to catch up on air now that he was off my back. It still wasn't easy, tied up and lying on the floor.

"Come on," Aiden said. "I saw that look in your eyes when I mentioned the dumbwaiter. That's when you knew *I* knew—that I knew every inch of this house, including the séance room. You know why I know the Blackwood house so well? Because I've been inside many, many times over the years.

Not because I was invited. I'm sure my father would never have allowed that. No, I had to sneak into a house that should have been partly mine."

Then it came to me. "You're Gracie's son!"

"Whoa, you're quick," he said. "Even Gracie doesn't know I'm her son since she gave me up for adoption. I was hoping I'd be named in my father's will, because he knew my mother was pregnant with me. But he never bothered to find me, so that didn't happen. I figured I'd show my birth certificate to the authorities, get a DNA test—and one from my father, postmortem, to prove his paternity. Then I'd at least inherit a part of my father's legacy and this house. But your aunts took it over and spent most of the inheritance on turning this place into an inn, leaving me with pretty much nothing."

"So what are you going to do now?" I barely managed to say with my face smashed against the attic floor.

"I don't have to do much," he said. "You've had enough poison to at least knock you out if not kill you right away. Once you've passed out, well . . ." He shrugged, but I knew what that meant—that I wasn't going to wake up.

"Aiden, you'll get caught. Noah is on his way to meet me here in the attic. He'll be along any minute."

"Yeah, about that," Aiden said, sighing. "I called him this morning and sent him on a wild goose chase to Santa Rosa to meet the lawyer I pretended to find. He'll be gone for hours until he figures out there's no such person. Not that I need that much time."

I wriggled and squirmed and tried to roll over, but with my wrists and ankles bound, I could barely move. I tried to reason with him. "Aiden, please don't do this. I'm sure my aunts will share the property with you once they know who you are. They're good people and if they knew they had a stepbrother, I'm sure they would welcome you."

"I don't think so, not after everything I've done."

Oh my God. The murders. "You poisoned Patty Fay? And the detective? Why?"

"Isn't it obvious? To get your aunts arrested. That would destroy the reputation of the inn and get them out of the way. Even if they don't go to jail, imagine trying to maintain a bed and breakfast inn without any guests. Can you imagine the reviews on Yelp and Trip Advisor thanks to the murders? I'm sure they'd have to put the house on the market—or give it to me if they want to keep it in the family, once I'd presented my birth certificate and DNA tests. And if they sell, well, then, I'll take a percentage of the sale. Oh course, your father still owns a third of it, but I plan to take care of him in the near future. After I'm done with you."

"Aiden, don't! You can stop now. It's not too late. Please! Like I said, I'm sure my aunts will want to know who you are."

"I doubt it." Aiden said.

I heard a distant noise, this time for real. It had come from downstairs. Someone was here. Runa? Marnie? Noah? The sheriff?

I could tell Aiden had heard it too. He stiffened, then walked quietly to the attic door, leaving me tied up on my stomach on the floor.

"Where are you going?" I cried. "What are you going to do?"

"Shh," he whispered. "I'll be right back, Carissa. I just want to make sure we're not disturbed."

I watched from my awkward vantage point, terrified, as he pulled out a key and unlocked the door, then headed out, closing the door behind him. I started to roll over toward the door, thinking if I could somehow get to it, I could try to sit up, open it, and work my way down the stairs.

Then I heard a click from the other side.

He'd locked me in. Now what?

I thought about Nancy Drew, tapping out "SOS" on the floor when she was bound and locked up in an attic. But I knew no one would hear me, three floors down. And I couldn't lift my feet high enough to tap them anyway.

But I could lift my head. I scanned the boxes and trunks nearby. Several of them had sharp, rusty hinges. Remembering a scene I'd written in a book called *Kidnapped by a Killer*, I rolled toward the closest trunk, bent forward, then twisted myself up to sitting. I scooted back against the hinge, felt for the sharp edge, and managed to cut my finger. I felt the sting and the warmth of blood dripping on my hand.

Get over it, I told myself through the pain. I located the hinge again and began using it to saw through the plastic tie. If it was sharp enough to cut my finger, hopefully it was sharp enough to cut the tie. As I sawed back and forth, I had a morbid thought: *if I didn't die from the poison, I'd probably get tetanus from the rusty hinge.*

Panic—or adrenaline—kicked in. I no longer felt the pain of the cut, only an urgent need to break free, knowing Aiden would be back any second. After a few more moments of sawing, the binding broke apart, freeing my hands.

I paused to listen for footsteps on the stairs.

A moaning sound. Coming from a few feet away. I didn't have time to try to free my legs.

I glanced around. The sound had come from the trunk that held my grandfather's séance stuff. I scooched over and lifted the lid.

I gasped as Pyewacket sprang out and disappeared behind another box. No time to think about how he'd gotten in this time. I dug around in the trunk as quickly as I could until I found the only thing I could use besides the divining rod. I really didn't want to stab Aiden to death.

Not unless I had to.

I picked up the large crystal ball. To my surprise, it weighed a ton.

Worried I was out of time, I set the ball down, then pushed myself up to standing. Trying to keep my balance with my ankles still bound, I bent down and picked up the crystal ball again. I held it tightly in my bloody hands as I hopped over to the attic door.

This would be the last and only chance to save myself—and the Blackwood Inn.

I stood to the side of the door and waited, trying to keep my breathing quiet. Seconds later, I heard footsteps.

Then the sound of the lock opening.

Then the doorknob turning.

I leaned back against the wall as I'd done before, and lifted the crystal ball over my head, hoping it didn't slip out of my hands.

As soon as the door opened, I watched through the crack as Aiden stepped in, holding a small bag of something.

More poison?

He stopped. "Carissa? Where are you?"

Before he could figure out my hiding place, I stepped forward and brought the heavy ball crashing down onto his head with all my strength. He dropped to the floor. I released the crystal ball and hopped over to the trunk again. Grabbing a handful of my grandfather's black silk scarves, I hopped back to Aiden. I figured I didn't have much time. While he was

Murder at Blackwood Inn

still unconscious, I used the scarves to tie up his wrists, ankles, legs, and arms.

After letting out a big breath of relief, I retrieved my phone. The screen was cracked, but luckily the phone still worked.

I called the sheriff.

While I waited, I realized something. Maybe crystals—and crystal balls—really do have protective powers after all.

Chapter Twenty-Five
The Power of a Crystal

After what seemed an eternity, I heard the sheriff's siren, then faint footsteps running up the stairs. I'd wrapped a scarf around the gash on Aiden's head, then sat beside him while I waited, rubbing my wrists and trying to figure out a better way to cut the binds off my ankles than a rusty hinge.

Seconds later, Noah burst through the attic door, beating the sheriff.

"Carissa!"

"Noah!" I smiled, relieved to see him. "I thought you were in Santa Rosa."

Before he could respond, the sheriff appeared and immediately took in the scene. Aiden lay near the door, tied up like a mummy in the scarves, and was now moaning and groaning. The crystal ball had rolled a few feet away, leaving dots of blood along its path—his and mine.

When the sheriff saw the blood on my hands, he asked, "Carissa, are you all right? You're bleeding." He pulled out his phone and called for the EMTs.

"I'm fine," I said, wiping the blood on my jeans. "It's not *all* my blood. But could one of you cut the ties off my ankles? Oh, and I think I've been poisoned."

"What?" Noah said as he whipped out a knife and went to work on the zip ties, carefully cutting through them.

"I'm pretty sure Aiden poisoned my latte. I only took a few sips, but I don't know how potent it was. So far I'm not feeling anything like hallucinations or breathing issues. My heart rate was up, but I think that was the adrenaline."

"Sheriff, you called the EMTs?" Noah asked as he gently massaged my ankles.

The sheriff nodded. "Should be here any minute." He looked down at the barely conscious body on the floor. "So what happened here?"

I sighed. "It was Aiden all along. He killed Patty Fay and the private investigator, then tried to frame my aunts for murder to get them out of the way so he could take over the Blackwood Inn."

The sheriff frowned. "What?"

"Turns out he's the illegitimate son of my grandfather," I added.

The sheriff's mouth dropped open. "Seriously?"

"Gracie Galloway is his mother." I turned to Noah. "Remember the letters we found signed 'Amen' and suspected that was a pseudonym for Gracie? I went to see her, and she admitted she'd had a relationship with my grandfather. He got her pregnant, but he wouldn't acknowledge the child, so she gave it—him—up for adoption."

Aiden began to mumble between moans. "My own mother gave me away. How could she do that to her son?"

Sheriff Lokey knelt down and rolled Aiden over. "You're really her son? And nobody knew?"

"I guess that's the way she wanted it," Aiden muttered, beginning to come to. "I had to hire a PI to find my mom and when he did, I found out her sister had set up the adoption for her. Turns out the family that raised me didn't really want a child, they just wanted someone to work their fishing boats. I ran away when I was sixteen, got a job a local newspaper, and found out I had a knack for writing. When I found out who my mother was, I moved here and got the job at the paper. That way I could keep an eye on her and the rest of the Blackwood family."

"Why didn't you just tell the Blackwoods the truth?" the sheriff asked.

"Once I found out, all I wanted was to be a part of the Blackwood family. But I knew my father would never let that happen, since he'd denied me in the first place. After he died, I started thinking about other ways to get my inheritance. Every now and then I'd sneak into the house when no one was home and discover where all the secret passageways and hidden rooms were. Sometimes, when the ladies came home unexpectedly, I'd go into the dumbwaiter shaft and spy on them. Eventually I decided to kill two old birds with one stone. I'd use Hazel's own poison garden against them. When they were out of the way, I'd show my birth certificate to the authorities, along with a DNA test, and tell them to order a posthumous test for my grandfather. Once that was done, I'd claim part ownership of the family estate as a rightful heir. Until Carissa came along and complicated things. When I realized she was snooping around and found out the truth—or at least most of it—I knew she'd eventually put two and two together. I had to stop her."

"So you tried to kill me with a poisoned latte," I said. "But why murder Patty Fay?"

"You don't have to say anything," the sheriff interjected.

"Read him his rights," Noah said. "Then if he wants to talk, he can."

Aiden scoffed. "I don't give a crap about your Miranda rights. What about *my* rights?"

"What gave you the right to kill Patty Fay?" Noah asked.

"Didn't you know? She was blackmailing me, along with a bunch of other people. Somehow she found out the truth—probably from the PI—and she used it against me. She threatened to put up an incriminating question about me on her website. I paid her off for a while, but she wouldn't stop pressing me for more money. So I had to shut her up. That's where I got the idea to use belladonna from Hazel's garden. It was the perfect choice—and that pre-party was the perfect opportunity."

"You also took one of Aunt Runa's crystals and put it under Patty Fay's bed. Was that to implicate her too?" I asked.

He half grinned. "Yeah. Like I said, killing two old birds with one stone—a crystal, actually—only by then it was three old birds. I had to make it look like your dithering Aunt Hazel poisoned Patty Fay, and your superstitious Aunt Runa was in on it. That was easy once I knew where all the skeletons—I mean keys—were. Like I said, I knew this house like the back of my hand."

"What about the private investigator, Herman Hicks? Why kill him?"

"Oh, come on," Aiden said. "He figured everything out, including who my biological father was. Unfortunately, he also suspected I killed Patty Fay, so he had to go."

"How did you poison Hicks?" the sheriff asked.

"Easy. First, I got ahold of Marnie's keys—she leaves them in her apron pocket a lot—and had my own set made. I entered the house when no one was around, went up to his room, and added crushed belladonna to his whiskey. It was obvious that he was a lush."

I looked at him in disbelief. He almost sounded proud of himself. But he'd been so charming, I never suspected he was capable of this.

"Hey, Carissa," Aiden said, grinning. "Guess what? You're my, what—half niece? I don't know. Something like that. Funny, huh?"

By the time Aiden's story was done, the EMTs had arrived. Noah asked them to check me first. After I explained I might have been poisoned, one of the EMTs asked the usual questions for belladonna poisoning—was I dizzy, hallucinating, have blurred vision, dry mouth, slurred speech. I answered "no" to all the questions. He checked my pupils, but they were only minimally dilated.

"Are you sure she's okay?" Noah asked. He gestured toward Aiden. "This guy poisoned two other people and they all died. Maybe you should pump her stomach or something."

The EMT turned back to me. "You said the poison was in a cup of coffee?"

"A latte," I clarified.

He nodded. "The caffeine acts as a sort of antidote to the poison. It's often used in combination for migraines. I guess he didn't know that."

"Wow," I said, grinning at Noah. Thank goodness I preferred caffeinated coffee over herbal tea. I thanked the EMT.

He and his partner treated Aiden's head wound, then took him away on a stretcher, handcuffed, with instructions to keep him under police watch at the hospital.

As soon as they were gone, Sheriff Lokey took off his hat, scratched his head, then replaced his hat. "I guess I better go free your Aunt Hazel before she has me taking any more of her special herbs for my IBS."

I smiled but couldn't manage a laugh, thinking about her in that cell. At least now she'd be coming home. I rubbed my wrists.

"You sure you're okay?" the sheriff asked.

"Apparently, I'll live. The worst he did was knock the wind out of me and chafe my wrists and ankles. Although I may get tetanus."

"We'll get you a shot for that," Noah said. "Meanwhile, I've got some duct tape that will fix your wrists and ankles right up."

"Ha. Ha," I said, not laughing.

"Well, then," the sheriff said, "I'll head back to the office, then bring Hazel home as soon as I've done the paperwork."

With that, he left the two of us alone in the attic.

"Want some tea?" Noah asked.

I grinned. "Only if it has caffeine. And can you put a little unpoisoned alcohol in it?"

"Normally I'd say it's a little early for that, but I figure we can bend the rules at this point."

We headed down the stairs and into the kitchen. Marnie was still out, no doubt buying more organic groceries, and so were Aunt Runa and Jonathan. I was sure they'd all be relieved when he heard the news about Aunt Hazel.

Noah put the kettle on, and I sat down at the kitchen table. He brought over a bowl of warm water and a cloth, then gently cleaned my ankles, wrists, and my cut finger. Finally, he added some antiseptic and covered the cuts with bandages.

"Make sure you get that tetanus shot if you haven't had one lately," he said when he was done. He emptied the bowl in the sink, then turned to me. "So, you actually hit Aiden on the head with your grandfather's crystal ball? How did you come up with that?"

I started to tell him it was thanks to Pyewacket, but that sounded ridiculous. There was no way to explain how he'd been in the trunk and alerted me to the potential weapon inside.

"Instinct, I guess," I said simply.

Noah brought two cups of tea to the table, along with a bottle of whiskey, and sat down. He poured a shot of the alcohol into the teacups and we both had a sip.

"Don't tell me you're becoming psychic like your aunts."

Psycho maybe, but not psychic.

I laughed. "Not a chance. I write fiction, I don't live it."

"Well, you've got some good stories to write now. I mean, you saved yourself from a murderer. You freed your aunt of a murder charge. And you probably put the Blackwood Bed and Breakfast Inn firmly on the map with all the publicity you'll get. Maybe it's time to give up ghostwriting."

"I still need to pay the bills," I answered.

A text came in. I checked the sender, recognized the number, then with a swipe, I deleted it.

"Spam?" Noah asked.

I nodded. My ex was definitely spam. But I was a little curious. What was Sergio's sudden interest in contacting me after all this time? Trouble in paradise? Not my problem.

Murder at Blackwood Inn

"By the way," Noah said, "I have a recipe for a Spam pasta I've been wanting to try. You in?"

I made a yuck face.

Noah laughed.

Then he slowly, slowly leaned in . . .

Chapter Twenty-Six
Unfinished Business

"Yoo hoo!" came a familiar voice from beyond the kitchen. Noah pulled back, grinning. I could almost read his mind: *nice timing*.

I smiled at him, then called out, "We're in here!" I rose to greet my newly freed Aunt Hazel, fresh from the local hoosgow.

Noah stood, too, and we both turned to welcome my aunt as she came through the swinging kitchen door. Behind her was Aunt Runa, carrying the two canvas bags I'd filled with comfort items for Aunt Hazel. Luckily she hadn't had time to use them.

I was so happy to see her, I rushed up and gave her a hug, probably squishing the air out of her lungs in the process. "You're free!" I said after I let her go.

"Yep," Aunt Hazel said. "I flew the coop. Made a jailbreak. Escaped incarceration." She turned and smiled at Jonathan, who had followed them into the kitchen. "I have to thank my attorney, Jonathan Duke, esquire. Perry Mason couldn't have done a better job."

Jonathan laughed. "Actually, I had little to do with it. You can thank your niece for her detective work." He looked at me. "By the way, are you all right? I heard about what happened. Sounded harrowing. You're lucky to be alive."

I nodded. "I'm fine. It'll take more than a poisoned latte to bring me down."

"Yeah, she's a tough one," the sheriff said as he joined us in the now crowded kitchen. It was becoming Grand Central Station in here. "Innkeeper, aunt protector, and amateur sleuth all rolled into one."

It was my turn to laugh. "Well, if it hadn't been for Noah—"

He cut me off. "Oh, no, Carissa. You're not going to pass the credit along to me. You were the one who figured out Aiden was the killer. He had me fooled. And you were the one who managed to take him down. He was already tied up like a package by the time I arrived. I missed all the action."

Now everyone was smiling. Marnie appeared from the back entrance, looking surprised to see us all gathered and grinning. She blinked, set down her grocery bag, and asked, "What's going on here?" Then she spotted Aunt Hazel.

Before Marnie could welcome my aunt, I intercepted her and gave her a hug. She stiffened, but to my surprise, she didn't push me away. "What was that for?" she asked when I let her go.

"I'm just glad you're still here," I answered. "I was worried you might have—"

"What? Quit?" she said. "Hmph. I do that at least once a week. Right, ladies?" she said to Aunt Hazel and Aunt Runa.

They nodded. "We've come to expect it," Aunt Runa said.

"Wouldn't be our Marnie if she didn't threaten to leave every now and then," Aunt Hazel added.

"Well, Marnie," I said. "I'm sorry I snooped into your stuff. I was only trying to help my aunt. I hope you'll forgive me."

She scoffed. "Already forgotten. By the way, you'll be happy to know I stopped by the jewelry store and worked out a deal with the owner. I don't want everyone in town thinking I'm a thief, even if I was only taking back me own necklace."

"I'm sure they don't," I said.

She went over to Aunt Hazel and gave her a side hug. It was the most affection I'd seen her give anyone. "Glad you're back. How about a cuppa?"

Of course, I thought. The magic elixir that solves everything at the Blackwood Bed and Breakfast Inn. Maybe if I drank more tea and fewer lattes, I wouldn't be so easy to poison. Then again, maybe coffee was its own special elixir. After all, it kept me from being poisoned.

Sheriff Lokey cleared his throat. "Ahem. If you don't mind, everyone, I still have a few questions."

"Come sit," Aunt Hazel said as she took the seat I'd vacated at the kitchen table. She patted the chair next to her for the sheriff to join her. Aunt Runa sat next to the sheriff and I took the last empty seat, still feeling a little sore and tired from my ordeal. Noah leaned against the wall, his arms crossed over his chest. Those biceps instantly reminded me of the kiss I'd just missed. The tea kettle whistled and Marnie went about pouring and serving tea to everyone but Noah, who held up a declining hand.

Once everyone was served, Sheriff Lokey turned his dark eyes on me.

I sighed. "You have questions?" I reiterated his words.

"Yes, ma'am," he answered.

I was fine until he called me "ma'am."

"Okay, Sheriff, go ahead and grill me. I've got nothing to hide," I said in my best gangsta voice.

I caught Noah raising an eyebrow. Apparently my gangsta imitation wasn't as good as I thought.

The sheriff pulled out his notebook and opened it. All I could see upside-down were scribbles. "So let me get this straight. Aiden killed Patty Fay because she was blackmailing him?"

I nodded. "Patty Fay set up a website called Pelican Point Privates, where she left leading questions and incriminating information about people in town, then sent them a link. Once they read what she's posted, she demanded they pay her if they wanted to keep her from naming names or giving any more details."

"And Aiden was one of her victims?" the sheriff asked, making a note.

"Yep. Somehow she knew his true identity, which he didn't want exposed. She knew a lot of secrets that I'm guessing she found out through hiring a private detective. So he paid her—to a point. After all, he had his own plan. When he got tired of forking over his money, he decided to poison her and make it look like Aunt Hazel did it, killing two birds with one stone, so to speak. He knew about the poison garden because he'd secretly been to the house and yard many times in the past, snooping around, hoping to find something that would help him claim his connection to the family."

"Did he kill your grandfather?" the sheriff asked.

"Good question," I said. I turned to Aunt Hazel and Aunt Runa for an answer since they'd hinted that there might have been something mysterious about his death.

"Yes," Aunt Hazel said.

"No," Aunt Runa said.

They looked at each other.

"Maybe," they said together.

"We don't know for sure," Aunt Runa said. "All we know is, Father supposedly died of natural causes. I mean, he was eighty years old. We never had an autopsy because we didn't question it. At least, I didn't."

She glanced at Aunt Hazel, who shrugged.

"I wasn't so sure," Aunt Hazel said. "I always suspected something else had killed him because he was perfectly fine up until that night, when he went to sleep and didn't wake up. Anyone—like Aiden—could have come in and put something—like poison—in his nightly hot chocolate. I'm just saying . . ." She drifted off.

I shuddered when I thought of my grandfather dying in the bed I currently slept in, especially if it hadn't been a natural death. The possibility that he might have been poisoned gave me a chill. But unless we exhumed him, we'd never know for sure.

Speaking about my grandfather's bed reminded me of the Mesmer book I'd found hidden in the bed slats, and its secret compartment inside containing my grandfather's journal that recalling coded notes about his séances. I'd meant to show it to my aunts and ask them about it, but I'd gotten distracted.

Where had I put the book? It seemed to have disappeared. Had one of my aunts found it and tucked it away so none of his "meetings" would be exposed?

Murder at Blackwood Inn

I had to ask. "Aunt Hazel, Aunt Runa, did you know anything about your father's séances?"

They looked at each other, no doubt reading each other's minds again.

"No," Aunt Hazel said. "At least I never witnessed anything like a séance. Did you, Runa?"

She shook her head.

I had my doubts. *How could they not have known?*

"We saw your father's black robe in the attic, from when you were a kid. I found it in one of his trunks with some other mystical stuff—a Ouija board, a divining rod, a crystal ball. Didn't he wear that robe to his séances?"

Aunt Hazel chuckled. "Oh, no. You must mean his magic shows. He wore a black robe when he did shows for us as kids. He loved to perform magic. But, no, not séances."

"The rumor that he gave séances was just that—a rumor," Aunt Runa added.

Hmm, I thought. *Did they really not know?* I hated to keep pressing. I didn't want them to think I suspected they were lying. But I had a sense they knew more than they were telling.

"But you must have known there was a secret room in the attic," I said. "With the round table in the middle and those chairs for the guests, it looked like the perfect place to hold a séance."

"That tiny room behind the far attic wall?" Aunt Hazel said. She shook her head. "As far as I know, that space was used for storage until it was finally boarded up."

"Why was it boarded up?" I asked.

Aunt Hazel sighed. "Oh, I was playing in there one day when I was a kid and nearly fell through the dumbwaiter shaft. When Father found out, he forbade us to go in there, and sealed it off to make sure it didn't happen again."

I was almost out of questions, until I thought about what Aiden had said. "Aiden told me he'd gone to one of your father's séances and planned to write a story about it."

Aunt Runa frowned. "Oh, I'm sure that wasn't a real séance. More like a kind of magic show for some of the locals, mostly women, I heard. When Aiden asked to join, hinting he was writing an article about séances, my father invited him, just for fun. I heard he put on a good show, hoping it would spread the word. But when Aiden turned it into such an exaggerated story just to sell his newspapers, Father was furious. He never forgave him for that. And he was never invited back."

"What do you know about the stuff I found in his trunks?" I asked, picking at one last thread. "The Ouija board, tarot cards, crystal ball?"

"All part of the act," Aunt Runa said. "Like I said, he put on a good show."

"And the old sea captain he supposedly channeled?" I asked.

Aunt Hazel smiled. "Father was very clever."

I had a feeling my aunts wouldn't budge on any of this, even though I sensed otherwise. Still, it wasn't worth getting into. The past was in the past. And at this point, it felt awkward asking about the possibility of his several affairs, so I decided not to ask about the love letters hidden in one of the trunks. If they didn't know about that part of their father's life, I wasn't going to tell them. Patty Fay was dead, and Annabelle would never admit to anything like this. It was up to Gracie to tell her story if she wanted to, and that seemed unlikely, now that her son had been arrested and accused of murder. And while Marnie had supposedly been in on the séances, I had a feeling that what happened at Blackwood Inn would stay at Blackwood Inn, as far as she was concerned. For now, the contents of those letters would go with my grandfather to his grave. As for the actual letters, I assumed Aiden had taken them along with his birth certificate. I wondered where they were now.

"Carissa, there's one thing you might not know about your grandfather," Aunt Hazel said.

"What's that?" I asked, hoping it wasn't anything more complicated than what I already knew.

"He was quite the poet," she answered. "Loved Robert Burns, the Scottish poet. Do you know his work?"

Before I could answer, Aunt Runa closed her eyes and began to sing:

Should auld acquaintance be forgot,
and never brought to mind?
Should auld acquaintance be forgot,
and auld lang syne?

The room was quite for a moment. Aunt Hazel broke the silence. "Father wrote a lot of love songs, too, you know, just like Robert Burns."

I glanced at Noah, but kept my mouth shut.

The sheriff tuned a page in his notebook. "What about the private investigator—Henry Hill? Do any of you know why he was killed?"

Noah spoke up. "Same thing, Sheriff. He found out about Aiden's background. I'm guessing he also learned about Patty Fay's blackmail scheme. Maybe he was blackmailing her?"

"I don't think he tried to blackmail Aiden," I said. "He didn't seem like that kind of person. Sloppy, maybe, alcoholic, full of bluster, but I think he was legit. I think Aiden saw his opportunity to make Aunt Hazel look even more guilty by using more poison from her garden on Henry. Plus, Aiden would have wanted to prevent Henry from snooping around. He certainly had plenty of opportunity. He'd had a set of the household keys made, which gave him easy access to the greenhouse and poisonous plants, the attic and the secret room, and all of our rooms, including Henry's. Who knows? Maybe Aiden suspected Henry was getting close and planned to share that information with you, Sheriff."

"What about the birth certificate?" the sheriff asked. "Why didn't Aiden present it to you all as evidence of his relationship to the Blackwood family?"

"The birth certificate didn't have enough information," Noah said. "The only readable name was Gracie's."

"He needed DNA proof," I added. "But that would have meant exhuming Grandfather's body for a match. I doubt my aunts would allow it unless there was a really valid reason for doing it." I turned to the attorney. "Am I right, Jonathan?"

Jonathan, who had been standing by the dining room door, sipping his tea and listening to the conversation, nodded. "You can exhume a body for DNA testing for paternity disputes but you need cause, and it's complicated, not like on TV."

"Even if the person has been deceased for a long time?" Aunt Runa asked.

"Yes," Jonathan confirmed. "Even if the body has decomposed, you can retrieve DNA from bones and teeth, even toenails and eyeballs. Those are the most common and reliable sources. But most people don't realize the process can be traumatic for the family after the deceased has been laid to rest. It's also expensive and takes time, depending on the procedure."

"Wouldn't he need permission?" Aunt Runa asked.

Jonathan nodded. "The request would have to come from the family or law enforcement, and you'd have to get permission from the court or another official. I doubt Aiden could have simply requested it because he didn't have proof of paternity. It's a Catch-twenty-two, of sorts."

Aunt Runa turned to me. "I'm curious, Carissa. When did you suspect Aiden might have been the killer?"

I shook my head at my cluelessness. "Not until he mentioned the dumbwaiter when we were up in the attic—and home alone. I mean, he was such a nice guy, tried to be helpful, it seemed, although he didn't accomplish much after promising to find a lawyer. I figured he was probably distracted, you know, working on the story? I guess I should have suspected him, but he didn't seem to have a motive. I had no idea he was related to my aunts. And since he was a journalist, I assumed he was impartial and just trying to find out what happened for his newspaper. He even shared some personal information about some of the people in town, which was helpful. Now that I think about it, he was probably trying to throw me off, and he did. I'm sure Nancy Drew would have seen right through him!"

The sheriff nodded and closed his notebook. "Well, those are all the questions I have, for now, anyway. I'm sure I'll have more after we interview Aiden again."

"By the way, does Gracie know about any of this?" I asked.

The sheriff nodded. "She called when she heard about her son's arrest. As you know, news travels fast in this town."

"Is she all right?" I asked, regretting that I thought she might be the killer.

"She says she's going to stand by him, now that she knows who he is and in spite of what he's done. I think she blames herself for giving him up for adoption to a family that wasn't right for him. Of course, she didn't know that at the time, but still. Anyway, she has a lot of friends who can help her through this—Harper, Annabelle, and you, Marnie."

Marnie nodded.

"Speaking of Harper and Annabelle, do you think they'll ever come around?" I asked Marnie.

"Doubt it," she said. "Most of the folks in this town are pretty set in their ways. They don't like change. I think Annabelle still resents the competition from the Blackwood Inn, and Harper still doesn't like what you all have done to the place."

"Hopefully they'll at least be civil," the sheriff said, "now that everything's been cleared up and they know the Blackwoods aren't responsible for the murders. Maybe they'll realize how much you all have been through and soften up a bit. I guess we'll just have to wait and see."

"I'll bake them some of my chocolate-dipped snickerdoodles," Aunt Hazel said. "You and the folks down at the jailhouse loved them, right, Sheriff?"

He smiled and patted his stomach. "A little too much, I'm afraid."

Everyone laughed.

"Well, I need to get back to work," the sheriff said.

"And I've got to pack," Jonathan added, "and pick up a few things for my wife to get me out of the doghouse. She's a little miffed that I didn't leave to go home. Are there any flower shops in town?"

"Yes," Aunt Hazel said. "The Red, Red Rose is a cute little shop downtown. Tell Missy I sent you."

The Red, Red Rose? I recognized that name from somewhere. I looked at Noah. He mouthed the name, "Burns."

Murder at Blackwood Inn

So the handyman was also a poet. What other mysteries was this man hiding?

"Bye, everyone," Sheriff Lokey said. He and Jonathan headed out of the kitchen.

Aunt Hazel sighed and rose wearily from the table. "Well, I'm pooped from all the excitement. Time for a nap."

"I'll join you," Aunt Runa said. "Haven't slept a wink since all this began."

I knew the feeling. A nap sounded pretty good.

"Will you be okay, Carissa?" Aunt Hazel said. "I know you haven't been sleeping well."

"I'll be fine. It's just taken some getting used to, what with all the creaks and flickering lights." I turned to Noah. "By the way, my lights—"

He held up a hand. "Sorry about that. I'll get right to them. Haven't figured out what's causing the flickering, but I need to make sure they're not a fire hazard."

Yikes. I hadn't thought about a fire danger. In fact, I'd started thinking more along the lines of messages from the beyond. I had to admit, this house was getting to me. As well as my grandfather's so-called ghost. And the mysterious Pyewacket, who always seemed to show up at an opportune time.

"Do you want a different room?" Aunt Hazel asked.

"Oh, no! I love pretending to be Nancy Drew! Honestly, I'm getting used to the quirks of the Blackwood Inn."

"Are you sure?" Aunt Runa asked.

"I'm sure," I said. "And good news. When I checked, the office phone was full of messages requesting reservations. I guess you were right about guests loving ghosts and everything that comes with them."

"I'm so glad!" Aunt Hazel said. "Maybe we'll change one of the rooms into a ghost-themed room, like Paranormal Activities or Poltergeist."

Oh boy, I thought. *What next? The Murder at Blackwood Inn Room?*

"Well, Aunt Hazel," I added, "you might consider getting rid of your poison garden—the root of all evil around here, so to speak."

Aunt Hazel gasped. "Oh, no! hat garden is my pride and joy. Besides, it has healing powers, too, you know. And now that only Noah and I are the ones with keys, it should be perfectly safe."

I shot her a look.

She frowned. "Fine. I'll think about it." With that, she and Aunt Runa headed out of the kitchen. Marnie looked at me, then at Noah, then said, "If you'll excuse me, I have some . . . cleaning to do."

Suddenly, Noah and I were alone.

I took a deep breath. "Where were we before were interrupted?" I said as he took the vacated seat next to me at the table.

He grinned.

Oh, yes. I blushed thinking about it.

Something under the table rubbed up against my leg. I thought it might be Noah's foot, but when I looked down, I saw Pyewacket staring up at me. I picked him up, set him in my lap, and petted him.

"Hey, cat," I said. "Thanks for saving my life." Pye continued to stare at me—a strange look in his eyes.

Noah began to lean over toward me.

I leaned in, too, the cat still on my lap.

Murder at Blackwood Inn

And then he kissed me.

I heard Pye make an unearthly sound. It was as if he were trying to tell me something.

But that's just crazy, right?

The End

Book includes brunch recipes (poison-free) and tasty tea additions (also poison-free.)

Dead and Breakfast Recipes

Caramel Pecan Brownies

Ingredients

- **4 oz** unsweetened baking chocolate
- **3/4 cups** butter
- **2 cups** granulated sugar
- **4** eggs
- **1 cup** all-purpose flour
- **1 cup** pecans, chopped
- **1** package, 11 oz caramel bits
- **1/3 cup** heavy whipping cream

Instructions

- Preheat oven to 350°F.
- Line a 9x13 baking dish with foil and spray with cooking spray.
- Microwave chocolate and butter until melted. Stir until well blended.
- Add sugar and eggs and mix well.
- Stir in flour.
- Stir in pecans.

- Pour half of brownie batter into prepared baking dish.
- Bake 20 minutes, or until top is firm to the touch.
- Combine caramel bits and whipping cream in a medium bowl. Microwave until caramel start to melt. Stir until caramel is completely melted.
- Pour caramel mixture over brownie batter in prepared pan, all the way to the edges. Pour remaining uncooked brownie batter on top of the caramel.
- Bake 26–30 minutes, or until toothpick inserted comes out clean and is firm to the touch.
- Cool completely, remove foil and cut into squares.

Raspberry Scones with Lemon Glaze

Ingredients

- **3 cups** flour
- **1/3 cup** granulated sugar
- **1 Tbsp** baking powder
- **1 tsp** salt
- **12 Tbsp (1–1/2 sticks)** unsalted butter, cut into pieces
- **3/4 cup** whole milk
- **1/2 tsp** vanilla
- **1 cup (3oz)** raspberries

Lemon Glaze

- **1 cup** powdered sugar
- **1 Tbsp** lemon juice
- **1/2 tsp** vanilla

Murder at Blackwood Inn

Instructions

1. Preheat the oven to 375°F.
2. Line a large sheet pan with parchment paper.
3. Whisk together the flour, sugar, baking powder, and salt until combined.
4. Add butter and use a pastry blender to form pea-sized pieces.
5. Drizzle the milk and vanilla over mixture, and stir until mostly combined.
6. Use your hands to fold in berries, until dough holds together.
7. Place dough on lightly floured surface and shape into a flat, **round** disk, about 1-1/2 inches thick.
8. Cut the dough into 6 wedges.
9. Transfer the scones to the prepared sheet pan, leaving space between them. Lightly brush the tops of the scones with milk, and sprinkle with sugar.
10. Bake for 20–30 minutes, until the scones are golden, gently puffed, and cooked through.

Glaze

1. Stir together powdered sugar and lemon juice until smooth.
2. Stir in the vanilla. Add a splash of milk.
3. While the scones are still warm, drizzle each with the icing. Let cool.

Tea Tips:

Spices like ginger, lemongrass, and turmeric are all fighters of toxic inflammation. Here are a few of Marnie's tips for making tastier cups of tea.

- Milk—tones down the bitter taste of tannins.
- Sugar, honey, or maple syrup—add richness to your tea.
- Spices—cinnamon, cardamom, ginger, and mint create aromatic teas.
- Lemon or lime—add zest to your tea.
- Coconut oil—creates a complex taste.

Acknowledgments

Thanks so much to my amazing agent, Laurie McLean at Fuse Literary, to my awesome editors, Holly Ingraham and Sandra Harding, to the fantastic production and promotion team, and everyone at Crooked Lane Books who worked on MURDER AT BLACKWOOD INN! What a great team!